THE ACRYPTUS TREE

"This book is dedicated to everyone who believed I could do it, and to anyone whose doubts inspired me to rise to the challenge."

PROLOGUE

It began in the early days of December, 1796. A humble British supply vessel had just set sail for the newly freed American coast. It was named the Diocles, and it was in awful disrepair. The weary beams creaked and grinded as waves crashed alongside its aged hull. Cold wind hissed as it battered the sails clinging to the ship's one solitary mast. The crew, a band of drunkards and misfits, came from destitute families with meager backgrounds. Even the captain was a surly oaf with fragile nerves and slothful posture. The Diocles rarely made good time.

Without warning, a destructive storm had consumed the skies. The bows of the ship heaved and groaned as the sails were quickly torn to shreds. Lethal winds and the shrill bite of freezing torrents made control of the Diocles impossible. Its crew and captain clung to their bunks and cried out for mercy, to no avail. It took only moments for the vessel to sink, pulling what supplies it carried down into endless oblivion.

Only four sailors survived: Francis Culver, the ship's cook and the oldest of eleven brothers; Peter Forsythe, the learned but prideful first mate; Joseph Gale, a zealous missionary intent on spreading faith amongst the growing nation; and John Cecil Rollins, the adolescent midshipman, cast out by his parents for want of food. Each had managed to grab hold of the same piece of floating debris as unrelenting currents carried them deeper into the chaos. The tumultuous waves rose to towering heights before crashing back down onto the survivors with growing ferocity. The skin of each man stung as if attacked by a thousand wasps. Their teeth chattered to the point of breaking and their hold on reality gradually grew faint. It was only a matter of time before their aching palms would loosen and they slipped away into watery darkness.

After what seemed an eternity, they each found the strength to open their eyes. The sound of deafening thunder still numbed their ears. All the clouds that had overpowered the sun for so long were now dissipating, and rays of hopeful sunlight beamed down upon the floating wreckage. It was at that moment that the survivors beheld a colossal island composed of solid rock looming in the distance. It rose up for what seemed two hundred yards, drawing closer as they weakly paddled their way towards it.

The four men had scaled the hazardous crag. Agonizing groans escaped their dry, cracking lips as they grasped each crevice with every upward inch. Though excruciating, the climb provided an undeniable sense of hope. This feeling, however, had evaporated as they finally reached the top, only to find a flat and barren surface where nothing could survive. Puddles of icy rainwater quenched the sailors' thirst, but the freezing temperatures and growing hunger in their bellies remained. It became clear that death would again come looking for them on that lifeless rock. This time there would be no escaping it. Not a single passing vessel was spotted, and it seemed unlikely that anyone might come searching for the wreckage of their ship. No one would grieve over the sinking of the Diocles. There would be no disheartened families, nor financial ruin. Life, for the rest of the populous, would go on.

The survivor, Joseph Gale, wished to explore the island more thoroughly before accepting it as his grave. The others stayed behind, calmly awaiting their impending doom. The missionary was not so easily defeated. For generations, his family had suffered long, nightmarish bouts with bad fortune, illness, and death. Some had interpreted it all as fate's cruel laughter while others considered it as an invulnerable curse. Whatever it was, the Gales had lived on, finding new ways to survive year after year. The decision by Joseph, however, to pursue a religious path had definitively ended their lineage. What precious time he had left in life he had sworn to make of use. His father had always said this was the only valuable action any man could do, and so he believed, with all his will and strength, that his ability to help the world wouldn't end that day.

Walking along, Gale discovered what appeared to be a brief incantation crudely carved into the ground beneath his feet. He called his comrades over to examine it. They all agreed that it had been inscribed long before their arrival. Peering closer, they each read one line aloud:

"I call upon that which was, and may be again

To rise up and be, as it was before

I accept the charges given, and the rewards to keep

Now never to pass on, now never more to sleep"

As they finished, a deep rumbling noise broke the calm. Out in the distance, from beneath the depths, there arose another mass of land. This one was larger, almost half the size of their beloved England. Fresh, green grass blanketed the ground, colorful plants blossomed, towering trees full of fruit grew bountifully, and serene beaches composed of the purest sand formed before the sailors' eyes. Birds could be seen descending from the clouds above to make their homes in the branches of trees, while the distant rumbling and mating calls of various land dwelling beasts resounded from beyond the coastline.

The survivors, struck with awe and fear, couldn't believe what they saw. An entirely new world was being birthed right before them. It could have been a hallucination brought on by the frosty air or insatiable hunger, but at that moment, it didn't matter. Whether what they saw was real or conjured up, it was far too beautiful to question. As they watched the wondrous phenomenon, each man felt whole again.

Four velvet flowers suddenly sprouted up from beneath their feet. They grew from the solid rock as if from freshly tilled soil. Overcome with hunger and fatigue, the castaways fell to their knees, devouring them without hesitation. Their aggressive hunger diminished and their bodies were soon rejuvenated.

The historical records of later years would show that the event would be forever known as The Swelling. The sailors made their way to the land mass and divided it into four equal provinces, which they named Amber, Daroon, Helite and Falcas. Helite went to Francis Culver. Daroon was given to Joseph Gale, while Falcas was claimed by Forsythe. The province of Amber was taken by Rollins. Together, the four men vowed unwavering loyalty to one another and to any who would help them colonize the land. The chances of being spotted were too monumental to ignore.

Hours of waiting turned into days. Days turned into weeks. No one came. It seemed as if the land was hidden from the view of passing ships. Hope soon turned into despair amongst the rulers, and all appeared to be lost, until one day the ocean was again consumed in a turbulent storm. When it passed, several ships lay cast upon the shore. The four lords came together once again to assist the survivors. Multiple families optimistically made their way across the land, creating small towns and villages while awaiting the search parties from home eventually sent to find them. Time passed on. With it came tempest after tempest, each bringing more crippled vessels to the shore and countless castaways seeking help. Soon the entire land was well populated and growing prosperously.

Apart from rich soil and bountiful harvests, the new residents soon made an exciting discovery. An accidental find during a routine mining operation revealed a collection of strange, glowing orbs buried deep underground. Some were the size of a mere egg, while others weighed in as much as a mountain boulder. Regardless of weight, each one seemed to offer an unlimited supply of wondrous energy. This led to the invention of various contraptions that improved everyday life. The origin of the glowing spheres, or "lorbs" as they came to be called, was never fully investigated. It never seemed curious to their finders that the caches of each supply appeared to be easy to locate, as if by design.

It became clear to the four lords that perhaps their destinies were not back in England, but rather in that strange new world that had saved their lives and supplied rare artifacts. They proclaimed the land an independent institution, and named it "Sanctumsea" for the salvation it had brought to all whose lives were shattered in the storms. Every new arrival chose a province to call home, and together the land grew in population and prosperity.

Each lord secured his province and ruled over it for several hundred years. This remarkable feat was possible because of the baffling flowers each sailor had eaten back on the stone island. They called it sunweed: a rare and powerful plant that granted its consumer extended life. Its magical properties varied, depending on who consumed it. Peter Forsythe died at the age of a hundred and twelve. The cook, Culver, passed away the day before his three hundredth birthday. Joseph Gale expired at age four hundred and nine. The midshipman, Rollins, was the last to go, making it to just over five hundred and fifty before the power of the plant finally wore off. Small clusters of sunweed had sprouted up from the gardens of each lord the day before his passing. No other sighting of the rare and powerful plant had been reported across all the land. Each lord instructed his chosen replacement to consume it as he had done. It became clear this was the manner in which rulers of Sanctumsea would reign to pass constructive laws and shield their subjects from harm.

The laws that were formed were modest and effective. All the provinces adhered to them.

They were as follows:

1) No lord of Sanctumsea may take aggressive action against his fellow rulers in any circumstance. Each shall rule steadfast in his province without interference in other provincial matters.
2) Any influences from "Memoriam", the land beyond Sanctumsea, should be strongly monitored.
3) Once a citizen of a province, always a citizen of that province. To relinquish one's citizenship can only result in permanent exile.
4) All crimes, including but not limited to slander, thievery, false statement, and the harm of a fellow citizen are expressly forbidden. Any participation in such actions will be swiftly dealt with as per the duties of the ruling lord.
5) Any peculiarities in Sanctumsea, whether resourceful or deadly, shall be weathered, but never investigated. Ignorance is kinder than curiosity.

The failure of these laws would result in immediate war amongst the provinces. This was an action no lord wanted to ensue. Violent conflict and bloody resolution were things of Memoriam. In Sanctumsea, it was avoided at all costs. The price of life was far too high. Because of this, most issues in each province were resolved diplomatically and without unnecessary force. And so, the people lived in peace, governed by their individual lord. This was the way things had been since The Swelling, and for over five hundred years, not much had changed.

CHAPTER ONE

Deep in the Amber province sat the pleasant village of Havendale. Like many others in Sanctumsea, it managed to rule itself without much influence or regard from its newly appointed lord. Though still subject to his rules, it stood in serenity and justice without incident or crime. Founded by Scottish, Italian, and German survivors over three hundred years ago, Havendale was a beacon of peaceful progress. Build on fertile ground with unhindered streams and rivers all within walking distance, there was little to complain about. Nestled against the quiet shade of the Wallowing Woods, the village had successfully grown over the years to accommodate its inhabitants.

What made Havendale stand out amongst its neighbors was the creation of the Guild of Promise. This was a compilation of its most intelligent and dedicated citizens, whose actions touched countless lives. The core virtues of a member were selflessness and heroism. Though multiple candidates could be elected, only one was selected to join the honorable guild per year. During this particular election, only five names had been entered. Of these five, one had generously declined. Another had been caught in the middle of a complicated love affair. Only three remained.

After each Guild ceremony, the residents of Havendale would take pleasure in the luxurious festivities of Wintersbane. This was a time for everyone in the village to gather to dine in celebration of spring and share their hopes for a prosperous harvest. Various committees and volunteers had already begun setting up tables, chairs, and banners in a large field just outside the front gate. The intoxicating aroma of various soups, broths, meats, and freshly baked breads carried high above the village streets. Every belly in Havendale ached with hunger as the time to celebrate drew near.

Invitations had been sent throughout Amber, encouraging other villages and nearby towns to partake in the wondrous festivities. This was just a formality. No one in Havendale had the slightest interest in being bothered by folk born from outside the village. To be from Havendale meant to be a living and breathing part of it, and not to be concerned with anyone that resided outside the village walls.

The Guild election was set for noon. The village square would be packed with all the citizens of Havendale, patiently awaiting the ceremonies. The mayor would give some opening remarks before allowing the nominated parties to give a short, eloquent speech. This would be immediately followed by the counting of ballots. Once the votes were tallied, the mayor would announce the winner before wrapping an aquamarine sash around the victor's arm. This was a symbol of the Guild, and every member was required to wear it.

One such individual was named Adelaide Stokes. As families in Havendale went, hers was one of the more reputable. The villagers knew her for her exquisite beauty and spirited demeanor, though she could have been blessed with a little more gratitude and grace, in her mother's opinion. She was exceptionally tall for a girl of eighteen. Her long strawberry blonde hair flowed down half the length of her back. She kept it straight and never braided. Her eyes were emerald green and her skin was light and fair. Sun kissed freckles dotted her nose and chin. She was fit in appearance but proper in manner, and all who knew her liked her well.

Adelaide lived in a two-story cottage near the center of Havendale. The outer walls were covered with lemon colored paint, and birds danced and nested cheerily on the chipped, white window sills. Thin puffs of wispy smoke escaped from the tar plastered chimney and drifted lazily along the cobble-top roof. Of all the houses and shops in the village, the Stokes's establishment was revered and longed for by any and all who beheld it.

The matriarch of the family was named Henrietta, but everyone called her Hattie for short. She was awkwardly slender with poor taste in clothes and hairstyle. Her face, which was small and tight, constantly had a nervous expression upon it. The sound of a cough could make her jump. A substantial portion of her parents' wealth had enabled her to live comfortably without lifting a finger to do anything, besides occasionally meander around in spiritless bouts of housework.

Adelaide also had two brothers. Many hours of outdoor labor had given her older sibling, Ronan, both rugged features and a muscular build. This had secured the fondness and dotage of several women throughout the village. It didn't hurt that he was a caring sort with funny jokes, a protective streak, and endless charisma. Gable, the youngest in the family, was spunky and swift. He had a legendary knack for getting into trouble, ever since the day he could crawl. Even so, his short scruffy hair and adorable smile had kept him in everyone's good graces. As a constant source of unlimited energy, there was no adventure too reckless, or grand, for the nine year old to tackle. No one in Havendale failed to acknowledge his potential for one day accomplishing remarkable things.

Adelaide's father, Bard Stokes, had been the casualty of a tragic hunting accident some years before. While on a family picnic on the outskirts of the Wallowing Woods, he had entered them to find Adelaide, who'd run off to play. While calling her name, he had stepped into the path of an unknown hunter, who had fled the scene after his weapon discharged. Adelaide herself had been standing not far behind and learned that if her father hadn't stood where he had, she may have very well died that day, instead. A thorough investigation into the matter had yielded no suspects and ultimately led to the banning of powerful firearms and other Memoriam-influenced weaponry in certain parts of Amber.

Born and raised in Havendale, Bard had always been considered to be an outstanding citizen by all. As a younger man, he had been nominated for a place in the Guild of Promise. He had lost, however, to a stubborn, irksome girl who often rebuked him for his unkempt appearance and lack of fashion. It had always humored the good folk of the village that, in time, she and Bard would one day marry and have three children.

Until his untimely passing, Hattie Stokes had always held her husband accountable for one particular vice: drinking. Though never excessive, some in the village believed it had driven a wedge between the two of them not long before his death. Hattie even went so far as to claim it was in a fit of drunkenness that Bard had lost his way in the Wallowing Woods and stumbled foolishly into the hunter's path.

"A real man would have commanded more common sense when his loved ones are concerned," she sometimes said at the breakfast table, "but your father enjoyed squandering our fortune in the hollows of ghastly taverns. He kept more company with babbling drunkards than he did with his own beloved family."

Adelaide had never once doubted her father, not even after all her mother had said. To her, Hattie seemed to remember only the bad things. Adelaide could remember much more. There were family picnics and outings. Sometimes she would return home from school to find a new, expensive dress waiting in her room. She could still hear Bard's laugh as Gable made funny faces behind Ronan's head at the dinner table. Her father's smile had never faltered. Whatever his faults might have been, Adelaide knew in her heart that Bard always considered his three children to be his greatest achievement. With these things in mind, it seemed unfair to only see his mistakes.

Any lingering memory of him had been pushed aside that day by Hattie as she prepared a hasty lunch of corn beef sandwiches in the kitchen. A tall pitcher of ice cold raspberry lemonade stood on the table next to a freshly baked loaf of banana bread, lightly glazed with honey. Gable was playing fetch in the living room with Pallard, the family beagle. Ronan had not yet returned home. After supper the evening before, he had stopped at the local floral shop. It was owned by the pretty and perky Jolene Ingram, whose reputation in the village held some questionable behavior. She had given Ronan several subtle invitations to pay her a visit after closing hours. The night had been quite strenuous.

Adelaide was upstairs, in her room, tending to a daily tradition. For an hour each day, she would lie flat on her stomach across her bed, which was hewn from oak and covered with hand woven blankets. The walls of her room were painted crimson with assorted white lilies adorned above the doorway. As she lay there, contently, she would pull a worn old binder out from beneath the bed. Once placed in front of her, she would open it, gaze fondly at a loving inscription from her father, and enter the newest story her mind had created. The journal had been a gift from Bard after her acceptance into the Guild of Promise. She had been nominated for writing a poem that was still considered a best seller in Havendale. It was about a love-torn warrior named Arcado, a man of pride and stainless honor. His quest for glory had always trumped his desire for human companionship, but a woman soon entered his life. She was Wendolyn, a cold and manipulative villainess. Together, they had lived and loved for a summer while all the wars in the land subsided. It was not long, however, before Wendolyn became involved with a political official, leaving Arcado heartbroken. In a fit of anger, he joined a final campaign against her new lover and was swiftly decapitated. The poem ended with Wendolyn attempting to steal from the official and suffering the same fate. The last thing she saw before the axe cut down was Arcado's face replacing those of everyone standing out in the crowd. She then closed her eyes, accepting her punishment, and whispered his name as death embraced her.

Though tragic, risqué, and occasionally graphic in design, the poem had become a local sensation, earning her Guild induction. When asked who had inspired her, she referenced Jonah Longstreet, Amber's most renowned and mysterious author, or "inkman" as they were often nicknamed. His countless novels, poems, limericks and short stories had charmed and encouraged thousands over the years. Adelaide had hoped to one day meet the treasured celebrity, but apart from hushed rumors and a few notable theories, no one had any evidence to suggest where the writer lived. His works had simply appeared across the land some years before, and all rejoiced in their discovery. Each one seemed to contain subtle messages of hope and inspiration, always pushing the reader to explore multiple theories and possibilities within. The richness and imaginative nature of his works fueled Adelaide to aspire to more than anyone in Havendale, including herself, believed it possible for her to attain. As far as she was concerned, Jonah Longstreet was undeniably the finest literary mastermind in the whole of creation, and she was unquestionably his greatest fan.

By now, her journal was full of colorful short stories, a few poetic fragments, and a sentence here and there about anything that crossed her mind. Every paragraph, no matter how trivial, was the beginning of something remarkable.

It wasn't until her mother started knocking at the door that she finally laid down her pencil and looked up.

"Addy? Adelaide?" Hattie called. "What are you doing in there? We have twenty minutes before the Guild's annual election. The mayor requested your presence specifically, as you are already aware, young lady. I do not approve of your laziness. You know how it makes me look. I swear you have your father's...."

Her mother's voice faded as she picked up her pencil and continued writing.

CHAPTER TWO

The downstairs door slammed shut, breaking Adelaide's focus on her journal. A low, harsh groan escaped her lips. If she had never been nominated and won that ridiculous sash, she might have been able to miss the election. Sadly this was not the case. Being a member of such a prestigious club limited how far back in the shadows one could stand.

With an exaggerated sigh, she pushed herself off the bed and began picking out an outfit. She had to choose something proper, or her mother was sure to fuss. It was horribly embarrassing how far the woman could take a tantrum, especially in public.

Adelaide had never been the "perfect daughter" Hattie always wanted. That was something she had only been to her father. Bard had always understood her, especially her creative mind. Since his death, Hattie had seemed more intent on turning her into someone else; someone her father had never demanded she be. If her mother wanted her to hurry to the Guild selection ceremony, then there was only one thing Adelaide could do. She decided that a few extra minutes preparing couldn't hurt.

After some deliberation, she selected a strapless teal dress with an egg white belt and grey cropped jacket. A comb was passed through her hair before she quickly slid on a pair of worn down running shoes. Wrapping her Guild sash around her arm, she begrudgingly made her way downstairs, stomping her feet on every step. Although she had always been mature for her age, it was difficult to act the part when dealing with a woman like her mother.

There was no need to lock up the house. In Havendale, prices were affordable and kindness resided in every home. Crime, as a whole, was almost nonexistent. The village was, to those who knew it, the perfect place to live. Every building was cleaned daily. Windows were washed, walls were painted, and not a speck of dust could be found on the efficiently polished floors. Not a single citizen was above cleanliness, and helping one's neighbor was a frequently performed ritual.

As Adelaide walked briskly down the cobbled street, admiring the streamers and banners hoisted over her head, she heard the hasty footsteps of someone following her. She gasped amusedly as she turned to see Ronan. His pants were wrinkled, he'd forgotten to put on socks, and his hair was suffering from the worst case of bed-head she had ever seen. Adelaide shook her head as he finally caught up to her. Her older brother smirked and gave her a gentle shove.

"I covered for you again," she informed him. "You can't keep this up without mom finding out."

"Come on, Addy, what is the big deal? I'll be twenty four in a few weeks. I'm hardly a squirm anymore, you know. Everyone in Havendale gets their own place at eighteen, and I'm well past due. It'll be your turn, now that I think of it. I'd be better off just packing up and moving in with Jolene."

"Ronan, she's twelve years older than you."

He smiled and wrapped his arm around her shoulder, giving her a gentle squeeze. Adelaide wrinkled her nose as the faint trace of Jolene's overwhelming perfume, "Sourbush No. 5", struck her nostrils.

"She is indeed, little sister, but I'm absolutely tossed over her. You'll see, I promise. One day soon enough...some fellow is going to make you as winked as I am."

Adelaide scoffed and rolled her eyes. In eighteen years, she had never felt remotely tossed or winked about guys in Havendale. It seemed safe to assume that wouldn't change anytime soon. The village was well stocked with eligible men, many of whom Hattie readily approved of. None of them, however, had made a staggering impression on her daughter. As far as Adelaide was concerned, her mother's eagerness to see her married off only made the taste of being unattached more flavorful.

The pair entered the village square just as the last seats were being filled. The three nominees could be seen in the distance, standing up on a makeshift platform before a handcrafted podium. The Mayor's office stood directly behind it, towering high above its neighboring structures. The square, normally barren, was completely covered with chairs. They were placed side by side in rows with a slender walkway cutting through the middle. Everyone from the village could be seen sitting down, comfortably awaiting the upcoming commencement. From what Adelaide could see, there were only two empty chairs left in the whole assembly. One stood next to her mother Hattie, clearly reserved for Ronan. The other stood all the way up in the front row, where all Guild members were required to sit. She groaned as Ronan patted her shoulder and wished her luck before walking off to join their family. Lowered her eyes, she silently made her way towards the front.

Every step felt infinite. Adelaide could feel the eyes of everyone in Havendale locked onto her as she slunk down the aisle. The thought of her mother's glare burning a hole into the back of her head made her grimace. She knew she would suffer Hattie's wrath after the ceremony. With any luck, she could avoid a public scene until after the party had subsided. Though Hattie Stokes enjoyed her prosperous reputation, an open rebuking didn't seem like something she would be afraid to pull. A shudder traveled down Adelaide's spine as she finally reached the front row. Clearing her throat, she took her seat and gazed up at the three nominees standing nonchalantly before her.

The one sitting closest to the podium stood out like a sore thumb; a thin, sickly thumb that hated everything and everyone around him. He had sad, lonely eyes, which clashed harshly with the proud expression stamped across his bony face. His skin was pasty white and his stringy butter colored hair was padded down with a slick, costly product. The three piece suit he wore was powdered and pressed, like something placed on a fresh corpse during a funeral display. Adelaide recognized him as Raoul King Jr. He was the sixteen year old son, and only child, of Havendale's wealthiest landowner and businessman.

The Kings were considered legitimate by many in their dealings around the area, but a large portion of their wealth was rumored to come from illegal productions. On the legal side, they had a province-wide enterprise mining and selling lorbs. In the past twenty years or so, however, a relatively harmless yet addictive substance known as "TOX" had surfaced. It was composed of small clumps of excess minerals found inside lorb quarries. The effects were fiercely intense and undeniably stimulating. The Kings were rumored to be its strongest peddlers.

As for Raoul Jr, he was known throughout the village for being a loner and often a trial to tolerate in others' company. It was possibly by pure accident, alone, that he had even found himself nominated for Guild membership. Four months earlier, an untamed horse had stampeded up and down the streets of Havendale, causing havoc and damages as it went. A young girl with a broken leg had been trapped in its path. Seconds before impact, however, she had been knocked out of harm's way by none other than Raoul himself. This seemed unusual to Adelaide. All she truly recalled about the nominee was his aversion to touching anything or anyone, due to fears of contracting deadly germs. This phobia had resulted in him wearing blue latex gloves nearly everywhere he went. Many in Havendale had suggested that his heroic action was merely the result of him running into the poor girl while trying to save himself. Enough voters, however, had ultimately deemed him worthy of nomination. And so there he sat, up on the stage, wearing his fanciest suit and smugly looking down at the crowd before him.

Adelaide had known the second nominee, Mimi Varrow, since childhood. Being the same age, the pair of them had, at one time, been almost inseparable. This had changed when, years ago, Hattie Stokes's jealous nature had caused a blunt accusation against Mimi's mother concerning Bard. Anyone with common sense could see that his loyalty rested with Hattie, but she disregarded the advice of her friends and ended her friendship with Mrs. Varrow on the grounds that she was too forward in Bard's company. This had been something of a troublesome issue in Havendale. More than one rumor had circulated about what Hattie had done to raise Bard's jealousy on the subject. The worst concerned Gable, whose slight genetic differences to his other siblings had been used as evidence to show that, perhaps, Mrs. Stokes had retaliated against her husband's supposed infidelity with some of her own. Adelaide often wondered how her dad could have endured someone like her Hattie throughout his life.

Mimi hadn't changed much since their mothers' dissolved friendship. Her dark, auburn hair was still voluminous and laced with shiny gold ribbons. She had the same dazzling eyes, plump cheeks, and sweet, tender smile. Always the rebel of fashion, her outfit was a tightly packed combination of tassels, polka dots, croqueted designs and eccentric logos. The Varrows were known as the sort of folk who didn't let the latest clothing trends dictate how they chose to dress. One item in particular caught Adelaide's attention: a shoelace bracelet tied loosely around Mimi's right wrist. It was a meager gift given to her just days before Hattie's final outburst. Adelaide smiled to know she had kept it.

She then turned her gaze to the final candidate, whose name was Finn Wessel. He was a tall, well kept man, around twenty five years old. His physique was flawless, and confidence seemed to emulate from him without interference. Wild, ebony hair peaked over the top of his brazen forehead and slid unhindered down to the back of his neck. The unblemished nature of his oiled, sunbathed skin and preservation of a short, stylish beard were things only a truly dedicated individual could achieve. As far as Adelaide knew, he was unattached, but for how long no one could say. His bachelor moments were always fleeting. Some in the village even claimed he had an illness that kept him hungry for a woman's touch. To all the damsels nearby, however, none of this seemed to matter. All they saw was his deep, piercing eyes, dangerous, smile, and flexible form. It was highly possible that these attributes were the only grounds for his nomination in the first place.

Adelaide's palms grew sweaty as her eyes slowly rolled along his hair and forehead, traveling down his resolute, hairy cheeks to his sharp, poignant chin. From there she studied the curve of his magnificent neck to the outline of his broad, powerful shoulders.

"What the rot is this?" she thought, her mouth growing dry. *"Am I sick or something?"*

These questions didn't prevent her from moving her gaze southward, dropping from button to button of Finn's freshly pressed white silk shirt. Once her eyes had reached the contours of his belt buckle, Adelaide blinked and forced herself to look away. Never in her lifetime had she been so enamored by someone. She couldn't understand what made her want him so badly. Finn Wessel was seven years her senior. He had a foul reputation and seemed to take pleasure in the discomfort and bad fortune of others. Even so, Adelaide couldn't control the ravenous craving rising up from her stomach, into her chest and flooding her brain. It was all she could do not to leap onto the stage and throw herself upon him, sending buttons flying across the stage as she exposed his noble, unshaved chest.

The intensifying thoughts growing in Adelaide's mind quickly dissipated as the doors to the mayor's office swung open behind the platform. All eyes turned to behold a short, balding man in his early forties making his way onto the stage. He was Horatio Hare, the twenty-sixth mayor of Havendale. A hefty fellow, he managed to bear himself with notable charisma. Stepping up to the podium, he took a deep, lingering breath before raising his hands and yelling out at the top of his lungs.

"Hello good and wonderful people of Havendale! We have the honor....no the privilege, of living in the finest village ever to be built in this marvelous land. We live in a place where we grow and prosper as one great community."

The crowd of villagers applauded.

"Makes you feel kind of special, doesn't he?"

This remark came from the Guild member sitting on Adelaide's left. She turned her head and recognized him as Clayton Hogg; another one of Havendale's emancipated young adults, almost two full years older than her. He had some impressive features: a head of wavy chestnut hair, charismatic green eyes and a sunny disposition. Adelaide casually glanced over his outfit and suppressed a giggle. He wore a pair of dusty trousers with hand-me-down suspenders. His shirt was shamrock green with fading brass buttons, barely visible under the leather duster that draped down to just above his knees. Adelaide's amusement was finally given away by an uncontrollable smirk. She started to turn her face, but restrained the urge when she noticed his unwavering smile directed towards her. Clayton genuinely seemed not to care about her opinion of him. She found this greatly annoying.

"If you please, good citizens," Mayor Hare continued, waving his hands. "We must prepare for this year's award ceremony, and the most fortunate nominee who will be today's winner. Today, we have some excellent individuals of our wonderful little village up here with me who are not only members of its citizenry, but marvelous additions to our future as well. Now, even though only one will be added to our Guild's inspiring long list of winners, I hope that each and every one of you knows, deep, deep, deep inside your hearts, that they are all winners, as is everyone sitting in the audience today. Together, you all make our village great."

Every person in the crowd leapt to their feet, clapping their hands with unreserved enthusiasm. Mayor Hare smiled and gave a humble bow. As the villagers took their seats, he shuffled over to the three nominees and extended his hand towards the podium.

Mimi Varrow was the first to go. She accepted a hug from the mayor along the way and blew out kisses to the audience as she moved along.

"Isn't she marvelous? A true definition of promise, wouldn't you all say?" Mayor Hare laughed. "Now could you please tell us your full name, young miss?"

"Certainly; my name is Mimieux Clemency Varrow."

"And I understand you go by Mimi, is that correct?"

The nominee nodded.

"Excellent," Hare laughed. "I imagine you must be just a little bit excited about all this, eh Mimi?"

"I'll tell you after I win that Guild position, Mister Mayor."

"Oh you are just delightful. I could just gobble you up! Now please tell us, Mimi, in your own excellent words, why should you be chosen as this year's Guild of Promise winner?"

Mimi cleared her throat as she looked out across the audience. Her eyes rested briefly on Clayton Hogg, who smiled up at her. She blushed with obvious flattery and began her speech. In it she spoke of how she didn't deserve to be nominated and thanked all those who supported her. This was an approach commonly used by yearly nominees in last minute attempts to gain respect and high regards from the viewing voters. She went on to say she was just an ordinary person trying her best to make a difference in the world. The crowd applauded generously as she wrapped up her dialogue and gave a pleasant curtsy.

Next up was Finn Wessel. He approached the podium with the sway and swagger of someone consumed and saturated with overconfidence.

"Hello everybody," he began. Adelaide felt goose bumps spread across her skin at the heavy, seductive tone of his voice. "How is everyone doing today? I mean, how could anyone in this town be anything short of wonderful? Am I right, Mr. Mayor? Am I right? And may I ask, have you been working out?"

Mayor Hare let forth his merriest laugh yet. Many people in the crowd chimed in. Throughout the course of his speech, Finn continued to lay joke after joke on his audience, fully grabbing their attention and causing riffs of uncontrollable mirth from row to row. Adelaide herself started shaking her head in delighted guffaw as he bantered on. He even rested his eyes on her for a brief second and winked before giving his closing remarks. The crowd gave him a standing ovation as he thanked them all and returned to his seat.

"The time has come, folks, to hear from our final nominee," Mayor Hare heartily announced. "His family is well known throughout our little village for their generosity and knack for wholesome business."

Adelaide rolled her eyes. Mayor Hare had clearly neglected to investigate the rumors circulating the Kings. It was just as possible that he was already more than aware of their activities. She shuddered as she pondered the possibility that Raoul's father might have secured this nomination with a sizable donation to Hare's private funds.

"Now, without further delay," the mayor continued. "Here is the one and only, Raoul King Jr!"

Adelaide watched the sullen nominee drag his feet across the wooden boards as he made his way over to the podium, receiving an unwanted slap on the back from Mayor Hare along the way. The heir to the King fortune gave a lazy wave towards the audience, frequently glancing down at his newly polished shoes. A moment of awkward silence followed. Mayor Hare cleared his throat, and several members of the crowd shifted in their chairs.

"Well," Raoul began, glancing out at the uninterested faces before him. "I, uh…I suppose…just vote for me… I guess. Thanks." He gave an exaggerated bow and returned to his seat as the crowd offer him a half hearted round of applause.

"What sort of rot is this?" Adelaide murmured, shaking her head. "He shouldn't even be up there."

"Come on, cut him some slack," Clayton whispered, nudging her shoulder. "He's a sad fellow and not well-liked. Let him have his few minutes of power."

Adelaide shot her pleasant companion a look of unflattering contempt as Mayor Hare once again took his place before the crowd.

"Well...was that not just the best group of nominee speeches?" he asked. "I think so. I certainly do. Now, it is time for moment we have all been waiting so patiently for: the vote tally."

Each member of the audience arose from their chairs. A pair of designated volunteers walked from row to row, handing out small slips of paper and pencils. All the citizens had to do was scribble down the name of their preferred candidate and fold it up to conceal their choice. With just three candidates, the votes were quickly collected back and counted by Mayor Hare. He finally approached the podium and beamed his biggest smile.

"There might be something seriously wrong with that guy," Clayton whispered with a chuckle.

Adelaide grunted and pretended to gaze around at the audience.

"Wait a minute! Why am I doing this?" she thought. *"Why do I even care?"*

Mayor Hare interrupted her train of thought.

"The votes, ladies and gentlemen, are in," he exclaimed. "The numbers are solid and the candidates well honored, I'd say. Now please, if all of you excellent people would stand, I will read aloud the results."

The nominees stood and took a step forward as Hare glanced down at the tally. Raoul smirked pompously at the audience. Mimi stood quietly and contently with a smile on her face. Finn waved his hand calmly with confidence. Adelaide found herself picturing for a moment what it would be like to invite him back to her room after all this was over....and then...and then...

"Outstanding," Hare declared. "These are simply outstanding results. Two nominees scored over ninety percent of the votes, a very close race indeed. The winner of this year's election and the next addition to our list of Guild members is...."

He took a second to compose himself. All his hopping about and shouting had rendered him short of breath. Finally, he held the slip of paper high in the air and exclaimed:

"Finn Wessel!"

CHAPTER THREE

The audience clapped their hands and cheered. A sharp, flirty whistle escaped Adelaide's lips. Her face burned bright red as Finn glanced down at her, his eyes full of gratitude and peaked interest. Mayor Hare ushered him down into the crowd to receive hearty handshakes and compliments from the villagers. Mimi laughed and joined him, receiving hugs from several loyal supporters who consoled her on her unfortunate defeat. Raoul stormed off in a fit with his fists tightly clenched. The squeaking noise from his latex gloves lessened as Adelaide watched him disappear behind the stage and out of sight.

It was tradition each year for the elected winner to lead the villagers down the streets of Havendale to the Wintersbane celebration. Clusters of ecstatic people were soon following Finn as he walked side by side with Mayor Hare. Songs and ballads concerning daring adventures and rowdy odysseys were boisterously chanted. The whole of Havendale was alive with uncontained happiness. Before long, the front entrance to the village came into view and the entourage passed gleefully through the gate.

Not far ahead, there stood a field of untended grass and freshly bloomed daisies. Directly in the center stood a tall, sloping hill that reached up against the towering tree trunks of the woods behind it. According to legend, the "Feasting Hill", as it was locally known, was where the founders of Havendale had first viewed the land upon which to build. In accordance with tradition, any event of notable significance was hosted there, from weddings and holidays to funerals and birthdays. Gable's last birthday, alone, had prompted a wild extravaganza full of raucous fireworks and marvelous party-games, not to mention a slew of his favorite desserts. These had included chilled pudding, strawberry ice cream, and moist, rich chocolate cake. An event like Wintersbane warranted spirits of a more staggering nature.

Several villagers had already broken company from the procession to carry bountiful trays heaped with assorted delicacies out towards it. The crowd quickly found their places along the long, adorned tables and took their seats, eager to begin the festivities. Mayor Hare ushered the Guild of Promise to the head table with one hand and, with the other, signaled the attention of everyone else as the food was dispensed from table to table.

From her seat with the Guild, Adelaide could see her family getting comfortable at a nearby table. Gable was bouncing excitedly in his chair next to Hattie, hungrily eying the feast before him. Ronan was somewhere nearby, most likely snatching a seat next to Jolene Ingram. Everyone was growing antsy and rapidly talking in fevered tones. The celebration was about to commence.

Adelaide fervently hoped Finn Wessel would end up beside her. Perhaps the two of them could play finger-tag underneath the table cloth. She was disappointed, however, to see him placed seven chairs down in the place of honor next to the ever jolly Horatio Hare. A loud groan escaped her lips as Clayton Hogg seat himself directly across from her. She tried to ignore his colorful smile and pretended not to notice him waving in her direction. He was becoming more irritating to her by the second with his tranquil demeanor. She was happy to be distracted when Mayor Hare finally leapt to his feet, causing quite a loud commotion as he did so.

"Now that we are all gathered together in good company," he laughed. "I say to you all...let the feasting commence."

There was steak, both rare and well-done, peppered and broiled, as well as tenderized lamb chops, a large tray of honey glazed ham, several baskets of breaded chicken legs, grilled venison with lemon juice, barbecued meatballs glazed in honey, chopped liver, shrimp and salmon bisque, tomato and bacon salad, and a dozen different forms of sliced lunch meats, ranging from bologna to pastrami. The bread table had a marvelous collection of baguettes, biscuits, and assorted bagels and muffins. Pastries, pies, puddings, and crèmes lined each row of the dessert tables, and all around the hill were wide stands covered with exotic fruits and homegrown vegetables. Two dozen wooden barrels had been rolled up the hill as well, their contents consisting of frothy Honeydrop Beer, perfectly aged Tart Wine, creamy Cinnamon Cider, and chilled creek water with half-sliced lemons and limes tossed in to sweeten the flavor.

No band had been hired to provide music for the party. In a village like Havendale, everyone had a masterful skill that contributed to some specific situation, including music. A couple Guild members could play an excellent fiddle. A mother of a previous nominee performed a series of jigs on her violin. Other townsfolk made drums out of pots and pans, while several more kept the beat with spoons, forks and ladles on their tables. In no time at all, there was merry music and dancing that resounded beyond the hill and over the walls and roofs of Havendale, carrying on across the farmland and bounteous landscape.

By the late afternoon, everyone's appetites were thoroughly satisfied. Whoever wasn't falling to their knees due to overindulgence of wine and freshly brewed beer was parading around the tables to fervent Havendale tunes. Adelaide danced with her brothers, Mayor Hare, a short freckled lad named Alec Tarr, and even secured several livelier numbers with Finn Wessel. More than once, she had cast her eyes towards Clayton Hogg, expecting to catch him checking her out. She figured he was thinking long and hard about how best to obtain a dance from her, perhaps a slow one, performed for all the romantics and loving sweethearts in the village. Instead, she saw him being cuddled on a bench by Mimi Varrow. She was attempting to inch her arm around his shoulder and whisper something seductive in his ear. Though his interest seemed minimal, Clayton was not openly rebuking her. The very sight gave Adelaide aggressive stomach cramps.

"*Honestly, the nerve of him,*" she thought. "*He doesn't even have to flirt with girls for rotting out loud. Well, what does it matter to me anyhow? So what if he wants to be a total rotter? What do I care? Where is Finn?*"

She saw the admirable Guild winner standing by himself across the party. His right hand was clawing at some food still stuck in his teeth while his left tightly clasped a partially full clay goblet. His stance was stoic and still, as if someone were sketching him nearby on a modest canvas. The expression on his face, however, was one of drunken stupor. From what Adelaide could recall, he hadn't had an empty glass since the beginning of the party. This failed to sway her as she moistened her lips and straightened her dress. Her body trembled as she noticed his eyes glancing invitingly towards her. Now was the time to move in, while everyone else on the hill was occupied. Adelaide chuckled quietly as she pictured her and Finn waltzing down the streets of Havendale, their arms locked and their faces mere inches apart. The image alone would drive her mother to winked hysterics. She started making her way towards where he stood, random thoughts of unquenchable passion stealing across her mind.

Their connection was abruptly interrupted by a distant sound. Adelaide turned towards it, straining her gaze outward down the winding road that led to Havendale from along the edge of the Wallowing Woods. The music and dancing stopped around her as, one by one, the people of Havendale caught a glimpse of the approaching noise. There were horsemen, around fifty riders in all, moving swiftly towards the hill from the north. They grew larger and more formidable with each lengthy stride. Several citizens took a nervous step backwards as the band of mounted steeds nearly trampled them before finally coming to a halt at the edge of the party. The villagers whispered amongst themselves in open concern. Adelaide inched her way to the edge of the bewildered crowd of spectators for a better look. She could feel Gable clenching her hand behind her as she stared up nervously at the unexpected arrivals.

The riders were covered from neck to toe in scaly armor. Each suit reflected in the fading sunlight, giving their owners an unsettling desolate glimmer. Their heads were bald, except for sweaty bandages and bloodstained wraps. The horses they sat upon were wretched, hairless beasts, with blood-shot eyes and sunburned skin. Peering closer, Adelaide saw that each animal's teeth had been sawed down into miniscule, protruding fangs.

Mayor Hare was first to address the ominous new arrivals. He did so with the same friendly attitude he always used, moving slowly from rider to rider with his hand extended and waiting patiently for one of them to accept it.

"My, my, gentlemen," he gleefully declared. "What…err…excellent animals you ride upon to our small and humble feast. We welcome all who desire to fill their stomachs and hear the sweet melody of music upon their weary ears. Please, rest your horses and enjoy some food while you regale us all with tales of your travels."

After finding no one to accept his handshake, Hare retracted it and turned his attention to one particular rider.

"Good sir, welcome to our little party. We do our best to accommodate any and all who enter the gates of Havendale, and entreat those to do to enjoy all our village has to offer."

The rider nodded his head and cast a quick glance at the crowd. Adelaide felt as if he was counting them. She gulped uncomfortably as nefarious reasons why racked her brain. Even Hare seemed taken aback by it.

"If I may ask...good sir...what do you call yourself?" the mayor asked.

"His name, you engorged buffoon, is Miltock," another rider said. Hare turned to face the speaker, who dismounted his horse and stepped ahead of his companions. Adelaide noticed the icy, pale complexion of his skin, as if all bodily heat had seeped through his pores long ago. His lips were bloody and raw from being frequently gnawed upon, and ink-colored veins reached out across his entire face like some horrific tattoo. Adelaide peered forward as the unnatural image seemed to shrink for a moment and then grow back to its original size.

"Well, I...." Hare stammered. The fact that he had been insulted was slowly dawning on him. "I am pleased to make his err....his acquaintance. Yes I am. You....you are, sir?"

"The one you seek. My name is Huglund. I command this rabble in the name of Lord Tibris Tiberion."

"Ah, I see, I see.....and who is that, sir?"

A quiet murmur passed amongst the riders. Their eyes immediately focused on Hare, who started perspiring.

"Who is he, you ask?" Huglund began. "Why, he is the one who governs your lands, who provides security for all your families at his expense. He grants you the privilege of living as free citizens in his realm without heavy tax or political influence. It is by his guidance, that all in Amber reap the bountiful profits that accompany successful business. Without him, your pockets would not be overflowing with shine. That is who he is. I would think someone like that would be first on everyone's mind now and again."

The ever pleasant mayor of Havendale lost his nerve. He glanced back and forth from one rider to the next, blabbering on as he did so.

"We are….a peaceful and self-governed community, sir, I can promise you. We…We make our own laws and abide justly by them. I have always known that, err, that our province had its own protector, but surely you must be aware that we have never met the man, nor met anyone who serves him directly…until this moment, of course."

Huglund sighed and shook his head. "The inappropriate manner in which you've acted here, tonight, is easily considered treason. I trust you can accept that. With that being said, our master and your lord is a just and forgiving man. I'm sure he would want me to allow this first time to pass as a warning in the understanding that there will never be a second."

"Well," Hare said nervously. "I surely do apologize about my inexcusable behavior, sir, I do. We have lived on our own for so long out here in the country we have forgotten who keeps us safe from any surrounding dangers."

"What dangers?" Gable whispered. "These rotters are the only dangerous thing I've ever seen around here."

Adelaide quickly shushed him.

"Well then," said the mayor, composing himself. "What is it that I can do for you and your men, Mister Huglund?"

"It's Captain," hissed Miltock.

"My apologies," Hare resumed with a frantic salute. "How can we be of service, Mist…Captain?"

Huglund looked over at Miltock, who pulled out a water stained scroll wrapped in red sash from the ragged satchel hanging from his saddle. He cautiously unrolled it before reading aloud its contents.

"By order of Tibris Tiberion, lord of Sanctumsea, protector of the Amber province, and successor to the revered John Cecil Rollins, the following letter has been approved:

All towns, cities, and villages within the boundaries of his lordship's domain shall be subject to strict and thorough investigation concerning matters of highest treason. These matters include and are not limited to: 1) conspiracy to lead or partake in rebellion, 2) low regard for any law passed on his Lordship's personal behalf, 3) use of unfriendly slander towards his Lordship, and lastly, 4) intent to do harm to his Lordship's person. Those found guilty of such improper behavior will be labeled "Red Hands" and dealt with according to the rights of law. This investigation shall be received and assisted by every true and loyal citizen of Amber, no matter the cost or personal sacrifice. It will not be taken lightly, and will be overseen by an officer of noble birth and unquestionable loyalty. This officer is to be shown both respect and gratitude, and should never suffer a lack in generosity from those he encounters. Please, therefore, give credence to Captain Huglund, elected officer in the Tibris Guard, and personal ambassador to Lord Tiberion himself.

In accordance with the laws and support of fellow lords of Sanctumsea:

-Lord Cassius of Daroon

-Lord Andromedes of Helite

-Lord Vaux of Falcas

Signed by:

Lord Tibris Tiberion of Amber"

As he finished, every Tibris Guard lowered his head in reverence. Miltock gently placed the script down in the edge of his saddle and looked to Huglund for further instruction.

"Well," said Hare. "As the mayor of Havendale and all its many excellent citizens, may I be the first to welcome all of you...err fine gentlemen to our humble village. On a personal level, Captain, I offer my sincerest apology for not giving proper...err umm respect and duty towards Lord Augustus...I mean Andromedes Cassius....Tiberius?"

Captain Huglund gave a malicious grin.

"Come now, let us put all that nonsense behind us and move forward," he slyly declared.

The mounted riders began to smirk and chuckle. At this seemingly kind recommendation, the mayor let forth a sob of relief. Everyone else in the crowd began to smile as well; everyone except Adelaide. She looked around skeptically and saw that several other citizens, including Finn, Clayton, and Mimi had the same concern look as her upon their faces.

"If you could just help Miltock, here, to hang up this scroll on that torch post over there, we can begin our investigation and soon be on our way," Huglund chuckled to Hare.

"Certainly sir...umm Captain. Yes, of course. Might I just say though, sir, that in my short career as an elected public official, not once has anyone in Havendale ever committed an act of treason mentioned on that scroll. You'll find no such Red Handed troublemakers here. Why, even this morning, we held our annual ceremony of excellence, which has become our most established event to take place in our humble village. We call it our Guild of Promise. I'm sure if you heard some of our members' feats you would see...."

"I suppose then," Huglund interrupted him, "that our investigation will be over before you know it. It is citizens like you who make our jobs all the more easier, sir, and I thank you." He seemed humored by the sound of his own voice, as if he was pulling off one of the greatest performances ever done. With that, he turned towards the other horsemen, scanning his eyes from one ghastly face to the next, finally resting on a jittery, undersized rider.

"Kobal, come forth," Huglund commanded.

The stunted man snickered maliciously. With a sinister cackle, he back flipped off his horse and eagerly approached the captain. A nasty scar curved out from above his upper lip and across his left eye, which was as white as milk. Adelaide shuddered as his gaze briefly passed over her, lingering just long enough to thoroughly look her up and down. Huglund placed his hand on the man's shoulder.

"Kobal; assist Miltock and the portly dip with their task."

The one eyed rider barred his teeth and bobbed his head repeatedly before hurrying away.

"Now," Huglund announced, turning back toward the crowd. "While my men assist your gargantuan official in hanging up the announcement, perhaps we could have someone read our progress into the investigation so far."

Several hands jerked up from the crowd.

"No. On second thought, perhaps one of my men would suit the task better." With that, he beckoned over to a third rider, who had been staring blankly at the tables still piled with food before him. It seemed as if he was trying to remember something from long ago forgotten. A loud growl from Huglund snapped him out of it.

"Read our progress, Ptolemi."

The Tibris Guard cringed in agony at the sound of his name and nodded. Huglund drew a second document from his belt and handed it over. The crowd stood in eager anticipation as Ptolemi cleared his throat and began to speak. His voice was joyless and wretchedly bleak.

"A census has been taken, in good measure, of all the many citizens in Amber, the wealthiest and most profitable province in Sanctumsea. I have, here, a short list of names of Red Handed citizens taken from that census that reside in Havendale. Though there is great unease in the heart of your ruler, Lord Tiberion, no act of treason can be dismissed. Therefore, for actions unexcused and punishable by the highest degree, this list of names, picked through careful and dedicated assortment, contains individuals who pose an immediate or future threat to our fine land's safety. They have been judged fairly for their actions, and will be subject to the full extent of his Lordship's law. The only outcome, in all accounts, is...."

Here, Ptolemi stopped, his lower lip starting to quiver. Huglund gave another growl, prompting him to finish.

"...the only outcome, in all accounts, is execution."

CHAPTER FOUR

"Gable," Adelaide fearfully whispered. "Run back to the house. Don't wait for me or Ronan. Just go home and lock the door until we get there."

The crowd started to panic. Scattered murmuring turned into fearful pleas as several villagers started running towards Havendale. Huglund nodded to Ptolemi, who continued reading.

"The accused are as follows:

    1) Marius Pint
    2) Lazlo Darden
    3) Jo Rullenham
    4) Dakota Browning
    5) Raoul King Jr.
    6) Mimi Varrow
    7) Tripper Wetherby
    8) Horatio Hare
    9) Lila Cussler
    10) Ripoll Stern
    11) Alec Tarr
    12) Ely Blath
    13) Pepin Grimsby
    14) Clayton Hogg
    15) Humphrey Hoast
    16) Charity Dodger
    17) Otis Lundeberg

18) Augustus Moll
19) Luck Keeper

And lastly,

20) Adelaide Stokes.

Your fates have been sealed in the eyes of Sorra above and Necrya below. Resistance is nonproductive. Questions are ill advised. Kindly accept your fates in a calm and orderly fashion. We, the Tibris Guards of Amber, and Lord Tibris Tiberion, thank you for your cooperation."

Then several things happened at once. Gable, and a dozen other children, turned and fled down the hill towards the front gate. Huglund unsheathed a long, jagged sword from beneath his saddlebag and waved it above his head. The rest of the Tibris Guards, seeing this, began savagely attacking the frightened partygoers. A handful of villagers foolishly tried to stand their ground, armed with wooden chairs and blunt cutlery. One by one, they were roughly captured or horrifically slain.

The Feasting Hill was in complete chaos. People darted away in different directions. Their colorful clothes were muddied and torn as they slipped and stumbled over one another. Many fleeing citizens met their fates as they fell into the path of maddened horses, while others dropped to their knees pleading for mercy. Mayor Hare, still standing in front of the post with the scroll in his hand, turned to face Miltock and Kobal.

"I say, do either of you fine gentleman have a nail? I mean, I just...hey, wait a minute....wait a minute I say. What exactly is going on...."

The last thing Hare ever did in his life was weakly grunt as he stared up at the two Tibris Guards. Their crudely sharpened swords stuck out of the delightful mayor's oversized stomach. His eyes rolled back as he slumped over, crashing through a table of desserts before landing on the ground with a deafening thump.

Three more named suspects lay twitching on the ground: Luck Keeper, a respected cabbage farmer; Marius Pint, the eccentric village mortician; and Lazlo Darden, the aged gate-watchman. Almost everyone else on the list offered themselves up in hopeful surrender. One was Lila Cussler, a middle aged widow with two small children and a successful packaging business. A passing Tibris Guard ended her life with a sharp thrust of his sword. The remaining suspects, to their disparaging chagrin, were quickly dispatched where they stood. All the while, Huglund looked around the macabre spectacle and smiled.

A few lucky villagers had managed to flee into the Wallowing Woods. As they disappeared, a sharp whistle from Huglund brought several horse drawn cages down the road. The last one contained five feral, rabid canines, their mouths foaming with ferocious bloodlust. Each creature bashed its head repeatedly against the iron bars, while their howls sucked the very hope and dwindling courage from all who heard them.

"Kill everyone you find," Huglund coldly commanded, unbolting the door. "Show no mercy. Tear every man, woman and squirm to bits. Now go!"

The dogs nodded in clear acknowledgement, their nostrils flaring with the scent of petrified human flesh. With ravenous snarls they leapt from their imprisonment and vanished into the woods. Scattered cries of agony sounded from beyond the trees, confirming the dogs were more than capable in hunting their prey.

Adelaide covered her ears as she zigzagged away from the onslaught. Ducking a wide swipe of a Tibris Guard's blade, she fully turned her attention towards the front gate of Havendale. It couldn't have been more than a hundred yards, with nothing blocking her path. Hopeless cries for mercy echoed behind her as she sprinted forward, intent on reaching the gatehouse. Only then would she be truly safe.

Each gatekeeper of a village, city, or town, when selected, was given a safe-phrase. Under threat of attack, they were instructed to recite it into the Flammeau-11, an audio-activated machine, to seal off the boundaries. Once spoken, the phrase would release an invisible veil of impenetrable fire that shielded all entrances and exits from invading forces. Anyone who tried to break through would be instantly incinerated. This modest piece of equipment was one of the earliest methods of defense created by the four new ruling lords, and had remained one of the most effective in all of Sanctumsea.

Adelaide leapt across the gate threshold and hurried into the gatehouse. As she struggled to catch her breath, she allowed her eyes to scan the walls. They were all decorated with rough sketches of budding plants, blossoming trees, and gentle landscapes. She secretly marveled at Lazlo's work, wondering if there could have ever been a possible collaboration between the two of them on one of her future projects. A loud banging noise from the corner caught her attention. She turned to see a mahogany desk. On top of it was a microphone attached to a long cord that led to the dust covered Flammeau-11 propped against the back wall. Tripper Wetherby, Finn Wessel, and Ely Blath, a sullen man in his mid fifties, stood around it, arguing harshly.

"I think it's got something to do with grasshoppers! Lazlo likes grasshoppers," cried Tripper. He was a lanky, spectacled lad, almost a full year younger than Adelaide. His hair was short and crisp, and the pitch of his voice could shatter glass.

"Well then, one of you two needs to find Lazlo and ask him," blandly stated Finn. He was leaning against the edge of the table, clearly trying to keep his wobbly balance. Adelaide could smell the Honeydrop Wine on his breath from across the room.

"Lazlo Darden isn't speaking so well right now," croaked Blath. He had crooked, tobacco-stained teeth, and his nose curved downward like a bent factory hook. Adelaide counted only four fingers on his right hand.

"What about the rest of the people on that list?" Adelaide threw in. Her voice startled the three survivors. "Did anyone else make it through?"

Finn smiled, nearly toppling over as he turned to face her. "Hey there, you're Adrianne, right?"

Adelaide's attempt to correct him was frantically cut off by Tripper.

"Mimi Varrow was first into the woods...I think...yes, maybe. That Dakota Browning...the one with really blonde hair...yes, she was with her. I don't know about the rest. Those rotting horsemen had everyone surrounded by the time I could make a run for it!"

"Who are they, anyhow?" Ely growled. "They just rode into our party and start offing innocent people. All on account of some...some list that we've never even heard of before. Calling all those people Red Hands? Who the rot does something like that?"

"They said we'd been accused," continued Tripper, turning his attention back to the Flammeau-11. "Accused and condemned on the new lord's say-so."

"I didn't even know we had a new lord," chuckled Finn, failing to suppress a burp.

"Get a hold of yourself, Wessel," growled Blath.

"Oh, for rot's sake," Tripper cried, throwing his hands in the air. "I don't know what to do. The veil's not activating!"

"Fine," Blath muttered. He picked up a shovel from behind the door, grasping it menacingly. "If they come inside, we'll take them on."

"And how, exactly, do you plan to do that?" asked a voice behind Adelaide. All eyes turned to see Clayton Hogg standing nonchalantly in the doorway. "You might be able to put up a fight once the defenses are set."

"We haven't got the phrase," moaned Tripper, rocking back and forth with his head cradled in his hands. "They'll be here any second."

"The phrase?" Clayton asked. "Don't you know? It's the first line of that poem Adelaide wrote, about the warrior and the givie."

"Who?" asked Finn.

Adelaide turned to ask Clayton why her award winning poem was being used as a defense for Havendale. Before she could, he was back out the door and hurrying down the street. The sounds of pleading and struggling could be heard just outside the gate. It was only a matter of time before the Tibris Guards came charging into Havendale.

"Now, Stokes!" yelled Tripper, pushing himself away from the controls. "Perhaps now would be a good time!"

Quickly organized her thoughts, Adelaide walked over to Darden's desk. Taking a long deep breath, she grasped the microphone in her hand and pressed the blinking red button at the bottom of the handle.

"I went to the lake to cast myself in," she recited, "to become like my father, a finer example of what may yet pass. My name is Arcado, and I war against many to become great in the eyes of one."

As she finished the stanza, there was a loud humming sound and a strong smell of kerosene. Adelaide peered outside the door. The open gateway briefly turned blue as the defenses swiftly activated. The heat waves emulating from it dried her eyes before she quickly turned her head away. Finn gave a loud whoop, head locking Tripper as he danced around the room.

"Well done, missy," Blath chuckled.

"Thank you. Now I'm going home," Adelaide announced. "My little brother is waiting for me and I need to find the rest of my family."

"Alright, I'll check the other entrances," declared Tripper, jerking his head free before dashing out the door.

"Well done on that whole gate thing, Angela," Finn threw in, staggering towards her. "You're a pearly fine lady."

Adelaide, eager to correct him, bit her lip as he gave her a passionate kiss on the cheek before slapping her rump. She grinned ear to ear and darted away towards her house, bashfully blushing as she went.

The front door was open when she arrived. Adelaide rushed inside and glanced about. It seemed that she was the first one to arrive. She was about to call out Ronan's name before he suddenly bolted through the doorway, almost knocking her over. Hattie followed close behind him. She was out of breath and in a state of shock. Her hands were trembling violently and her face was sprinkled with drops of blood. Adelaide watched dumbfounded as her mother stumbled over to the nearest couch and sat down, her eyes darting from side to side. She reached up towards her face, dabbing the tips of her fingers as she began to hum an eerie tune.

"Ronan, relax!" Adelaide exclaimed, turning her attention back to her brother. "It's alright, we're safe now. The defenses are up. I activated them. We're safe."

"Where's Gable?" he shouted.

"I'm here," cried a muffled voice. Gable's head popped up out of a laundry basket set up next to the kitchen door. A towel and a pair of nylons hung draped across his face.

"Are we safe now, Addy?" he asked.

Ronan ran up, cursing under his breath and roughly yanked Gable out of the basket.

"No, we aren't. Those rotting Tibris Guards made it through the defenses."

"Wait…..what?" Adelaide cried. Her stomach felt queasy. "How is that possible?"

"Three minutes after the veil was activated, a handful of them charged in. The second their horses hit the wall they were instantly vaporized. But not their riders, oh no, they were just fine. Got right up off the ground and started detaining anyone they could find. After that, the rest of them dismounted outside and just…just walked right on through the gate. The whole village is crawling with them. They're knocking down rotting door after rotting door, looking for survivors and killing anyone who resists."

"Cut them down, cut them down," Hattie murmured. A peculiar, goofy grin leaked onto her face as she rocked back and forth and started to cackle and blink uncontrollably.

"Addy, what's wrong with Mom?" Gable asked nervously.

"Just ignore her. I don't understand, Ronan. How..."

"I don't know either. It was like there wasn't any fire there to hurt them. I would have assumed the defenses were down if those horses hadn't puffed away right up in front of me. Now here, take this. You're going to need it."

Ronan returned to the living room, handing Adelaide a bag he'd packed in the kitchen. She took a look inside.

"This won't be enough supplies for all four of us."

"That's because it's for only one."

Adelaide gave him a horrified look and shook her head.

"No," she cried. "I won't leave you all to be killed off like Hare and Lazlo."

"Hare and Lazlo were on the list. So was Ely Blath."

"Yeah, but I....Blath is dead? I just saw him."

Hattie squealed behind them, rambling off random numbers and slapping her palm against the side of her face. Gable rushed over to her, grasping for her hand with salty tears brimming in his eyes. Adelaide ignored all this as she repetitively shook her head at Ronan.

"Don't worry about us, Addy," declared Ronan. "You take that bag and get the rot out of Havendale. Head for the east exit, disarm the defenses and slip away. The Wallowing Woods are vast and it'll take them weeks to cover it all. You can avoid detection and stay ahead of them until someone figures out what's going on."

"Just promise me you'll all stay alive," Adelaide pleaded. She gave him her most intense stare. "Promise me."

"You can be such an adult sometimes, Addy."

"Promise me now!" she yelled.

"Ok, I...."

A bright flash from outside cut him off. Adelaide screamed as the front door flew off its hinges, ripping through the wall as if being yanked by some invisible force. Gable dove back into the clothes bin as Captain Huglund entered, followed by Kobal, Ptolemi, and an unnamed Tibris Guard with a broken nose. Hattie Stokes stared up at them, her face now twisted in a peculiar grin and her teeth chattering loudly as her head started to bobble. She began waving her hand back and forth in a welcoming fashion, even standing up and briefly curtseying before falling back onto the couch. Huglund took one look at Adelaide before turning to Kobal.

"Kill her."

The Tibris Guard turned his one good eye on Adelaide. She looked in horror as his tongue poked out of his mouth like a snake, licking around the edge of his lips. He unsheathed his sword and advanced upon her. She had only a second to brace herself before Ronan shoved her towards the stairs, receiving the blow of Kobal's weapon on his left shoulder. He went down, his shirt soaking with blood. Hattie started laughing hysterically as she looked on.

"Find the young one," Huglund ordered Ptolemi.

"Leave them alone, you rotters! Fight me," Ronan groaned loudly, grabbing out at Kobal's wrists as he struggled to his feet. "You got....you got nothing."

"Ronan, no," Adelaide sobbed, stumbling backwards up towards her room.

Kobal struggled to break free from Ronan's grip. His feet were slipping in small puddles of blood accumulating beneath him but he kept his hold on the one eyed Guard. As Ptolemi successfully located Gable, the young boy let out a frightened cry. Ronan turned, breaking his focus just long enough for Kobal to push him back into a wall, knocking the air from his lungs. The Tibris Guard raised his blade and lunged forward.

The last thing Adelaide heard her brother say before Kobal decapitated him was: "Keep running, Addy. Stay alive."

CHAPTER FIVE

Adelaide retreated to her bedroom. Kobal and the unnamed Tibris Guard were close behind her. Clenching her eyes shut, she locked the door and leaned against it. She heard the nameless Guard curse angrily as he stumbled forward, and Kobal snickering behind him.

"*He must have tripped on the top step,*" she thought.

Ronan had always promised to fix it. Adelaide desperately tried to wipe her eyes dry on the shoulder of her jacket. The image of her brother's head toppling off his neck flashed repeatedly across her mind. Finally, she bent over, her stomach aching to release a deluge of vomit. Several seconds of painful dry heaving followed. A low, threatening growl informed her that Pallard was hiding under her bed. Adelaide shuddered as she heard Kobal slowly drag his fingernails down the other side of the door.

"Come out, little givie," he hissed. "Come out and play with us."

Straightening herself upright, Adelaide towards her bed and pulled Pallard out of his hiding place. She glanced about before putting him inside her closet. Maybe in there he wouldn't be a threat, and the Tibris Guards might leave him alone. She scrambled to locate her journal as Kobal continued his taunting.

"Please, please, pretty please open the door, tiny flower. Don't make me break it down. Break it down on your tiny, pretty head. Do you want that? Do you?"

Adelaide opened the bag Ronan had prepared in the kitchen. There was a sharpened, carving knife with a redwood handle, four fresh, green apples, a loaf of rye bread, and a thick slab of ham leftover from supper the night before. As she stuffed her book and a blanket in with the rest of the supplies, she hurried to the window. Her body shuddered uncontrollably as Kobal started hacking his way through the door. Bit by bit, his blade sliced through the wooden frames. Another few seconds and he'd be through. Adelaide took one last view of her bedroom before closing her eyes and leaping outside. A sharp pain shot up through her legs as her feet smacked down onto the ground. She stumbled forward, falling flat onto her stomach. Her knees and elbows scraped against the cobblestone street, causing her to whimper in pain. Years ago, in a moment like this, her father would have come running with a bag of ice and a shoulder to cry on. Those days, tragically, were forever gone. Adelaide lay there, unable to move, expecting to black out at any second.

"She's outside!" Kobal screeched from above. "The givie is trying to escape!"

Adelaide struggled to her feet. She managed to stand upright just as Ptolemi leapt through the open doorway, just a few feet away from her.

"You…think you can take me?" she groaned at him, clenching her fists and blinking away a tear. "I can still kick your rump, you murdering rot."

Ptolemi stared at her, his expression blank. It was the same way he had looked back up on the hill. His hand moved slowly to his sword-handle where it stayed. Seeing this, Adelaide inched her way backwards, trying to give some distance between her and the Tibris Guard. No matter what happened, she wouldn't be taken so easily, not without a fight.

Ptolemi's lips moved. No words came out; nothing but a low, ghostly moan, followed by a sharp shudder as he tightened his face. Whatever he wanted to say was causing him unfathomable pain. He stopped trying as the sound of Kobal crashing down the stairs resounded behind him. Staring intently at her, he cocked his head to the side, and jerked it violently. His message was clear: Run.

Adelaide hobbled off as quickly as she could. Her legs buckled and stung, and still she went. Limping along, she glanced back to see Ptolemi still standing there, his hand gripping tightly onto his sword handle. The expression of pain on his face was still noticeable, even as Kobal and his unnamed companion brushed past him to give chase. Thinking quickly, she ducked down an alleyway, stepping along until she found the side-door to one of the neighboring houses. She instantly smelled smoke as she hurried inside, slamming the door shut behind her and stumbling through what she interpreted as a well-kept laundry room. This had to have been Jo Rullenham's house. Jo and her fiancée, Garvey Brahl, had just moved into it less than a month before, a wedding gift from Garvey's parents. The wedding itself couldn't have been more than a few weeks away, but given the present circumstances, Adelaide couldn't recall. She turned abruptly into a hallway and tripped over what felt like someone's body. Struggling to her feet, she rushed towards what appeared to be the front door. Wisps of thin, grey smoke were carrying down the nearby stairs, followed by the hopeless screams of a young woman.

"Jo," Adelaide thought. She was trapped upstairs to die by some passing Guards. She had to help her before it was too late.

"Ha! Got you now, little givie," Kobal exclaimed, his face peering from the entrance of the laundry room. "Where will you hide now?"

Adelaide screamed, falling back against the door. She knew that it was only a matter of minutes before the fire upstairs consumed Jo Rullenham. She closed her eyes tightly together as she struggled with her conscience.

"*I....I can't,*" she thought. "*I can't.....leave her.*"

"Enough of this pitter patter," Kobal yelled, advancing swiftly upon her. "Come and join your brother in the bleak emptiness beyond."

With that, Adelaide reached for the door handle beside her and shoved it outward. She heard a loud crunch as it struck the face of the unnamed Tibris Guard on the other side, patiently awaiting her attempted escape. She didn't wait to see how badly she'd hurt him as she limped along down the cobblestoned road. Quickening her pace, she ran past several Tibris Guards who were too distracted pulling out struggling, screaming villagers from their homes to notice her. Nearly every building in Havendale was on fire, sparked off by unstable lorbs cast by Tibris Guards to drive out hiding survivors. The smoke rose up high into the air, blacking out the sun and coating the village in a bleak, shifting atmosphere. The one eyed Kobal and his companion appeared to have become lost in the commotion. Adelaide hopelessly pressed her palms to her ears in the hope of drowning out the chaos, but to no avail. The noise followed her as she stumbled along, narrowly avoiding colliding with Tibris Guards or tripping over the dead and wounded. She passed several more blocks of agony and terror before maneuvering her way down an alleyway and finally arriving at the east gate. It appeared deserted from what she could see.

Glancing outside the open gateway, Adelaide saw a hundred yards of untended field, mostly covered in wildflowers and neglected weeds. A couple hundred feet beyond that stood The Wallowing Woods. There were no Tibris Guards in sight.

She entered the gatehouse and picked up the microphone sitting on the desk. A distant cry briefly diverted her attention before she quickly spoke the poem-passage and waited for the humming sound of the Flammeau-11 to stop. With an afflicted sigh of anguish for Ronan and all the others who had died that day, she shouldered her bag and passed through the gateway. Hobbling along, she cleared the fields and finally entered the woods, leaving the sounds of death far behind her as she stumbled into the dark of nightfall. With no lorb to guide her, she found herself blindly rushing past sharp branches with thorns that poked, slashed, and prodded her from every direction. It seemed so different from when she was a child. With her father holding her hand, nothing had frightened her. Now there was nothing calming about the woods. Every tree, bush, and stone appeared nightmarish and deadly. It was as she ran through it all that Adelaide started to remember how her father's death had come about. It had been years ago, back when she was just around Gable's age. The family had taken a stroll to their favorite clearing at the edge of the woods to enjoy some of Hattie Stokes' gourmet sandwiches and homemade lemon cake. Once the meal had concluded, she had darted off to chase dancing butterflies. Sunbeams had penetrated the foliage above her head as she made her way deeper and deeper into the woods. Her mother's calls for her swift return had fallen on deaf ears as she laughed and skipped her way out of sight from the safety of the clearing. It was only when she nearly tripped over a log concealed by fallen leaves that she realized her blunder in wandering away. Growing nervous, she had hurriedly tried retracing her steps. It was at that moment, when all seemed lost, that she saw her father appear not ten paces away. He smiled and started walking towards her before a loud, cracking noise that stung Adelaide's eardrums shook the air. She saw her father stop, shudder, and slump to his knees, his hands clutching his chest. She had rushed over to where he knelt, reaching him just in time to see his eyes close and feel his final breath on her tear stained cheek. No one had come forward to confess to the horrible accident, and a thorough investigation had yielded little else. Since that tragic day, all firearms had been banned in Havendale, and many surrounding villages had done the same.

Adelaide had never given much credence to this action, since doing it had no ability to bring her father back. Ever since his death, she had done her best to move on, gradually going a day or two without bursting into tears. The view from her bedroom window just narrowly missed the village cemetery. She had to sit sideways on the window ledge to get a view. Sometimes she would sit for hours there, staring out at where her father lay buried. If only he had been around that day. She had no doubt he could have kept their family safe. All five of them would surely be together on the run, armed to the teeth and hauling enough food and drink to last a month in hiding. Adelaide smiled at the thought before choking back a disparaging sob as the truth washed over her. Her father was dead and buried. Her mother was now a blubbering wink. Her little brother was dead or soon to be, and Ronan...oh Ronan.

Above the treetops, dark storm clouds were hastily forming. Her legs throbbed painfully and her feet felt swollen inside her shoes. Her mouth tasted like blood as her lips and face were constantly scraped and scratched by passing branches. There was neither path nor trail to lead her along. Only blind terror and the hope she didn't end up back on the hill or somewhere close to Havendale.

A loud crack of thunder sounded high above her head. In her growing delirium, Adelaide couldn't help but let her mind wander. She considered how the approaching storm might have affected things if Huglund and his Tibris Guards had never shown up. Perhaps Mayor Hare would have laughed his heartiest laugh, prompting Finn to tell some more jokes. Gable and his friends would have scurried along to the nearest table and sought shelter beneath it. Maybe Finn would have grabbed her hand and pulled her along to that old shack near the front gate, or further along to the abandoned barn down the road. Some place with just enough room for two people to stand close together, or maybe....maybe even lie down. A bolt of lightning might have struck Clayton Hogg just as he was finally submitted to Mimi

Varrow's eccentric seductions. Her brother, Ronan, would have danced with Jolene Ingram, and everyone on that rotting list of names would still be alive.

Then she tripped over something. It was crouched down directly in her path, and well concealed from sight until it was too late. Everything went silent as her head struck the ground. Darkness consumed her as she slipped away into unconsciousness.

CHAPTER SIX

Nightmares plagued Adelaide's mind. She found herself drifting high above people from Havendale being slowly tortured and killed, all together in one great bloodbath. Struggled to close her eyes, she found them pulled open by some invisible force. Out of the corner of her eye she could see Ronan. She could make out his bloody, shuddering form bending beneath a glistening blade, held in the hands of none other than the dead-eyed Kobal. He was grinning maliciously, rubbing the edge of the blade aggressively against the raw skin of Ronan's neck, hissing and spitting down on his face. As he raised the sword to strike, he suddenly jerked up his head towards her. Though she felt invisible to his gaze, she still could feel his cold, murderous, solitary eye focusing on where she was floating. She saw his teeth start to crumble in his mouth as he spit and sputtered.

"This is on you, lovely givie. Cringe under the scourging glare of Necrya. Be cast with all the little squirms screaming, all the pretty women weeping, all the fiery men fleeing. Be alone now, without hope, and see your brother die slow."

"No...." Adelaide whimpered. Her voice sounded small and muffled, like she was speaking into a pillow. "No, Ronan. I...I didn't mean to....you promised. Please....Oh please."

The image of Kobal's sword slicing down jerked her back awake. A layer of cold sweat covered her face and a freshly made tear started to fall warmly down her cheek. The rain had stopped above her head and everything around her seemed freshly illuminated.

"*It must be morning,*" she thought. The sky was still grey from the night's storm. Dark, scattered clouds floated overhead. Stray drops of water fell from the tips of the branches and leaves, some landing on or around her. There was a certain magic in it all, not that Adelaide knew much about the magic of Sanctumsea. Her educator, Miss Imelda Barnum, had taught them all about the four castaways, sunweed, the distribution of land into four provinces, and how the discovery of lorbs had greatly simplified living. When it came to issues of other magic and the ability to wield it, however, Miss Barnum had skipped a chapter or two. Then again, perhaps there had been no chapter to skip. In the remote regions of Sanctumsea, where towns and villages like Havendale existed, people brave enough to study such items were difficult to find. The abundant lorbs provided all necessary functions to those who handle them. Those who mined them seemed rarely interested in the radiant qualities they possessed. At the end of the day, each unique sphere performed its duty without fail, and for the people of Sanctumsea, that was enough. The only person who had ever been intrigued by seemingly magical fossils of Sanctumsea before The Swelling was Adelaide's own hero, Jonah Longstreet. His stories were always full of such things, inspiring the imagination and creating debatable thoughts for his readers. He demanded curiosity without apology and seemed intent on educating those who turned his pages with more fantastical ideas than how to farm produce or hem clothing. Any myth or legend concerning Sanctumsea had been successfully woven into his tales. Adelaide found herself wondering just how much Longstreet could have truly known about the time before the rising of their land, and where his information came from. Its fictional background only enticed her more as she debated the odds of how much of it was real and what parts might be purely made up. If only she could meet him…just once.

As Adelaide pondered all this, a sharp, shrill whistle sounded in the distance. It was immediately followed by a fevered bark and the sound of something with four legs running swiftly towards her. She winced as she pictured one of Huglund's savage dogs bounding in her direction, intent on ripping her to pieces. Reaching into her knapsack lying beside her, she withdrew the sharpened kitchen knife, grasping the handle tightly. The mangy beast wouldn't take her easily. Not without a fight. She pulled herself upright and raised the blade in anticipation. A few more seconds and the vicious animal would be in sight. Adelaide took a deep breath and thought about everyone in Havendale she had ever loved, and how she would be with them soon.

Suddenly, a loud yelp from where the creature would have been drew her attention. A sickening whimper and a loud gurgling noise immediately followed. Then, all grew silent. Puzzled, she slowly crawled towards where the snarling had stopped and peered through a raspberry bush blocking her view.

Five yards away, hanging from a long strand of wire, were the mangled remains of the savage canine. Its head had been crushed in some sort of homemade wooden vise. Its eyes bulged from its sockets, and its neck was almost completely twisted around. The snare, though crudely made, was clearly effective. The animal had died instantly.

"Ah. Like my trap, do you?" a friendly voice asked.

Adelaide swung around.

Clayton Hogg stood before her. His hair was disheveled and his party clothes were crusted with mud. In one hand he held a satchel brimming with supplies, and in the other he clutched a hand carved wooden mallet from one of Havendale's tool shops.

"Easy there," he chuckled, taking a step back. "I didn't mean to startle you."

"Well, I..." Adelaide started, trying to seem nonchalance. "I thought you were a Tibris Guard."

Clayton smiled broadly and started sorting through her bag.

"Wow, you didn't really plan this out, did you? Some bread and fruit? That wouldn't last you two days out here."

"My brother made that for me," Adelaide snapped. "Right before he was killed by a Tibris Guard."

Clayton, clearly apologetic, cleared his throat and changed the conversation.

"Oh...well, you know I doubt you would have made it much further if you hadn't bumped your head last night. Lucky thing I found you when I did."

"You used me as bait, you rotting dip," Adelaide snorted angrily.

"I did do that, I confess, but from what I can see it worked perfectly. One less beast hunting us down, wouldn't you agree? Also, you need a better weapon. That knife of yours will cut skin alright. Put it up against a Tibris Guard's armor, and you're going to need a little more power to strike your killing blow. That weapon can slice butter well enough, but it can't penetrate Firetongue scales."

He grinned at Adelaide's puzzled expression.

"Firetongues: big, bad rotters out of Lumos Island on the western side of Sanctumsea. You've heard the stories, I'm sure. Two hundred foot long carnivorous worms with bodies as wide as tree trunks. They shoot flammable venom through fangs protruding from the tips of their tongues. Stand close enough to one and you'll wind up deep fried with a side of barbeque. Their scales are thick and protect them from various means of harm. I think that's why those Tibris Guards walked straight through our defenses without flinching. They found a way to turn Firetongue scales into a suit of armor."

"Well, how exactly are we supposed to kill them then?" Adelaide snidely asked. "Maybe you could try milking a Firetongue's fangs and see how that goes."

Clayton smiled at her blatant sarcasm.

"And how the rot did you even escape from Havendale?" she pressed on.

"I took one of the side gates, same as you. When I realized the Tibris Guards were inside the village, I filled up some bags with as much food and camping supplies as I could carry. Some years back, my old man told me about an abandoned well a few miles into the woods. Along the way there, I discovered some scattered dog tracks. In fact, I was investigating them when you tripped over me and knocked yourself out last night. Once I made sure you were still breathing, I decided to lure one of the mongrels in close enough to snare it. As you could see," he beckoned to the carcass hanging from the trap, "I succeeded quite well."

"You still used me as bait," Adelaide begrudgingly reminded him. "Besides, there are still four of those things left out there."

"Not quite. I came across one with its brains bashed in last night. Figure it was Mimi Varrow who'd done it, on account of a bloody earring I saw lying nearby. I guess the dog tried lunging for her throat and got a piece of her ear instead. At least she's still alive, probably still running with Dakota Browning. I saw them head off into the woods before I reached the gatehouse."

"How could this even happen? We've been accused of crimes and labeled Red Hands! What crimes could possibly warrant immediate annihilation? It makes no sense."

"Look, if we want answers, then this Lord Tiberion would be the one to have them."

Adelaide groaned and threw up her hands.

"Fine," she declared. "Let's go ask him."

Clayton laughed and shook his head.

"Look," he told her. "I understand your anger and want for vengeance, but this won't be easy. All I managed to scrounge together in the tunnel were a few blankets, some food rations, and a wooden mallet. All you have is a butter knife and a snack. I just don't want the possibility of you or both of us dying before we figure this thing out. Surely, someone could provide you safety until I return. And when I do, I intend on bringing Tibris Tiberion along by his nose hairs, if need be, to witness his unjustified misdeeds. But I plan to do it alone without hindrance."

Adelaide scoffed and took a step towards him, their eyes locked in a powerful stare.

"If you plan to make your way to Reignfall to confront Tiberion," she boldly stated, "then you will have me in your company. That is all there is to it. Though my family rests in Sorra's bosom, I will see every Tibris Guard in Amber suckle the teats of Necrya! Don't you even think about trying to stop me."

Clayton smiled.

"Well...I guess I underestimated you, Stokes. I expect a few extra hands might even come in handy. Who knows, there might be some other survivors waiting at the old well."

"Well then, let's be off," Adelaide exclaimed, shouldering her knapsack. As she did, Clayton reached into his pocket and pulled forth a freshly folded handkerchief. She eyed him curiously as he handed it to her. It was at that moment that she realized she still was crying. Not loud blubbering like her mother did when craving attention, but a gentle stream of tears progressing since she'd awoken after the storm. She hastily dabbed her face and desperately tried to put recent events out of her mind. She could still hear the screams of terror and agony, see the lifeless forms sprawled out along the streets, and smell the fire and ash as her village had burned. Adelaide's eyes brimmed, again, as she remembered Ronan's fall and reminisced about her winked mother. And what had happened to Gable? Poor, terrified Gable. He was so young. The chances of him being alive seemed so miniscule. She jumped as Clayton's hand gently touched her arm. His fingers gave her goose bumps, causing a warm, glowing sensation to spread throughout her entire body. It was a wholesome feeling of trust, something even Finn had never made her feel.

"Miss Stokes...Adelaide, I lost my dad a long time ago. Never had brothers or sisters, and really never knew my mother. But if I had and they were taken from me, I don't know what I would do. I give you my word...no, my most upright vow, that if there is the smallest chance your brother and mother are still alive, we will get them back. I swear on my life."

His voice was soothing and kind. Adelaide found herself almost smiling before abruptly pulling away from his touch. Another second and she feared she would have leapt into his arms for comfort. And it frightened her how tempting that sounded. She merely shrugged her shoulders and dried her face.

"My...my, uh, I....I don't think my mother will make it. She was winked when Huglund came to execute me. I don't think he even gave her a second glance."

"Winked or not," Clayton laughed. "We will do everything and anything we can for her. As for Gable, I wouldn't worry too much. I reckon he'll know how to keep safe until we can figure out what to do."

"How do you know?"

Clayton smiled and shrugged.

"No, wait. How could you possibly know for certain?" she asked more aggressively.

Clayton shrugged again, causing Adelaide to angrily grind her teeth. Without warning, she struck him roughly on the shoulder with her fist. Clayton winced in pain as a look of disbelief crossed his face.

"You wink!" she cried out. Her voice grew louder with every sentence. "How can you stay so calm after everything that has happened to us? What the rot is wrong with you? You can't know that Gable's alive! You rotting can't! My brothers are both gone. My winked mother is gone. Every rotting person in Havendale is gone. We are never getting them back, so stop wasting your breath trying to make me feel better by giving me fairy tales about rescue and getting payback against Tibris Guards. I don't believe you, and I won't be pulled into your foolish dream where everything is lorb-light and happiness. This is real. And the reality of this is we are both going to die, just like everyone else, and no one will shed a tear over our bones."

A horrible sickness seized her stomach as she finished her rant. She instantly wanted to fall to her knees and plead with Clayton that all she'd said was a lie. For her entire life, Adelaide had possessed the occasional outburst of anger that seemed impossible to control. While her mother had deemed it a worthless trait, her ever caring father had attributed it towards her artistic passion. In that moment, however, it did nothing but fill her with shame. She lowered her gaze, half-expected Clayton to leave her there, giving her exactly what she had just asked for. She certainly deserved it. Part of her didn't even care.

"Did you really mean that, Adelaide?"

No response.

"Well," Clayton went on. "As much as I realize I must pester you, with my calm demeanor and positive thinking, I can assure you it is taking all of my strength. I had no family to lose, but Havendale was my home too. If I don't stay optimistic and give in to despair, then I worry about what sort of rotting state I might find myself in. It's been a battle, you see, all my life, and I've worked hard to conquer it. I suppose if I did leave you here all by yourself, I would be riddled with guilt. I don't enjoy feeling guilty. You don't have to thank me, but you are coming along. Please understand no matter how hard you make the experience, I can and will endure it. Now, if I could please have my handkerchief back, we should probably start for the well."

CHAPTER SEVEN

The chilled morning air kissed Adelaide's skin as she and Clayton walked along. Both of them had been going for an hour without exchanging a single glance or word. The foliage grew thicker around them as the sunlight danced through the tree branches above. A passing chipmunk scurried across their path, pausing briefly to scrub its nose before darting out of sight. Freshly grown grass and old dried twigs littered the forest floor. The hungry calls of baby birds layered the hurried rush of their mother's wings. The entire world seemed to be waking up around them with a gentle ease. Adelaide's anger subsided enough to enjoy the lush atmosphere around her, and an awkward feeling of shame crept over her as she stared up at her companion several paces ahead. She wanted to apologize, but held her tongue as he stopped suddenly. Glancing about, his eyes rested on a nearby tree stump.

"We're close," Clayton finally announced. "That used to be a marker of mine when I came out here exploring. You can see my initials carved into the side of it."

"Exploring?" asked Adelaide. "You know it's against the law to be out here."

"Well, after everything my dad taught me, it seemed a waste not to. There wasn't a thing in all these woods Thatcher Hogg couldn't catch. He taught me how to set that trap this morning."

Adelaide nodded. She had never met Clayton's father, though rumors of his brawling nature had passed in everyday conversation. Her dad had been, to an extent, something of a friend to him, which her mother often criticized. It was one of the few things Adelaide and Hattie had actually agreed on. The idea that Bard, a respected citizen, could stand the company of a boozing womanizer like Thatcher, seemed impossible. The man's only success in life had been as Havendale's doctor, and even that hadn't always worked out well for him. As she pondered further, it suddenly dawned on Adelaide that Thatcher hadn't even bothered to attend Bard's funeral. She knit her brow and furiously informed Clayton.

"That is wretched, to be sure," he meekly replied. "I imagine, however, that he didn't know. My old man up and left some years ago without as much as a rotting goodbye. No one in Havendale took any notice, except your dad of course. The name Bard Stokes was a popular one in our household."

"He would never say a word in anger about anyone unless they deserved it," Adelaide stated proudly.

"I've heard nothing different," Clayton laughed. "You must be proud to be his daughter." Before Adelaide could thank him, he stopped in his tracks and pointed ahead. "Well, look at that," he laughed. "We have arrived."

A small clearing lay before them. Pure white rose-buds were dotted across the ground, still moist from the night's drenching torrents. Not a bush or tree was around to disrupt the seemingly perfect circle of natural utopia. Directly in the center stood the well, composed of gray bricks and mortar slowly being engulfed by green moss and twisting vines. A wooden bucket with rusty hinges lay overturned on its side nearby.

Leaning against the well, was Finn Wessel. His flowing hair was slicked back, revealing a nasty bruise across his scalp. The top three buttons of his shirt were missing, allowing a generous view of his glistening chest. It was in that instant, Adelaide found herself experiencing an inner hunger which only a wild animal could relate to. It was stronger than anything she had felt during the election ceremony, and certainly more intense than what had overcome her on the Feasting Hill. Her body jolted and shivered mercilessly as she succumbed to the pulsating impulse. Rudely shoving Clayton aside, she ran forward and leapt into Finn's arms. Without thinking, she placed a long smothering kiss on his lips, closing her eyes and squeezing her arms tightly around him as she did so. The inside of his mouth tasted of Honeydrop Beer and Tart Wine, but she didn't care. Clayton cleared his throat and turned away as she struggled to enclose her mouth entirely over his, sucking and pulling at his tongue in the process. Finn, though surprised, did not pull away.

"Oh, well isn't that just precious."

Adelaide would have known that glum, nasally voice anywhere. Raoul King Jr! She leapt back, half in embarrassment, half in surprise. Finn noticed her puzzled expression and laughed as Raoul rose to his feet from behind the well, roughly pressing multiple wrinkles out of his pants. His blue gloves were ripped in several places, revealing his hands to be even more pallid than the rest of his body.

"I found him sobbing like a squirm under some bushes," Finn remarked. "So I yanked him away before those Tibris Guards could hear his girly cries. I remembered Clayton saying something about this old well a while back and thought I'd come check it out."

"I wasn't crying," Raoul stated defensively. "I keep trying to tell you, I stubbed my…my toe on something sharp and….look, I was merely reacting to the pain."

"Ok, sure," Finn laughed harshly. "Blondie here claims he was going to follow the tree line all the way to the next village, only he didn't know what village that was, or how far it was to get there. So, I told him if he wanted to survive the night, he could follow me."

"Don't call me Blondie. And I didn't know we'd be having a givie along for company."

Finn quickly turned and gave him a rough shove. Raoul sneered and pushed him back. The pair began pacing around each other, with fists clenched and eyes locked. Before either could strike a blow, Adelaide jumped between them, throwing her hands up against their chests.

"Stop it!" she yelled. "Two days ago, the idea of two fellows fighting over me would have turned my squeezer raw, but right now I am not in the mood. Do you hear me? We have just lost everything and everyone we care about. They were taken by Tibris Tiberion, the rotting lord of Amber. Clayton and I are going to confront him right now and find out why we have been condemned as Red Hands. The two of you are welcome to join, but don't think for a second that I'll tolerate any outbursts of hormonal rage. Have I made myself perfectly clear?"

Finn grinned and nodded sheepishly. Raoul pursed his lips and glared intently at Adelaide. She returned his glare with one of her own.

"So," Finn chuckled. "How do you both plan to accomplish that?"

Adelaide looked to Clayton, who stepped forward.

"These woods are impossible to navigate, unless you've spent quite some time in them," he stoutly announced. "If Huglund is at all brainy, he'll understand that. So he'll move along the border, and wait for us to expose ourselves out in the open. If we can make our way through it all, and come out before Huglund reaches us, we can raise an alarm that awakens all of Sanctumsea. But we need to move soon and fast. Is anyone else armed?" He drew forth his mallet.

Raoul and Finn shook their heads. Adelaide held up her knife.

"Well I snatched more than just blankets and grub on my way out of Havendale," Clayton announced. He lay down his knapsack and drew forth a brand new single-bit hatchet with the price tag still stamped on the handle. Finn's eyes lit up as Clayton handed it over to him.

"What about me?" Raoul snapped.

"We could always use you as dog bait," chuckled Finn.

"I also nabbed this," Clayton said, offering Raoul a letter opener carved out of ivory. The edges were dull and the tip of the blade was worn down to a nub. Even with applied force, it would take several jabs for the item to draw blood. Raoul accepted it with an exacerbated sigh.

"Thanks a bunch. Now I can scratch our names into tombstones before we get ended."

"Maybe you can use some family shine to buy them off," Finn snorted. "Isn't that what your lot does?"

Raoul advanced once again with fists clenched. Adelaide stood before him, her face resolute. Her eyes told an unspoken tale of unpleasant consequences should he choose to defy her. He shuddered beneath her unwavering stare.

"Now," Clayton threw in. "If we stay alert, and take notice of every safe plant, berry, and passing creek, we might just make it. Anyone have any questions?"

The trio glanced at each other in growing discomfort, obviously unprepared to face whatever lay in front of them.

"Alright then," Clayton declared, shouldering his bag. "Let's get moving."

CHAPTER EIGHT

Clayton led the way, walking along with all the confidence he could muster. There was a slight touch of uncertainty in his face, which he hid well under a mask of determination. He glanced back occasionally at the rest of the group, beckoning them forward in hopeful spirits. It was clear to him that no matter what lay ahead of them, the last thing any of them could do was start to panic.

Adelaide trudged behind him. She felt exposed and intimidated as she moved through the untended vegetation. Every branch, leaf, and drop of dew gave her pause as she struggled to keep agonizing memories at bay. Ominous laughing bounded from behind every tree trunk. Eerie whispers darted in and out of her ears, chilling her through to the bones. She desperately clung to the dwindling hope that, unlike her mother, she hadn't gone completely winked.

Finn followed close behind. His gaze drifted from the back of Adelaide's neck, down to the small of her spine, and finally rested on the shape of her rump against the back of her dress. He gulped and swallowed intensely. Even then, walking along in fervent haste away from the maddening pandemonium behind them, his mind flickered sparingly from one lusty fantasy to another.

Raoul trailed several yards behind the group, grumbling and groaning with every pace. Occasionally, he reached down to the dampened earth and picked up a fallen acorn. A plotting smirk crossed his lips as he aimed the tiny missile directly at the back of Finn's head before ultimately chucking it lazily at nearby songbirds or a darting squirrel.

Every half hour, Clayton raised his hand to signal a short rest. The group would sit and rub the calices growing on the soles of their feet before again pressing on. Each resting period gave them all a chance to learn more about each other. More than once Adelaide's love of literature became a focusing issue. She ranted on about Jonah Longstreet, and always scoffed at her companions' lack of interest in him. Finn would humor her with flirtatious indifference, while Clayton humbly took her berating and insulting regarding lack of proper intelligence. Raoul stayed out of the conversation, contributing an occasional grunt or sarcastic sigh to get on Adelaide's nerves. She'd merely cast him another warning glance, and continue on.

"I love Longstreet's work," she proclaimed during one such break. "The man isn't afraid to go there, you know, and challenge the very history of our world. According to Jonah, there might very well have been a Sanctumsea before us. You know, like a fully inhabited land that had people, and magic, and a society that we could never understand. Then, obviously, something terrible happened. You know, like a natural catastrophe or consuming struggle amongst the natives, or whatever the case might have been. Ultimately, the whole land sunk beneath the surface and eventually was recalled by our founders, the Four Lords."

"What about the natives?" Clayton asked over his shoulder. "Does he mention what happened to them?"

"Not really," Adelaide replied. "I expect they were wiped out by the catastrophe or moved on to a better life. Whatever the case was, we have become the new inhabitants of Sanctumsea."

"Wouldn't that be something if it was true," Finn said with a sigh.

"Well, it is true," Adelaide laughed. "The way he describes it all is just so eloquent and clear. It's like he was there to witness it."

Raoul snorted loudly at her remark.

"Hey," Adelaide brashly declared, turning around to face him. "There has been sufficient evidence to support magical properties in Sanctumsea. Just look at our lifestyle now. What about using orbs with strange power inside to fuel our machines and light our homes? What about all the fast working medicine and peculiar inscriptions? I mean, for rotting out loud, this land exists because four ordinary men recited poetry chiseled into stone. You can't honestly believe it is all just a coincidence?"

"I believe in what I see and touch," Raoul declared. He reached down into his satchel and drew forth a pair of tiny red pebbles. "These…are TOX. You stick them in your mouth and suck until your senses dull. Then your jaw starts vibrating, and a cool sensation travels down your limbs. Your eyes pulsate, your ears itch, and every hair on your body stands rigid for hours. There's no magic here, I can promise you."

"You've had some all this time!" Adelaide exclaimed.

Clayton shook his head, and Finn spat in disgust.

"Don't judge me," Raoul laughed. "If Havendale's citizens hadn't partaken in our supply, we wouldn't have sold as much as we did."

"No one in Havendale would support your family," Adelaide yelled angrily. "You should be locked up just for carrying those!"

Raoul rubbed the tips of his pinkies against his chin, the rudest gesture one could perform in Sanctumsea. Finn nearly attacked him on the spot, but a humorous antidote from Clayton quickly calmed the situation. The group shouldered their supplies and moved on.

The daylight started to fade above their heads. The sky's bluish hue became overlapped with thin shades of crimson. The first of the evening stars started to peak out from the infinity above, just as the sun started creeping stealthily out of sight. Adelaide sighed at the progress they had made during their first day, and wondered when Clayton would announce his intention to set up camp. She jumped suddenly as she felt Finn's hand suddenly slip into hers. His fingers moved gently up and down her palm. She smiled broadly, hoping he didn't notice the deep blush growing in her cheeks. What did it mean? Was he just being flirty? Did he want something more? The thoughts of what that might be made her knees weak. She wished Clayton and Raoul could depart their company for just a short while, just long enough for him to show her.

Soon, the group came across a small clearing with enough fresh, green grass and open space to set up camp. The fading twilight provided a serene atmosphere. Eager fireflies danced between the tree branches while crickets and toads inhabiting a nearby brook announced themselves with unrelenting chirps and boisterous croaking. The group laid their blankets out in a close circle and dug a shallow pit. After counting the lorb supply, Clayton decided that three lorbs would suffice for the first night. As they were dropped inside, each one emitted a bold, unwavering glow that illuminated the faces of everyone huddled around them. A hearty supper of corned beef hash and sliced carrots was shared from person to person along with generous sips of chilled creek water from Clayton's canteen. Though the food tasted of sealed packaging, a long day of trekking through the woods had rallied everyone's appetites beyond picky selection. As they ate, Clayton complimented the group on their covered ground. He estimated they would be out of the Wallowing Woods before long, and on their way to Reignfall.

"Do we even have a plan for when we get there?" Raoul asked grumpily. "I doubt they'll let us march right through the rotting front door."

"We'll find a way," Clayton assured him.

"How have they gotten away with it for so long?" Adelaide piped up. "Maybe it's a conspiracy. Something the four lords have secretly buried under a landslide of rumors and superstition. I wonder if there will be something about it in Jonah's next book."

Raoul shook his head with a sneer.

"Plug it, King," Adelaide retorted. "I'm telling you it's so familiar. Jonah has used eerie beings, secret motives, and runaway heroes in his work before. It's almost like he could see this coming. Maybe he even wrote some of his works to prepare us for what's to come."

"If that's the case, I'd love to sit down with the gentleman and divulge some truth," Clayton laughed. "Where does this wordsmith reside, anyhow?"

"No one knows," Adelaide admitted. "Not being seen by his greatest fans anywhere in Sanctumsea has only enhanced his reputation. His books and poems just appear out of nowhere. It's really quite something."

"Well, if we're going to change course to hunt down some invisible scribbler, then count me out," Raoul grunted.

"We're not changing anything," Clayton said. "The plan is to reach Reignfall and confront Lord Tiberion, and that is precisely what we are going to do."

"Well not without a good night's sleep we aren't," said Finn. His hand reached over to playfully massage Adelaide's shoulder.

Raoul grunted in disgust. Clayton smiled and suggested the group take turns keeping watch in case trouble should arise. He and Raoul stood first guard, while Adelaide and Finn rested before relieving them. The night passed on in uneventful ease.

Adelaide found herself nestling closer and closer to Finn, whose arms reached out in a dreaming state to pull her in. She didn't fight it, and sighed with open pleasure as she felt his hands clasp together across her trembling waist. The slight chill of the night air failed to hinder the growing warmth she felt exploding throughout her entire body. Until that spontaneous moment back at the well, she had never found herself so hungrily attracted to someone before. Never in a thousand years, could she picture being sought after by anyone as fit and reputable as Finn Wessel. However, as she felt his gentle breath strike the back of her neck, a craving for whatever feelings he might stir inside her eliminated any chances of getting sleep. Before she knew it, Clayton was politely rousing the pair of them to begin their shift. Rubbing the sleep from her eyes, Adelaide allowed her head to rest on the edge of Finn's shoulder as they sat comfortably beside the dancing lorb light. Time seemed to leap forward as the sun soon rose over the distant tree line and the group slowly roused themselves.

"Givies and winks," Raoul groggily groaned as he opened his eyes. "How could people ever sleep outside?"

"My joints feel like they're made of glass," Adelaide sighed. "I'd give a lasting plug to have my bed back."

"I'll certainly take you up on that, Abigail," Finn chuckled.

"Abigail?" Raoul inquired with a smirk. Adelaide shot him a cold glance.

The group settled down as Clayton quickly prepared a modest breakfast of rye bread and some assorted fruit. After they had eaten, the pit was refilled with dirt and the supplies packed away.

Raoul sat on a nearby boulder, casting acorns at chattering squirrels while Clayton and Finn cleaned up the campsite. Adelaide wrote away into her journal, desperately trying to distract herself from the lingering memories of the horrors she'd witnessed back in Havendale. Several unchecked tears fell onto the pages, blurring multiple sentences. Finally giving up, she roughly wiped her eyes and slammed the journal closed.

According to Clayton, the only way around the outside of the Wallowing Woods was an old country road which bended and turned without proper maintenance. There were a dozen dilapidated bridges and steep chasms which would add several days to anyone's journey, even Huglund and his riders. With that in mind, the group could edge slightly northward from their current location, taking random trails blazed before the founding of Havendale until they exited the woods with time to spare. Once they had done so, it was only a question of finding the quickest and safest way to reach Reignfall before their pursuers managed to overtake them.

As they pressed onward, Raoul began speaking more openly with his companions. Not a single word out of his mouth, however, was pleasant to hear. Following breakfast, he immediately started ranting about poor etiquette within Havendale. Not a single villager was left untainted, nor a single establishment skipped over. The line at the bakery had always been too long, the barber's scissors too dull, and the law passed against givies was utterly absurd. It became apparent that the wealthy heir didn't have a single compliment to share about anyone. In between hurtful comments, he managed to uncover some forbidden trinket from Memoriam hidden on his person. They were exceedingly rare, usually too expensive for everyday folk to purchase. This only fueled his criticisms concerning individuals and establishments less fortunate than his family and their abundant enterprises.

Clayton, Adelaide and Finn gradually grew accustomed to his rants, and even found them somewhat entertaining. It gave them ease to reflect and debate on ways of life before the Tibris Guards came. It was almost as if everything they knew was patiently awaiting their return.

The sun burned brightly above their heads as the group trudged along. Although spring was still in its infancy, the day proved to be unconventionally humid. As a result, Finn and Raoul exchanged harsher words than usual, and twice as often. Clayton's canteen emptied before lunch, with no creeks or ponds anywhere in sight. Even the wildlife around them seemed to lose its breath. Birds stopped chirping. Rabbits and squirrels retired to shady sanctuaries. The air itself grew heavy with moisture, and caused many beads of sweat to roll down the cheeks and foreheads of the four walking travelers.

Adelaide wiped her brow profusely with both hands, desperately attempting to maintain the look a lady of Havendale would strive for. She felt grimy and odorous, still wearing the same clothes from Wintersbane, and without access to cleaning supplies or bathing salts. Her hair grew frizzy and mangled as the day progressed, giving her the unrelenting desire to duck out of sight and wallow in self-consciousness. It was only when she witnessed Finn candidly removing his shirt just ahead that her image concerns flittered away. He had done it merely to avoid heatstroke, without realizing the blossoming urges his action placed inside Adelaide. She licked her lips, as those ever passionate fantasies involving the pair of them crossed her mind again and again. It was all she could do to contain herself. In that moment, whether her desire for Finn was love, pure as cotton, or savage, animalistic, fleshly hunger, she didn't care. Something had to be done, and as soon as possible.

"Say, Clayton," she remarked, trying desperately to sound nonchalant. "Wouldn't it be a fine idea to send someone out in search of a fresh water supply? Maybe there's some just up ahead."

"A mighty fine idea, Adelaide," he replied, smiling. "I suppose I could check it out."

"Excellent! I'm sure Raoul here would be happy to go with you."

"Like rot I would," Raoul grumbled indignantly. His opinion quickly changed as he quelled under Adelaide's icy stare "Then again…maybe a walk would do me some good. My feet can't get much more bruised up, now can they?"

"You'll live," Clayton laughed. "Come on. I could use the company."

"Good luck, you two," Adelaide called out as the pair walked away. "We'll keep guard while you're gone."

The sounds of their footsteps grew faint before she turned to Finn with the most seductive smile she could muster. She felt naughty and exposed as his eyes moved up and down her trembling form. With a burst of passionate energy, Adelaide took a step forward and locked her hands behind his neck. Finn didn't pull away. He tilted his head, ever so slightly, before connecting his lips to hers. She actively ignored the fact that his saliva still tasted of various intoxicated beverages as she gave herself entirely up to the heat of the moment.

The two of them were quickly on the ground. They rolled about passionately from one blanket to the next. Their lips pressed and locked repeatedly as Adelaide groped his arms and pulled him closer against her. Finn caressed her neck and shoulders while gently moaning out every name that started with the letter A except for hers. Though she found his noises unnecessary and his patterns awkward, Adelaide beamed and blushed at the realization that her fantasies were at last coming true. She felt herself tremble as his fingers intensely latched onto the hem of her dress. Before he could proceed further, a loud snapping noise sounded from behind some nearby bushes.

Adelaide glanced about suspiciously.

"What's wrong, Antoinette?" Finn whispered.

"Did you...did you hear that? I thought I heard something."

"It's probably just Blondie catching a peek. Haven't you ever had someone watch?"

Adelaide scoffed and shoved him back before sitting herself upright and straining her ear.

"I'm serious Finn, I think I heard..."

Her sentence was cut short. Three of Huglund's dogs, their eyes as black as coal, leapt from behind the bushes. Two placed their paws on Adelaide's back, holding her down, while the third circled Finn, who started swinging his hatchet wildly from side to side. Reaching down for her knife, Adelaide realized she had left it tucked away inside her knapsack several feet away. Any attempt to grab for it could result in her losing her hand.

She gasped as the third dog managed to dodge a swipe of Finn's axe before leaping at his throat. Its jaws were open and spit spewed from its gums as it flew. Finn pulled his weapon back just in time. The dull edge of the blade caught the brute on the side of its face. The animal grunted and collapsed to the ground, his legs twitching wildly and his eyes rolling back. Finn brought the hatchet down one more time, smashing its skull with a sickening thump.

Seeing this, the dog nearest Adelaide's ear pushed her head firmly into the ground with its paw while placing its jaws on the back of her neck. Finn understood its message clearly.

"Finn," Adelaide hissed through clenched teeth. "Don't you drop that axe. If you do, we're dead. They'll kill us both."

"Don't you fret, Addison," Finn told her, his hand shaking as he slowly began to lower the weapon. "Just trust me."

"Finn," she cried out. Her voice was muffled with dirt. "Don't you let go of that axe. Don't even think about it!"

Once again, the dog growled in her ear. The second dog arched its back, fur bristling in the breeze. Leaning back onto its hind legs, it prepared to jump. The first dog kept its jaws locked on Adelaide's neck, waiting for Finn to make his move.

"Well," a voice behind them said, "what have we got going on here?"

The animals turned abruptly to see Clayton standing behind them. Raoul walked up beside him, a sharp walking stick brandished menacingly in both hands. The second dog snarled and leapt toward them. Clayton stepped aside as Raoul thrust out his newly found weapon. The tip pierced the brute's hide underneath its left leg, cleaving its heart in two. The dog fell, its chest caving in and lungs closing up before it reached the ground.

The remaining creature loosened its grasp on Adelaide as it witnessed the death of its companion. She took the opportunity to place her palms squarely on the earth and push upward. The beast yelped as it flew onto its back. Regaining posture, it stared at Clayton with barred teeth. Then it redirected its attention to Adelaide. Its eyes grew dark as it balanced itself, staring coldly towards her. Suddenly, it pounced.

Adelaide couldn't back away. She stood paralyzed as certain death flew towards her. The last thing she saw before blacking out was Clayton's mallet smashing into the creature's jaw. She heard a sickening crunch before her vision grew blurry and she fell to the ground.

Kobal returned to her dreams. His dead eye stared towards her as he butchered Ronan and all the citizens of Havendale a second time. All the while, she was forced to stand there watching, her body trapped in invisible strains floating above them. Unable to cry out, unable to leave, she continued to watch her family and friends be murdered again and again before her.

"Adelaide..." a faint, yet looming voice hovered over the blackness.

She wanted to answer, but found herself choking on her own words. Kobal smiled as he beckoned to yet another figure kneeling beneath him as he raised his sword once again.

"Adelaide," the voice repeated, this time more clearly. "Wake up!"

A loud boom resounded overhead. The blackness vanished and suddenly a stinging sensation struck her nose.

"Told you this would bring her around," said Raoul as he removed the TOX pellet from beneath her nose.

Clayton sat beside her, his hand pressing a cold, damp cloth to her forehead.

"We were worried you were done for good," he informed her.

"Finn," she groaned weakly. "Where's Finn?"

"Of course, we save her life and she wants that rotter," Raoul muttered.

"He's out collecting more aqua," Clayton informed her. "He wanted to make sure you had plenty when you came to. We found a creek not too far ahead. Once you're rested, we'll head there together. If we're lucky, we will make it to the edge of the woods by sunset. Then it's off to Reignfall for a word or two with the Lord Tibris Tiberion. But for now, just rest. Sorra knows you need it."

Adelaide nodded and closed her eyes. She desperately hoped that for just once since the attack on Havendale, she would be able to slumber in tranquility. Her hopes were unfortunately dashed as woeful horrors plagued her mind once more.

CHAPTER NINE

At Clayton's request, Adelaide made her way to the fresh water supply shortly after rising from her nap. She heaved an uneasy sigh as her three companions urged her onward, remaining out of sight to give her some small amount of privacy. The gentle current babbled along, carrying fallen leaves towards an undisclosed location, far away from the security of their arborous masters. Rays of sunlight bounced off the dancing ripples, reflecting themselves against the surrounding tree trunks and slippery moss-covered stones.

Weak as she was, Adelaide managed to remove her dampened, stained party dress. The gentle current caressed her exposed flesh as she submerged herself into the cool, refreshing water. Melodious songbirds fluttered from tree branch to tree branch as she scrubbed the dirt and grime off of her arms and shoulders. Shapely clouds drifted casually above as she dipped her head backwards, letting the grease wash away from her hair. In that serene moment, Adelaide found herself succumbing to the light touches of hope. Fleeting as they were, she allowed them to consume her body, slipping unchecked into her emotionally raw psyche. After what felt like an eternity, but couldn't have been more than a few minutes, she dunked her entire head underwater before returning to dry land to redress. She turned, one last time, to witness the perfect beauty surrounding her. If only they could all have stayed there, where mayhem and suffering seemed nonexistent. Adelaide shook her head as she permitted the harsh reality of her situation to resurface. She called out to her companions to rejoin her, and soon the group was on its way.

The scenery around them soon started to change. The shrubs and trees lessened in density, and the animal wildlife became more abundant and braver in revealing themselves. Various woodland creatures popped their heads out of holes and from behind tree trunks. The sharp chattering of squirrels up on the branches above them, quarreling over nuts and other assorted foods became frequent, and every now and then a bird's song could be heard from the top of a branch.

Even with her moment of ease back at the creek still fresh in her mind, Adelaide again found herself submitting to inner fears. The earlier attack, combined with the lingering effects of the nightmare that followed, had left her entirely vulnerable. Each snap of a twig made her jump. Every gust of wind made her shudder. Her companions faded to mere shadows dancing along beside her as the world started to shrink dimly away. She struggled to rationalize her thoughts as they darted from one side of her mind to the next. Time enveloped her as every step she took seemed to resound throughout the woods. Quietly, she whispered each pace until the numbers reached the hundreds. Now and then she shook her head, as if all the thoughts and memories she contained inside were pieces of a complicated puzzle, just waiting to be put together. Her skin felt cold as bouts of ringing noises struck her ears. She found herself oddly smiling, much like her mother had done back In Havendale. This caused her to cringe and blink her eyes before muttering out an incomprehensible stanza. It was almost agonizing to feel Finn's hand suddenly touch her shoulder and release her from the trance.

"Ariadne," he whispered. "Look. We're here."

They had finally reached the edge of the woods. A rough, country road stood before them, stretching along from east to west. Beyond that, as far as the eye could see, were rows and rows of corn stalks.

"Well," Finn said, rubbing the back of his neck uncomfortably. "What now?"

"No Tibris Guards in sight," Adelaide stated.

"We don't know what's out there," Raoul muttered. "They could be waiting for us."

"Whatever is out there," declared Clayton, "we will find out tomorrow. The sun's almost down and I don't intend on striking out into the farmlands under nightfall. The stories you hear about those seeders and what they do to lost travelers makes my skin crawl. We stay put till morning."

The group agreed and they retreated back into the woods to make camp. Clayton prepared a second pit and tossed three more lorbs into its center. Finn helped Adelaide organize dinner while Raoul surprised everyone by laying out some blankets. The conversation stayed light that evening. Plates of cold bacon and homegrown tomatoes from Havendale's public garden were passed around and quickly devoured. Many darkening thoughts and concerns weighed on the group's mind, preventing the break out of their normal lively debates. It wasn't until Raoul cleared his throat and rose to his feet that the night took an interesting turn.

"So," he began. "Do any of you know what feelings taste like?"

His remark was met with stares of confusion, so he continued on.

"You might consider me a rotting wink for tasting the occasional pellet of TOX. That being said, I have to say it will blow your rotting minds. Once all the side effects fade away, you get a chance to understand yourself a whole lot more than you could on any amount of Cinnamon Cider or Honeydrop Wine. I must also add that with all this, recent tragedy befalling us, it certainly helps to take the edge off. I cannot put it any simpler than that. Care for a sample?"

With that, Raoul extended his hand, revealing three TOX pellets. Finn shook his head while Adelaide scoffed in distain. Clayton stared uneasily, stroking his chin in unmanageable curiosity.

"You are pathetic, Raoul," Adelaide snorted. "No one here is going to indulge in your little vice."

"I...uh...I doubt they'd even work on me," Clayton laughed hesitantly. "I am already quite content in all things."

Raoul smiled.

"Your first time is always the best," he assured them. "You'll wink out almost immediately. Sorra herself couldn't give you so much pleasure. I'd give anything to have my first taste again."

Clayton hesitated briefly before snatching it out of Raoul's hand.

"You rotting wink," said Adelaide, aghast. 'I don't believe you."

"What do you say, Stokes?" Raoul asked gingerly. That unnatural smirk was growing on his face again as he waved his hand from side to side.

Even as she shook her head, Adelaide could feel the painful sensations from earlier starting to return. She quickly thrust her hands behind her as they started to tremble.

"I can see you're a little on edge," Raoul chuckled. "Here. I promise this will help."

Adelaide cast a quick glance to Finn, who shook his head in defeat and held out his hand. Raoul tossed him one, which he dropped into his mouth with an indifferent sigh. Clayton was already easing back and casting his eyes towards the sky. Whatever the TOX was doing it seemed to be working quickly. Seeing this, Adelaide muttered something unintelligible and snatched the remaining pellet. Biting her lip and closing her eyes, she dropped it into her mouth.

CHAPTER TEN

The sky was littered with clusters of stars swirling around the emptiness within. It was a vast infinity without name or legend that reached into the very fabric of existence. As Clayton Hogg stared up into that formidable void, he sloppily wiped away the vomit from around the corners of his mouth and started to speak. His voice broke and his lips quivered. Whoever he believed he was talking to, it was clear he had no control over how devastated he felt.

"I see you...I...I can see you up there. Why are you hiding from me? You think I cared? I didn't then and I don't now. You left me. You abandoned your only son to...to go chase some winked theory about what makes Sanctumsea tick. What did...did it...did it get you? Where are you now? Did you find what you were looking for?"

"Hey," a voice behind him hissed. Finn was standing a few feet away, a blanket tied loosely around his waist. His face was clammy and glistened in the pale moonlight. "Clayton, Clayton, Clay...Pig...Hogs, Clay Pigs, I mean Clayton Hog-pig...your name is so rotting catchy. Listen, Piggy, we got to trod...yes, trod on. Blondie's magic beans only keep us invisible for so long. We need to go find Gobblegut, the king of the Thunder-giants, so they can give us protection against the rising Rainmakers. Are you listening to me? Mr. Pig? Mr. Hog-pig, you must listen to me. Hey, have you...you...you seen my blanket? I think some rotter snatched it."

Ignoring his rant, Clayton stepped cautiously away and walked back to camp. He could see Adelaide squatting over the glowing lorbs, her hands resting firmly on her knees. She was making various animal noises at Raoul, who sat beside her with his arms crossed and legs spread as widely as they could go.

"Hey King," she whispered seductively, after belting forth the mating call of some exotic bird. "Hey, come on, King. What do you want, huh? I can bark like a chicken. I can squeal like a cat. What does your royal plugger crave?"

Raoul looked up at her, licking his lips hungrily.

"Oh you want me to shed my skin like a Firetongue?" she laughed. "Flick my licker out at you? Wriggle my body free? You want to plug my rump till the sun comes up, don't you?"

Raoul nodded.

"Well come on then!" she exclaimed, throwing out her arms. "Show me what you can do."

The disagreeable heir lurched to his feet, only to lose his balance and slump back down. A low, grumbling snore passed through his lips as he rolled onto his side and coiled himself into a tightly coiled ball. His eyes, though glassy and cross-eyed, stayed open as he drifted away into a highly medicated sleep.

Adelaide threw her hair back, laughing melodiously. She turned towards Clayton as he approached her and addressed him in a poorly practiced accent.

"I knew he'd topple, the over invigorated dip. He wants me bad. Everyone wants me. Everyone...except you, of course. What's wrong with you, Clay? May I call you Clay? Ha, as if your opinion means anything to me. Close your rotting mouth. You think you're so mighty and stout, with your grand shoulders and noble pelvis...not that your pelvis crossed my mind. I think you might be making me say these things with your oblivious expressions, you rotting statue."

It was then that Adelaide noticed Clayton's gaze was focused on the three lorbs still glowing inside the shallow pit. He seemed thoroughly entranced by them and had completely missed her dialogue.

"They're so...bright, and illuminated," he murmured, more so to himself than to Adelaide. "We have no idea what makes them tick or how they even came to be. And yet we rely on them for so much. You know who was really curious about them was my father. Oh the way he went on about theories, legends and whispers from before the founding of the four provinces. The winked dip was convinced they possessed more qualities than we already knew. That's why he left, you know. To chase a couple raw leads fueled by obsession and untended paranoia. I haven't heard from him since."

"Lorbs is lorbs," Adelaide murmured, rolling her eyes. "Lorbs is lorbs is...is lorbs and lorbs is lorbs...well they just are."

"Miss Stokes, I think you might be wiser than your actions...oh my, excuse me...give you credit for."

Adelaide blushed. From Clayton, this was the closest thing to a compliment she had ever received.

"My mum...momma...mommy would disagree. Sorra above, she could be a pest...yes, a pest. She was always going on about me being more like a lady. As if she was any rotting better! I tell you, Clayton...I'll tell you...I'll...I have this glimpse of her when I was a small girl, sitting down to tea with Mr. Van...Arrow...Varrow. You remember him, I'm sure. Everyone started talking, and my dad defended her, but...but you know....Gable was born not...well he...never mind. I'm sure it was nothing."

"Of course," Clayton assured her. "I'm sure it was. Could you kindly keep an eye on Raoul there while I return Finn to our company?"

Adelaide burped loudly before giving him an exaggerated nod.

The search proved to be easier than expected. Clayton had barely set out into the woods before the sound of shameless whimpering rose from behind a nearby tree. Finn was slouched against the bark, his head in his hands and his eyes red with sorrow. It was the first time anyone had seen him cry.

"Finn, why don't you come back to camp? The group's missing you."

Finn choked back a laugh and shook his head. His hand slowly rose and pointed out towards a patch of ground some yards away. From what Clayton could see there was nothing there.

"Why doesn't somebody help him?"

"Help who, Finn? What do you see?"

"He's just laying there….he is hurt. Won't someone make sure he's ok? I…can't do it myself. Then everyone will know my secret."

"Who are you talking about?" Clayton pressed.

With that, a low sigh escaped Finn's lips and he arched himself upright.

"I…I think Gobblegut isn't coming, Pigs. We'd better retire for the night."

"Are you sure you're alright?"

"Sorra above and Necrya below, I'm dandy. I'm...resolute. I just had a little itching of the mind, that's all. Come on, let's head back to camp."

With that he stumbled back towards the campsite, leaving Clayton to puzzle over his friend's strange hallucination.

CHAPTER ELEVEN

The next morning began awkwardly. Finn awoke to the image of Raoul's naked feet grazing his nostrils. Adelaide groaned in agony with her stomach in knots. Clayton struggled to his knees before toppling back onto his face. By the time everyone could sit upright without vomiting, the sun had already reached the center of the sky.

"So, that was TOX," Clayton remarked dryly. His bones felt brittle and there was a disdainful taste of chalk in his mouth.

"I think I'll do without a second serving," Adelaide whispered, cradling her head in her hands.

"Oh you dips can't handle a little lawbreaking now and then," Raoul sneered. "Some Red Hands you are."

A moment of silence passed. The group shared glanced with one another before Clayton suddenly broke out laughing. Raoul joined him, soon followed by Adelaide and Finn.

"Aye," Clayton exclaimed, rocking from side to side. "A bunch of rotting troublemakers, we are. No wonder we've been condemned to die."

"I don't know how we managed to hide it so well," Adelaide threw in humorously.

"A gang of givie-loving dips," Raoul croaked.

The erratic merriment commenced for a few seconds more until Adelaide finally forced herself to stand up and waddle clumsily out of sight. The sounds of gagging and light vomiting soon became audible. She was gone for only a moment before swiftly returning to the camp. There was something small clasped in her hands as she walked. A closer look from the group confirmed it to be a locket. Small, worn, and second rate, it appeared to have been left outside for quite some time. Inside it was a rough carving of a young man's face. Scratched beneath the image were the words, *"From Hollis"*.

"It's been here for at least a week," Clayton said, examining the item. "Maybe dropped in haste by someone on the run."

"Whoever it belonged to left tracks," Adelaide stated, pointing ahead. Scattered footsteps had disturbed the untouched soil. Unlike hers, each footprint wove a tale of life threatened desperation, harshly imprinted by its maker.

"Where do you suppose they come from?" Adelaide continued.

"Only one way to find out," replied Clayton, stuffing the locket inside his pocket. "Let's clean up here and retrace them. Maybe there's shelter and better food up ahead."

The rest of the group, though skeptical, ultimately agreed. Their rations were dwindling, and the thought of resting their burdened heads on something softer than a coarse knapsack filled their minds with unyielding resolve.

Afternoon folded into evening as they packed up their supplies and made their way back into the woods. The sun, like a nosy neighbor slyly peaking over the top of a fence, lowered itself from sight. Darkness creeped steadily over the sky, exposing its twinkling stars like an army of hives consuming a nervous face. Adelaide, shivering, wondered how long it would be before Clayton decided to set up camp for the night. She ultimately decided to mention it to him. Before she could, however, her thoughts were interrupted by a pair of faint voices stemming from the growing darkness ahead. Adelaide unsheathed her knife. Raoul clasped his letter opener menacingly while Finn pulled out his hatchet. Clayton bade them all to crouch down as flickering lights appeared just up ahead.

The voices soon became clearer. One appeared to have a stutter.

"I'm t-t-t-telling you, P-Puck, that last c-c-critter we had was sp-sp-spectacular. Hunted him down and k-k-killed him myself. So all I'm saying is you c-c-c-ca-can't have my leftovers if you were t-t-too busy sleeping t-t-to help."

What the one called Puck said next was inaudible.

"N-n-now there's no c-c-c-call for that k-k-kind of language. You know there'll be p-p-plenty of more ca-ca-critters out there to c-catch."

"Wath is that to me, huh? I'm still hungry," replied Puck. His voice was painfully muffled, as if his jaw was swollen.

"What are they arguing about?" Adelaide asked, a little too loudly. Clayton's finger shot up to his lips.

"Hey," the stuttering man said. "D-d-did you hear that?"

"Sure did," Puck replied. "We'th got spies wathing us."

The group froze. No one dared to breathe.

"W-w-w- oh rot it, w-w-what d-do we d-d-do?" the stuttering man exclaimed.

"I'll tell you whath we do; we attath them by using the elelent of suprith!"

"Not if we attack you first," Raoul boldly yelled. He leapt from behind Clayton and darted into the bushes, swinging his blade side to side. There was a quick yelp, followed by a momentary struggle and the continuation of Puck's cursing.

"I g-g-got him," the stuttering man cried, his voice mixing with loud cries of pain from Raoul.

"Well hoth him down," Puck growled. "So I can beath him for hithing my fath!"

"Well?" Adelaide hissed. Clayton nodded and gave the sign to attack. All three jumped out into the open.

The stuttering man was not to be feared. He was five foot-two and couldn't have weighed more than a hundred pounds. The one called Puck, was slightly taller and more built. His jaw was wired with some homemade dental contraption and both his hands were cupped to his nose with a stream of blood dripping down his clenched fingers. Both the men were dressed in white slacks and white robes. Their hair was greasy and unkempt. Each of their faces was clean-shaven, and their postures were absolute. Raoul was trapped in a headlock, courtesy of the stuttering man. His weapon lay on the ground beside him. At seeing Clayton, the man immediately released Raoul, throwing up his hands in surrender. Puck took one look at the armed trio and toppled backwards, his hands still clasping his nose in muffled agony.

The sight of two grown men sitting on the ground, their arms waving in the air and their faces livid with fear, was too much to bear. Finn started chuckling while Clayton and Adelaide tried to quell the massive smiles growing on their faces. Raoul, however, was far from humored. Picking himself up, he began fumbling around in search of his letter opener.

"I'm going to slice your rotting throats," he hissed.

"Now, now, Raoul," Clayton said, grabbing his arm. "It was you that attacked them first, don't forget that."

"Yeah," Adelaide laughed. "They don't seem so dangerous to me."

"Oh, we aren't mith, we aren't ath all. Are we, Boras?"

The stuttering man struggled to his feet.

"Oh n-no miss," he began. "We're as friendly as they c-c-come. Just a c-couple of hunters out in the woods t-t-trying to c-c-catch us some game."

"Well then," Clayton sighed, sheathing his sword as he helped up Puck. "I suppose we should introduce ourselves more peacefully then."

"Oh sir, I assure you the mist-t-take is all our own. We are simple dwellers of these woods, and must be c-c-careful of anyone we do not know. I am Boras, and this fine fellow right over here is P--P-Puck. We are residents of the excellent town of P-p-p-p-p oh rot it all… "

"Pinewood," Puck finished. "We come from Pinewood."

"What is Pinewood?" Adelaide asked.

"Oh it's an excellent place to b-b-be," Boras laughed. By now the weapons had been sheathed and the two men seemed peculiarly at ease, given the very recent exchange of blows and rude comments. "We pride ourselves on our lumber skills. The mayor, you see, he has a p-p-plan, a masterful p-plan, and he will see t-t-t-t-to it that the plan goes ac-c-cording to schedule."

"Perhaths," Puck said. "They should all meeth the mayor."

His companion beamed at the idea. He started ranting on about the perks of Pinewood as he headed into the woods. Puck stood there, extending his arm towards his friend's retreating figure, encouraging the group to follow his friend.

Had Adelaide been less tired and hungry, she would have been discouraged from the idea of following complete strangers into the darkness. That being said, she was not alone in thinking that whoever these odd characters were, they both seemed pleasant enough. It was also likely that this town they had mentioned would have beds with fresh linens and hot food laid out on real plates with silverware. Perhaps a nice hot bath wasn't completely out of the question, either. With this thought consuming their minds, the four fugitives decided to follow their newfound guides. They each kept their weapons ready, just to be safe, but both the hunters were too occupied praising Pinewood and all its glory to really notice.

A beach soon appeared in the distance. The sand seemed dark and coarse in the growing dusk. Stretching beyond it was a large body of water, green as pea soup, with thin wisps of mist rising up from the surface. A raft lay floating just off the shore, tied down to a rock sunk securely in the shallows of the lake.

"This," Boras said, "is our way to P-P-Pinewood."

"Why can't we just walk around?" Raoul asked, gazing uncomfortably at the liquid mass before them. "I can't....I mean I don't...I don't like water."

"Ah," Puck chuckled. "Well, if you fell like taking a chath in thath part of the foreth, you'd for sure be dead. For safethy issues, the mayor hath filled the woods with old mines and bear traps, to keep out dangerous people. He's a smarth man, the mayor."

Together, he and Boras untied the raft and bade the group to board it.

"T-T-Take your chances on this, or t-t-t-t-try your luck in the w-w-woods," Boras warned them.

Raoul looked to Finn, who looked to Adelaide, who looked to Clayton. Darkness had fully set in around them. A lantern containing a single lorb hung from a pole, illuminating the entire raft. Boras and Puck had already gotten on and were patiently awaiting the group's decision.

"Alright," Clayton finally said. "Let's go to Pinewood."

CHAPTER TWELVE

The lake looked eerie as the raft moved along. An occasional bubble broke the surface, as if some underwater dweller was watching them out of the murky depths. This caused Adelaide to close her eyes and tightly clench Finn's hand. It was just easier to ignore the water as they floated along into the growing mist.

The raft was wobbly and unpredictable. More than once, Raoul and Clayton were forced to move closer to the edges in order to balance it. Boras looked up at the group and smiled, as if he felt overly obligated to make them feel welcome. Puck kept poking his swollen jaw and cursing under his breath as he paddled along. There was nothing around them but mist and green water.

"You sure we're heading in the right direction?" Finn finally asked.

Puck grunted and rolled his eyes. Boras started nodding his head vigorously.

"W-w-w-we are c-closer than you think; only a matter of sec-c-conds now."

"What is Pinewood like?" Clayton inquired.

"Ah," Boras exclaimed. "It is a wonderful p-p-p-place. Full of t-t-t-terrific p-people that c-c-care about each other. We share all our food, we protect the weak and d-d-defenseless, and we d-d-d-do our best to uphold all that is g-g-good and right."

"Have either of you ever heard of Tibris Guards?" asked Adelaide.

A tiny splash was heard behind them, followed by one of Puck's curses.

"Roth," he groaned. "Dropth the thupid oar again."

Boras giggled. It was hard to ignore that he was enjoying all this a little too much.

"Well be more c-c-c-careful then, my friend," he told Puck before responding to Adelaide. "T-t-t-t-Tibris Guards......No, no, c-c-can't say that I have. What are they?"

"Winking dips," stated Clayton. "They're led by a heartless son of Necrya named Huglund. They've been ordered to massacre innocent people all around Sanctumsea on account of some investigation by Lord Tiberion, sitting all pomp on his throne in Reignfall."

"G-g-goodness," Boras exclaimed. "They sound extremely d-d-dangerous."

"We were fortunate enough to escape with our lives before," Clayton continued. "I figure they'll walk around these woods a dozen times before giving up their search."

"Oh rewally," Puck jumped in. "How do woo figger that?"

"The Wallowing Woods are vast. Even a bunch of Tibris Guards can't maneuver their way inside it without a map. So, we can resupply in your town, and head out before they have a chance to stop us. Then it's just a matter of finding help to get north."

"You all will be safe once you g-g-g-get inside Pinewood," Boras declared. "The mayor is not one t-t-to t-t-t-t-turn away innocent p-p-people."

"I'll believe that only when I see it for myself," said Finn. "We haven't exactly had a very pleasant experience the past few days."

"Well," Puck grunted, as he pointed ahead, "there ith your proof."

Out of the rising mist there appeared three faint glimmers of light. Below them were the faint outlines of long, flat structures standing just above the surface of the lake.

As the raft drew closer, three men could be seen holding lorbs. They were all hooded and cloaked in white.

"Those would be our d-d-dock k-k-k-keepers," Boras said. "They p--p-protect us from d-d-danger of all sorts."

"Don't the mines around the lake already take care of that?" inquired Adelaide.

"They d-d-do, but every town needs m-m-m-m…oh rot it all. Every town needs muscle t-t-too."

"We very rarely hath visitors," Puck informed them. "Your arrival will cause massith excitement."

As the group gradually made their way off the raft and onto the dock, a large cluster of people wearing white garments gathered before them. Boras and Puck did their best to hold off the growing numbers, but to no avail.

"Thank you," cried a nearby mother of two. "Thank you for what you're doing."

"We will survive" an elderly man chimed. "They have saved us all."

"Let me hug them! Please, let me through," exclaimed a pretty maiden.

Adelaide looked about and tried her best to smile. It was difficult to accept the thanks when she hardly knew what on earth they were talking about. Clayton was acting as humble as he could while Finn took every handshake and embrace as warmly as it was given. Raoul, being his usual self, struggled to avoid contact with the grateful hosts, even shoving them away as forcefully as he could.

"Quiet, everyone!" a loud voice exclaimed. "I said shut your gaps."

The crowd grew silent. All turned towards the speaker. He was a man in his late thirties, with a gruff complexion, including massive broad shoulders and sinewy forearms. He had dark, bushy eyebrows, a short, blunt nose, and a thin strip of beard running from his lower lip down to the bottom of his chin. Unlike the townsfolk, he wore a pressed grey business suit completed with a vest, a pocket watch and an aqua blue necktie. The crowd bowed their heads slightly as they saw him approaching the docks and made way to give him space.

"Now that you lot can finally breathe," he began, addressing Adelaide. "Allow me to introduce myself. My name is Freud Blankis. I'm the right hand man and personal bodyguard to our great mayor of Pinewood. What's your business here, tonight?"

Clayton cleared his throat and stepped forward.

"Sir, my name is Clayton Hogg, recent resident of the village Havendale and proud member of its honorable Guild of Promise. These are my friends and companions: Adelaide Stokes, Finn Wessel, and Raoul King Jr. Together, we have eluded capture and certain death at the hands of a barbaric officer of the law and his murderous troop, who seek to execute innocents of all ages without a fair and public trial. We have come here, tonight, to beg sanctuary in the hope you can aid us in our escape and offer us protection."

"We found them in the wooths tonight," said Puck. "They told uth they were running from Tibrith Guardth."

"Ah," Freud exclaimed, rubbing his hands together. "The notorious Tibris Guards. Aye, I've heard a thing or two about them."

"You have?" asked Adelaide. It seemed odd that the first people they met outside of Havendale would be more informed on the subject.

Freud laughed. He had a creepy smile, which was difficult to hide.

"Perhaps," he said. "You all would enjoy the details a little more while being fed with some of our excellent food. Maybe even some fresh clothes and a warm bath would appeal to you?"

"Well we certainly wouldn't enjoy them less," Clayton chuckled.

"Excellent," Freud declared. "Puck and Boras here will run ahead and inform the tavern to prepare four rooms, unless of course any of you lads and the young lady would prefer to share?"

."Well…"started Finn, gazing lustfully at Adelaide.

"I think four rooms will work out just fine," Clayton cut him off.

"Maybe something to drink a little stronger than water or cider as well," Raoul mumbled.

"Fresh clothes for me," Adelaide sighed. Her dress was hardly visible under all the grass stains and patches of mud.

"All in good time, I promise you," Freud assured them. "But first, the mayor is quite adamant in meeting you all personally.

We don't often get visitors here, as I'm sure your guides have informed you. If anyone in Pinewood knows anything important about your Tibris Guards, it would be the mayor."

Boras and Puck shuffled on ahead as Freud led the group into town. The townsfolk from the docks stayed close behind, wide smiles on their faces and quiet weeping arising from several of the women.

"We are an isolated community here," stated Freud. "These forest dwellers aren't very socially experienced with folks outside our little community. Give them time to adjust."

The town of Pinewood was a pinnacle of art and true craftsmanship. Though built in the heart of the woods, the structures and materials were shockingly modern. Every building was made from stone and plaster, with complex wooden foundations stained in dark glaze that gave them all a richer shine. Every roof had fading green shingles that blended nicely with the surrounding wildlife. With all the modern designs and the number of structures standing in Pinewood, it seemed puzzling to Adelaide and the rest of the group that they had never heard even a rumor of it.

"We're a lumber town," Freud said. "As you can tell, business isn't what it used to be. People started moving out to these parts back when Sanctumsea first rose from the depths and all those ships started crashing on the shore. The first settlers here figured the wood trade was going to make everyone a handsome fortune."

"What happened?" Clayton asked.

"The future happened. With the completion of Reignfall and lorb caches being discovered to the north, business all but died here."

"That's terrible," Adelaide said. "But, this place....these buildings? How can you afford such modern repairs?"

"The mayor," replied Freud. "He's been running this town for nearly a decade. He's done a rotting fine job, too. We were practically in the dust when he happened along and got elected. Without him, we would have been starved out or run off by now."

"And you say this mayor has knowledge of Captain Huglund and his Tibris Guards?" asked Clayton.

"I would assume so," Freud laughed. "He's a Red Hand, just like the four of you."

This fact took all four of the group by surprise.

"So," began Adelaide. "It's been going on for quite a while now, this whole list of names and execution law?"

"About ten years would be my guess, but it has never been this bad," Freud replied.

"How do you come and go from town?" Clayton asked. "Do you only use the raft?"

"We usually use the raft, unless a larger group of people have to leave in a hurry. In that case we use a series of maps drawn up a couple years back that navigate through the more dangerous parts of the woods, keeping us off the mines and away from any hidden explosives."

"Why would people have to leave here in such a hurry?" asked Adelaide.

"We've had a few incidents where people got winked from living in the woods too long and took off with limited supplies or small valuables. Just last week we had a fellow cross the mines without a map after snagging some important documents from the mayor's office after one of his shifts. I imagine he thought they'd be worth something on the outside. Personally, I believe he spent most of his time working in the mayor's office just to study those rotting maps in the first place. He was a cleaner; always dusting things off and sweeping up floors. Not too bright, if I recall. The fact he was able to keep employment was nothing short of the mayor's unending kindness."

"And?" asked Clayton

Freud looked at him puzzled.

"What happened next," piped in Adelaide. "Did you ever catch him?"

"Oh, aye," Freud said. "A search party caught him in the woods beyond and buried him there. No one takes from the Mayor of Pinewood and gets away with it. Never did find those documents though, probably buried them somewhere before making a break for it. Good thing he was only a cleaner, we might have ended up losing someone special."

"That's...that's a horrible thing to say!" Adelaide exclaimed. "How could you say something so heartless?"

"Yeah, Augustine is right," Finn declared. "Not a very friendly remark, Blankis."

"I apologize," Freud chuckled. "I can seem a little...heartless at times. It's just the way I am I suppose."

With that he turned and gestured to the house before them.

The group found themselves standing before a great, elegant structure. Red shingles covered the roof and black laced curtains draped the inside of the windows. The door was the color of custard and the walls were eggshell white. Freud casually walked to the door and knocked twice before stepping back.

A thin, wheezy voice arose from inside.

"Enter."

CHAPTER THIRTEEN

A narrow corridor led the group into a large living room. The floor beneath them was made of stained oak, with a long, shag-rug stretching across it. The walls were covered in various paintings depicting intense actions of hunting and outdoor sports. Against the walls stood rows and rows of neatly stocked books, numbering somewhere in the hundreds to thousands. Piles of illuminated lorbs cast light out from inside a giant fireplace hewn from marble and stone. To the right of it was an armchair, in which sat the huddled form of a wrinkled, old man. He wore the same pearly garb as his fellow townsfolk. A brown-beaded necklace hung down his neck and a crimson rope tied loosely around his waist. His face was sullen and dry in the flickering lorb light. His long, flowing hair was white as snow, with a hint of grey edged along the temple. As the group processed in, he lifted his head and proceeded to look over each of the four travelers, starting with Raoul, then Clayton, then Finn, finally resting his long gaze upon Adelaide.

"So," their host began. His voice was unnerving, yet gentle, as he struggled to stand to greet them. "You are the newcomers I have heard so much about this evening. The town is practically giddy over your presence. Then again, I suppose with the way we live our lives in solitude here, a little company is precisely what we need from time to time. I am Oderheim, Mayor of Pinewood. Forgive my lack of speed; I fear anyone who knows me must learn the virtue of patience. I may be young inside, but alas, my body has outrun my spirit."

"We appreciate your generosity," Clayton said as he took his hand and shook it gratefully. "We certainly didn't expect this luck on our travels."

"My pleasure, dear boy, my absolute pleasure," Oderheim laughed. He continued on down the row, shaking each hand until he reached Adelaide. He ushered her to hug him, an action that caught her slightly off guard. She accepted his embrace and gasped as she caught a quick peak of his arm.

"What is it, my dear?"

"I'm...I'm sorry. It's just your arm, sir. There's something wrong with it."

Oderheim looked down.

"Yes I'm afraid there is."

With that, he rolled up his sleeve to give them all a better look.

A haunting image stretched down from beneath his wrist down to the elbow. It appeared to be some kind of tree. Its branches were decayed and wrapped around one another in a twisted, mangled form. The skin beneath it was irritated and worn, as if its bearer had rubbed it raw trying to remove the ghastly impression.

"What the rot is that?" exclaimed Finn.

Oderheim shook his head.

"That, son, is a cruel twist of destiny." He then turned to Freud and waved his hand. "Thank you, Blankis. You may leave us for now."

Freud nodded and exited the house, closing the door softly behind him.

"A useful foreman," Oderheim sighed. "I found him just when good help around here was impossible to locate. I've been told he was a boxer of sorts, in another life, of course. He's an excellent worker and a fine friend."

"Excuse me, sir, but that mark on your arm," pressed Clayton. "What did you mean when you said it was a curse?"

Oderheim sighed and looked down at the ghastly image. "Well, son, what I meant by that was that it was given to me for reasons I've yet to fully understand. But please, do sit down and rest your feet. Leave your bags by the hallway."

Finn and Raoul moved towards the fireplace. Adelaide sat down on a small chair nearby and took in the view of the room. A glass chandelier hung from the ceiling directly above her head, thin shiny crystals dangled down from the three brass rings that composed its center. Two banners stood against the wall, each bearing a large oak tree with two axes crossed before it. The entire room was full of wooden figurines, big and small, each one depicting a lumberjack in one of the many stages of his job. One stood with his back arched to the side and his arms outreached, as if an imaginary axe was in his grasp. Another showed the lumberjack hunched over on a fallen trunk with his hands cupped to his mouth as if a sandwich was supposed to be there. Perhaps the most interesting was the one behind Oderheim's chair. Its arms were crossed and its eyes seemed focused on the chair Adelaide sat in. The lorb light gave it a looming and formidable stance, one that made her feel pretty uncomfortable. Oderheim crossed his arms just like the figurine depicted and glanced out at her. Clayton stood beside his chair, awaiting his answer patiently.

"Now," continued Oderheim. "To fully answer your question, Mr. Hogg, you should know that you four are not the only unfortunates to bear the title of Red Hands."

"What does that even mean?" Raoul asked in a frustrated manner. "We haven't done anything wrong. We aren't traitors of anything if we haven't committed any rotting crimes, right?"

Oderheim smiled. "Ah, but with that being said, Mister King, do you not recall what was spoken by The Tibris Guards when they read you that scroll?"

Raoul scowled and looked away. Clayton thought about it for a second before responding. "It said we had already been tried and found guilty, of crimes either past or future."

"That is precisely right," Oderheim exclaimed. "We may not know how ourselves, but by malicious intent or ignorant participation, all Red Hands have become dangers to the very structure of Sanctumsea."

"Either that or they're blowing smoke out their rumps" Raoul muttered.

"I can't imagine an execution of this mass and magnitude being approved and taken into action because of some random notion, young man," Oderheim told him. "In the minds of the Tibris Guards and Lord Tiberion, we are all threats to Amber's security. Frankly, I can barely lift a cup of water to my lips these days, let alone wield a sword with which to strike someone down. But according to them, somehow, I either have been, or soon will be, a danger to the land and many of its inhabitants. And that ultimately, my friends, is why I have this mark on my arm: to inform anyone who crosses my path that I am a Red Hand and not to be helped or trusted."

"How did you get it, Mayor Oderheim?" Adelaide asked. "How did you get that terrible mark?"

"A Red Hand becomes imprinted over time with the mark once in the company of another bearing it," the mayor replied. "No one really knows how it happens. They just appear. I imagine yours became visible soon after you walked through the front door. Usually an outside bearer can trigger its creation."

Finn found his along his right bicep. Raoul's was situated squarely across the palm of his left hand, hidden well by the tattered remains of his latex glove. Clayton's sat squarely in the center of his chest. Try as she did, Adelaide couldn't locate hers.

"I don't have one!" she finally exclaimed gleefully. "I'm not one of them. There's been an error."

"Adelaide...." Clayton said.

"No look, there isn't a mark. They made a mistake!" she cried happily. "I can....I can go home. I can get out of this. Don't you see? They have to understand. They have to."

"Hey," Raoul threw in. "Look behind you."

Adelaide turned around.

Behind her was a wall, and on that wall hung a large gold plated mirror. As she cranked her neck, Adelaide could see the mark as clear as day, stamped squarely just below her hairline. Even in the reflection it appeared bigger and more distinct than any of the boys put together. Her long hair had done its job of hiding it from sight. A solitary tear rolled down her cheek as she felt her last glimmer of hope fade away.

"I'm so sorry, my dear," Oderheim said.

"Oh Sorra no," she moaned, shaking her head. She rubbed the mark anxiously until Clayton laid his hand down on her shoulder and the scrubbing stopped.

"I'm afraid they never fade," continued Oderheim. "Mine still looks as rotted as the first day I found it ten years ago."

"What is it supposed to be?" asked Clayton.

Oderheim sighed and slowly rose from his seat.

"It is called The Acryptus Tree. I don't suppose any of you are familiar with the writings of Jonah Longstreet?"

Adelaide's eyes widened at the mention of his name.

"I take it from your expression you might know a thing or two about his works," the mayor chuckled. "Talented fellow, I must admit, but perhaps a little too solitary for someone of his artistic stature."

"You mean these arborous blisters are the doings of some rotting inkman?" Raoul yelled.

"I don't...I don't understand," Adelaide stammered. "I've acquired every book he's ever written. There's never been any mention of something called an Acryptus Tree."

"Ah," Oderheim sighed, striding over to his engorged bookshelf. "You see, my dear, some of us more shined fellows can secure items not publicly sold in the common markets. I expect Mr. King here knows a little about what I'm saying."

"Rot off," Raoul retorted.

"I thought so," Oderheim chuckled. "Well, to prove my point, I managed to uncover the rough draft of Mr. Longstreet's latest work last year. Bearing this thing on my arm for so long had greatly embittered me. But when I saw a familiar image illustrating the cover, I felt hope for the first time in annuals. Here you are."

He handed Adelaide a pencil thin manuscript. It was loosely bound and slightly singed at the corners. She bit her lip at Oderheim's poor treatment of it.

"The entire story rests at exactly thirty three pages," the mayor informed them. "A harrowing, if not hurried, tale concerning Sorra and Necrya, the Two Mothers."

"I'm sorry, but what exactly do those two pompous givies have to do with this rotting imprint," Raoul bitterly asked.

Oderheim gasped in surprise.

"I say, young sir, please watch yourself. That sort of slanderous offense will not be tolerated in Pinewood. I imagine if Freud had heard you just then he wouldn't have been able to contain himself and violence would ensue."

"He apologies, I assure you," Clayton said, giving his companion a warning stare. "Now tell us, sir, what does the story say about our predicament?"

"In the beginning," Oderheim continued. "There were two sisters, this we all know from our learning days. One was Sorra, the mother of all that was good and pure in existence, and Necrya, her malevolent sibling whose only desire was for chaos and wicked deeds. Together they lived and ruled over everything, constantly quarreling over how much influence each held over life itself."

"And they continue their squabbling to this day," Raoul growled. "We all know the stories."

"Much more than stories in the minds and hearts of those who call Sanctumsea home," Oderheim told him. "Even you much have felt their presence in times of need or want."

"Hardly," Raoul scoffed.

"Mayor Oderheim, please, go on," Adelaide pleaded quietly. Her face was turning milky white and her lips quivered in uncontrollable misery.

"According to Longstreet's tale," the mayor progressed, "Sorra bore a son whom she named Acryptus. For his first birthday, she bestowed on him a seed, which he planted in the earth and tended until a tree started to grow. Sorra cautioned Acryptus to always treat the tree with love and tenderness, so only good fruit might be yielded. He did so for many years, and as he learned the ways of kindness and compassion, his tree bloomed without tarnish. But as he lived the life his mother taught him, his cunning aunt watched from the shadows, plotting away. It wasn't long before she began whispering alternate ideals into her nephew's ear, whenever his mother's focus was elsewhere. Now and then, as he gave into his aunt's suggestions of malice and greed, a single leaf would fall from his precious tree. Any and all things done in her favor rewarded him with earthly pleasures, but little peace or modesty. As he became corrupted and unjust, the tree slowly withered away."

"Did Sorra do nothing?" Clayton asked. "How could she let her son go so wrong?"

"Ah, Mr. Hogg, as you should remember, Sorra does not control us," Oderheim reminded him. "She merely illuminates our path with a gentle light. What we decide is up to us."

"So what happened next?" Adelaide pressed him.

"After years of succumbing to bad judgment, his health started to decrease," Mayor Oderheim morbidly replied. "The tree twisted and knotted itself so terribly that all hope seemed lost. As he lay on his deathbed, his senses failing, he managed to utter one final sentence before expiring."

Oderheim then fell silent, as if in deep contemplation.

"Well, rot it? Raoul barked out. "What was it?"

The old man smiled and shook his head.

"I'm afraid I do not know," he admitted. "You see, that is where the story ends. It seems Longstreet never finished the story, or at least not in the draft that I received."

Raoul jumped to his feet, cursing aloud and scuffing up the carpet.

"Is it possible to make contact with Longstreet?" Adelaide sharply threw at Oderheim. "Have you heard any news on his whereabouts?"

"What about other Red Hands on the run?" Clayton inquired. "Have you met any besides us these past ten years?"

Oderheim sat in deep contemplation, folding his hands against his mouth before struggling to his feet.

"I know you all have many questions to be answered," he began, "but I am a tired old man, and you all have traveled quite far these past few days. If you will permit me my rest, I swear on my life to answer as many of your questions as I have knowledge for first thing tomorrow morning. We have a tavern in town where you will find food and drink, as well as four rooms prepared by your guides, Boras and Puck. Anything Pinewood can offer is at your disposal. And now, my dears, I bid you goodnight."

With that, Oderheim escorted them back outside. Freud Blankis was waiting for them as the door slowly shut behind them, locking itself with a series of loud clicks and thuds.

CHAPTER FOURTEEN

"Quite the gentleman, isn't he?" Freud chuckled.

"To be sure," Clayton said.

"I must say he was pretty rotting set on asking us to leave," Raoul said, "especially when we had questions to be answered."

"Well, he's a tired man," Freud replied. "He needs sleep, as do we all. In fact, once you four have eaten your fill, I encourage you all to retire to your rooms and get some rest. It is seven hours to sunrise and half the town is already put to bed."

As he spoke, Freud turned to face one of the passing buildings. It was nostalgic to behold. The timber walls were coated with rich sap residue that glimmered in the light of a cloudless moon. Lorb light danced behind the stain glass windows, accompanied by the sounds of playful laughter and harmless goading.

"What is this place?" Clayton asked.

"This is somewhere to loosen one's belt, let your beard grow, and drink off a day of frustration," Freud heartily responded. "Inside here, you will find enough Honeydrop, TOX pellets and even a givie or two to supply the whole of Amber."

"TOX, you say?" Raoul inquired.

'We never had such a place in Havendale," Adelaide remarked. 'I don't think any village around us did either."

"Such libations aren't always welcomed outside of town," laughed Freud. "We believe our visitors should be pampered and plugged until them can take no more. Just think of it as more ways to enjoy your newfound security. Welcome, my friends, to The Lambshead."

The air inside the tavern was thick and stifling. Every floor, wall, staircase, and ceiling appeared to be completely hewn out of wood. Various carvings depicting magnificent hunts, inebriated brawls, and uncensored fraternizing littered the beams and pillars that kept the establishment intact. A solitary bar stood opposite from the door. The bartender, a portly gentleman with wisps of golden hair padded down around his sweaty head lazily moved behind it, restocking as he went.

Sitting in a nearby corner was a young woman. She wore the traditional clothes of Pinewood, but had considerably altered them to appear more sensual. The sleeves of her robe had been removed and her pants were hiked up to just above her knees. The bottom half of her shirt had been cut off to reveal a lean, taut midsection. Her short, shaggy, auburn hair had bright, pink tips, which was a common method of coloring in the givie profession, or so Clayton had heard. She must have been a couple years older than him, but looked strikingly young for her age. He found it extremely difficult to take his eyes off her.

"As you can see, my fortunate Red Hands, we have food and drink as well as pleasurable entertainment," Freud informed them. "Anything you order is on the house, compliments of Mayor Oderheim. I recommend a bottle of our finest Honeydrop. I'll have the barkeep scrounge one up for you."

"Sounds good to me," laughed Finn.

"I'll just have a Cinnamon Cider," Adelaide announced.

"Make that two," Clayton said.

Freud looked momentarily puzzled.

"My friends, I don't understand, I was led to believe you all have had a long, harrowing journey."

"We have," Adelaide replied.

"So," Freud continued, "after taking you in and offering you our finest stock, you deny our hospitality? Is what we have not good enough for you? Is that what you're saying?"

"No!" Adelaide exclaimed, taken aback. "We certainly do appreciate all you and Oderheim have done for us; I just like to have my wits about me."

"I certainly hope not," Finn whispered seductively in her ear. Adelaide laughed and gave him a playful jab in the ribs with her finger.

"I see. Any particular reason why you wouldn't trust us completely?" continued Freud. "Maybe we haven't proven our worthiness to you, eh?"

"It isn't a big deal if she doesn't want to drink, plugger," Raoul growled, taking a stand directly in front of Adelaide. "Stop trying to guilt her into it."

Freud continued smiling, his jaw hardening as if he had no choice. His hands were clinging to his belt, twitching and squeezing. The intent of violence was growing in his eyes.

"You misunderstand me," he growled. "I'm merely suggesting you all might enjoy one of our stronger beverages better on account of the trouble we went through preparing it for you. Don't get in my face for that. You won't do well."

"I'll take my chances," Raoul growled.

An awkward second of silence passed before Freud took a step back with a sigh.

"Well, personally it makes no difference to me," he declared. "I would just have figured that given how kind we have been to you since your arrival, a small glass of our best Honeydrop wouldn't be too much to offer."

"Well Mr. Blankis, that is quite kind, but I just don't drink that stuff," Adelaide stated. "I'm sure you understand."

"Perfectly well I assure you," he replied.

Adelaide heard a hint of a sneer in his voice, though none of her companions seemed to notice. She wondered how something as small as what they each preferred to drink could irk him so badly.

"Now," he went on, "if you all will excuse me, I have the duty of checking the town boundaries each night. Your rooms are upstairs, the first four you see. Hot baths and clean towels are available, and your breakfast will be served promptly at eight o'clock over at the bar. I expect Mayor Oderheim will call for you sometime around eight thirty. I bid you all good night and pleasant dreams."

With that he departed, slamming the door roughly behind him as he went.

"Did we offend him in some way?" Adelaide asked.

"I don't know, and I don't rotting care," laughed Finn. "You all can sip squirm beverages until the sun comes up. There's a cup of Honeydrop with my name on it. Do I smell roast beef and baked bread too? Is anyone else hungry?"

"I could eat," Adelaide remarked.

"Food sounds good to me," Clayton joined in. "What about you, Raoul?"

Their companion shrugged.

"All I can think about is that rotting bath and bed," he told them. "I think I'll get some sleep. See you all in the morning." With that he grabbed a nearby bowl of TOX pellets and marched upstairs.

"Well," said Finn, "I don't know about the rest of you, but I have a feeling. A feeling we are safe and sound. Maybe Pinewood could be our new home."

"Even with our friend Freud Blankis?" Clayton asked.

"A little impatience isn't that terrible. I'm for seeing how long we can make this last. With only the lake to gain access and the surrounding woods protected by hidden mines, I can't see how Huglund could even get us, even if he tried. Blondie needs to stop being so winked and see that, the broiled squab."

Clayton shook his head.

"What?" Finn asked.

"He's trying. He is genuinely trying, Finn. Give him time, he'll surprise you."

With that, Clayton walked over to a nearby table. Adelaide took Finn's hand and clasped it gently as he smiled at her. She was just about to make her way over to join Clayton when the bartender walked from behind the counter and approached them. His breath smelled appallingly of liverwurst.

"With compliments of Mayor Oderheim, I've been ordered to…."

"Yeah, yeah we know, supply us with Honeydrop," Finn chuckled. "I'll have one, thanks. Aurora here will take a Cinnamon Cider."

"I don't understand," the bartender said. "I saw Mr. Blankis speaking with you."

"What is it with you people and drinking?" Adelaide exclaimed. "If I want to drink, then I'll rotting drink."

The bartender frowned, his bushy eyebrows arching up as he did so.

"Well, I suppose if you don't want any, you don't want any."

"Thank you," Adelaide laughed. "Now do you have any good musicians in this town?"

"Ah," the bartender sighed smiling. "You will find we have something much better."

He cautioned them over to the side of the bar. Something was sitting on the surface, hidden under a duty blanket. He pulled the covering off to reveal a peculiar looking device molded out of shiny, light metal, much like a typewriter. On the front of it was a series of buttons with letters on them. A pair of stereos, connected to the device by a thin strand of cord, sat against a nearby wall.

"What is it?" asked Adelaide.

"The next stage in music," replied the bartender. "Though somewhat outdated in Memoriam, this contraption is the newest means of enjoying music in the whole of Sanctumsea. It allows you to listen to a series of favored songs from multiple lands beyond our own. You simply push any two buttons, one after another, and a song will emit. Try it out."

Finn pressed down on the letter A, and then played with his other choices before finally resting his finger on the letter P. The box made a subtle whirling sound and a quiet cackle rose from each of the stereos.

"Wait for it," the bartender said.

The cackling soon turned into a pleasant, forgotten ditty from a time long past. It rolled and danced swiftly from ear to ear as a dozen different instruments and melodious voices chimed in together. No one could tell what it was about, and no one seemed to care. It was impossible not to smile and imagine a better time.

Finn started to sway his hips along to the beat. His overabundant confidence masked his lack of talent very well. Adelaide laughed heartily before joining in. She turned to see if Clayton was planning to dance as well, but shook her head as she witnessed his gaze lingering on the givie sitting on the chair beside him.

"Unbelievable," she thought, *"and with someone of her profession."*

Her brows unfurled as she allowed Finn to wrap his arms around her shoulders and plant a kiss on her lips. The pair was soon dipping back and forth to the rhythm of the song.

Clayton watched them both with a tranquil smile on his lips. He found himself, however, shifting uncomfortably in his chair as the young woman next to him leaned closer in, studying his face intently.

"Didn't your folks ever teach you it's not polite to stare?" he finally asked her.

"They aren't around to teach me anything these days."

"Perhaps they didn't like your choice in career."

"Well" she laughed. "A girl has to eat."

"Maybe you should change your diet."

The givie pulled back for a moment.

"You're different than the rest."

"What do you mean?" Clayton inquired.

"Any Red Hand who comes through this town can hardly wait to down a glass of Honeydrop or bed the nearest givie. I take it you haven't completely fallen for Pinewood's charming façade?"

"I don't know about that," Clayton laughed. "It seems well enough."

The givie shook her head.

"It's a web," she whispered. "Once you're in, it's hard to see what's about to happen until it's too late."

Clayton turned to face her.

"And what is about to happen, exactly?"

"I…" she stammered. "I shouldn't say."

"I disagree."

"Why should I trust you?"

"I'm having a similar debate."

"If you tell Blankis about what I'm saying to you, they won't just make me lie on my back. They'll peel it off my spine."

"I reckon my companions and I can keep our mouths shut. Freud Blankis isn't exactly our friend at the moment."

"Because you declined his offer of spirits?" she chuckled. "Yeah that never happens when your kind come running. There'd be an empty bottle and a satisfied customer by now. Honeydrop is a funny thing. The chemistry of it is so rich you can hardly notice the laudanum lacing the rim of the bottle. These people need you all unconscious and awaiting your fate."

Clayton tilted his head curiously.

"What fate would you be referring to?" he asked.

At this point, the givie cleared her throat and glanced out the window. She seemed adamant that no one catch what she was saying.

"Look," she began. "I've already been warned about helping you people out, and I figure if you're too winked to see it yourselves, then I can't do much else except sit and watch it all unfold. So I'll just say this: Just run. Don't stop, don't think. Find a way out of this place. Oderheim may have brought us back from poverty ten years ago, but what he did has cost us all our humanity. And the town doesn't interfere as long as it keeps food on their plates and breath in their lungs. Just pretend, for a moment, that everything that's happened since those two rotters Puck and Boras found you in the woods have been part of a plan, a plan to do something truly unforgiveable to you and all your friends."

The bartender was giving her an odd glance, his eyes darkening intensely. Seeing this, the she grabbed Clayton by the collar and pulled herself onto his lap. Before he had time to react, she was placing kiss after kiss on his lips, allowing them to linger before granting him the chance to contribute as well. When she finally let him up for air, the first thing Clayton saw was Adelaide's brightly flushed face as she stared at him, her cheeks starting to quiver. She immediately snatched Finn's face in her hands and planted a series of quick but passionate pecks on his mouth, checking every now and again to see if Clayton was watching. He did, for a second, but then turned back to the givie with confusion on his face.

"Not bad, Red Hand. I think he's convinced. Unless you think a trip upstairs would help?"

Clayton remained silent.

"Well?" she whispered, softly breathing into his ear.

"I'm thinking," he chuckled.

"Well," she sighed, removing herself from his lap. "When you decide, ask for Tazme. People around here call me Taz."

"What kind of name is Tazme?"

"It's short for something, a place in Memoriam, I think. My dad told me once it was where his ancestors came from. Anyways be careful. I doubt this calm will last much longer. Try and stay close to your friends and leave by sunrise. It doesn't bode well for your kind. Oderheim considers you a rich payday, nothing more."

"Oderheim is one of us," said Clayton.

Taz shook her head.

"He might have the mark, but he's in the clear as long as he keeps at his plan. I can't say anymore. Just keep your group safe."

She turned her head to see Adelaide and Finn leaving the dance floor to retreat to a bench outside, where their actions were swiftly cut from view.

"She does realize she isn't fooling anyone, right?" Taz chuckled.

Clayton looked at her curiously.

"Wow," she laughed, rolling her eyes. "I guess you are winked after all."

With that, she smiled and leaned in to give him another kiss on the cheek, but then changed her mind and planted it on his lips. As she finally walked away, the bartender gave Clayton a suspicious glance. Thinking fast, the Red Hand jerked his thumbs up with an obnoxious grin. The bartender smirked and nodded in agreement.

"I've got to warn the others," Clayton thought. He got up and started moving casually towards the front door. Once outside, he could see that Adelaide and Finn were nowhere to be found.

The streets of Pinewood were deserted. Clayton felt nervous standing there; the only breathing body on the street and visible to anyone who might care to peak outside their windows. Not a sound emitted from any of the buildings nearby, making his nervous breathing the loudest thing to be heard. He was just about to start looking for his friends when a rustling noise from two houses down caught his attention. Glancing about to see if anyone was watching him, Clayton slowly crept along the walkway, wincing as the boards beneath his feet creaked with each carefully placed step. He hastily ducked down beneath the window as a loud crash sounded from inside the house.

"Winking rot, Jade; don't be attracting any attention. We need to keep a low profile."

"Well," a woman's voice responded. The shrill, penetrating sound of it made Clayton cringe. "We couldn't possibly attract any more with your ear-splitting mouth breathing."

A third voice spoke. It didn't take Clayton any effort to know who it belonged to.

"Well now thath the liths are on, we cath see where we're going."

Clayton crouched down as low as he could go. Puck couldn't have been standing more than a couple feet from the window pane.

"Alright, so we are all agreed," Jade stated. "No mistakes this time. I'm sure I don't have to tell you what Freud would do if he discovered that grave out in the woods, where Hollis is supposed to be buried, is actually rotting empty."

"He'll kill us all," the first man said.

"Exactly," continued Jade. "I still can't believe that rotting cleaner actually ran off without saying goodbye to the givie. He adored that sack of silky flesh."

"She wath always trouble," said Puck. "She probably ith trying to warn those four Red Haths me and Boras found in the wooths."

"She wouldn't dare," growled Jade. "Not after what Freud did to her parents last summer. She knows to follow the rules he set when Red Hands are brought to town."

"Even so," the first man said. "I reckon we should go secure them now before they get suspicious. I heard they didn't drink."

"Everyone drinks the Honeydrop," Jade muttered. "It's almost tragic how easy it is to get them all to do it."

"Well they didn't," the man announced. "No Honeydrop means no sleep. So we might have to get a little rough if we want to be done before those riders arrive tomorrow."

"Tomorrow?" asked Puck nervously. "They're that cloth?"

"Right on the heels of those naive squirms," cackled Jade. "Freud says they will be here by first light. After we tear this place apart, we'll get Boras and head over to the tavern. They should be asleep by now, with or without the drug."

"And Oderheim will uphold hith deal thith time?" asked Puck. "I don't want juth Boras getting all the tasty snacks again."

"Shut your hole you rotting wink, you'll give me night scares," yelled the first man. "I swear, I'll never understand how you two can do that stuff and still sleep at night."

"Ith a choice," Puck chuckled. "Frankly, ith you ever find yourselves with the option to consume some yourself, I highly recommend it."

The girl, Jade, spat in disgust.

"I'm with Garrick," she said. "I've done a few unnatural things in my day, but to do that is....ugh I cannot begin to describe it. And to call them critters, like they are mindless beasts you just pop from a rabbit hole and cook over a fire. I swear, only a sickly beast can rightly consume his own kind like that. It isn't natural."

"Enough chatter," Garrick said. "Let's make sure the cellar is ready to go downstairs and get over to The Lambshead. I want to have a little fun with that girl before we lock them up. I imagine Tibris Guards don't mind getting them a little used, as long as they're still breathing."

Clayton didn't hear Garrick's remark as he nearly tripped backwards in shock from Jade's comment to Puck. He stayed in the shadows as he quickly snuck his way back towards the tavern. It was clear to him now what Taz had meant. He knew it was time to leave Pinewood.

CHAPTER FIFTEEN

Raoul was surprised as he approached his room. There seemed to be a peculiar smell rising from behind the door. It was foreign and exotic, like a lost flower sprinkled with various spices and a touch of orange-scented perfume. It was repulsive, to say the least. Cautiously, he edged his way up to where the door stood partially ajar, and poked his head inside.

The room was mostly empty. The only pieces of furniture were a table covered in a hand-stitched quilt, a pair of wooden chairs, a master desk by the window, and a twin-size bed across the room. The wallpaper on the walls was worn, portraying an assembly of countryside images including rolling hills, small ponds, white board fences and a series of old dirt roads. The source of the intensely female smell, however, did not come from any of these items. The source came in the form of a young girl lying directly in front of him, her legs curled up at the foot of the bed and her tiny head resting on the palm of her hand. She blinked her eyes a lot, all the while trying to appear alluring from beneath the blankets wrapped loosely around her shivering form.

Raoul looked at her curiously, not completely sure how to react to the situation. Was it some kind of joke? The little girl certainly wasn't laughing. In fact, she was doing her best to hold back a tear as he stepped inside, closing the door behind him.

"Umm…..hello," he said.

The girl smiled and shook her hair back, an act which was supposed to appear alluring, but ended up just looking sad and unnatural. Raoul was less than comfortable.

"Hello yourself," she replied in a low voice. Raoul felt disgusting just for listening to it.

"Can I....I'm sorry but can I...um, help you...with anything?"

He certainly didn't mean that the way she took it. The words were hardly out of his mouth before she slid seductively to the end of the bed and slowly arched herself upwards.

"I don't know. Do you think you can?"

The blanket slipped away.

Raoul should have averted his eyes. He knew he should have. For a good ten seconds he stood there, his gaze wandering the girl's scrawny form, studying her twists and curves. A single thought crossed his mind, which he quickly quelled before turning away.

"I...umm....I don't know what it is you expect me to do here, but....umm...oh boy. As flattered as I am, I have to tell you there won't be anything happening here tonight. Sorry."

The girl looked at him strangely, as if she didn't understand his response.

"So, if you could please put some clothes on, I would really appreciate it. It's not that you....you know, aren't attractive, I just don't feel well, that's it."

This seemed like the appropriate road to take, and Raoul felt pleased with the way he had handled the situation. He was, however, horrified to hear the girl start sniffling and rocking back and forth as she grew more and more upset.

"Oh rot, um, I'm sorry, I know you were probably…um…looking forward to it, but I am sorry. I'm just not in the mood, and quite frankly, I feel a little uncomfortable just having this conversation. Please stop crying."

"I know," she moaned, her head falling into her hands. "And I know why."

"Ah," Raoul said, sighing in relief. "Good, then it isn't just me."

"Yes, and I am sorry," she continued. "I know I am quite ugly, but I have to try regardless."

"Well I hope you…..wait, sorry what?"

"I am ugly. I know I don't have pretty features; like beautiful eyes with fluttery eyelashes, or a nicer and larger pair of…"

Raoul coughed loudly to cut her off.

"Well, you can see," she continued. "I am not fit to serve you tonight, or anyone for that matter. I should have known you would have been displeased."

"I beg your pardon?"

"It is true that I have no prior experience, but I was told very specifically what to do. I would not disappoint you, especially if your eyes were closed."

"I…..I mean what the…what?"

"It would mean a day of good eating for my family," she pleaded, her tear stained eyes beaming. "They aren't my real family, of course. I was given to them after my uncle was killed and eaten in the woods by a couple of wild animals, or so that man Boras told me. They may not love me and make me clean and cook, but I still hate to see them live off crumbs and watered down soup all the time."

Raoul's expression was that of extreme discomfort. He wanted to leave, badly, but here before him was a scared, sad little girl who was speaking as if she had no choice but to act in this manner. He felt sorry for her, a strange thing, since he had never felt sorry for anyone at any point in his entire life, except maybe himself.

"Look," he started. "It isn't that you aren't….well, attractive. I mean how old are you?"

"I'm not sure. We don't celebrate birthdays at my home. Well, not mine anyways. I can recall at least thirteen years."

She seemed so sweet, so innocent; completely unaware of the action she was adamantly pursuing and what it would mean for her. Standing there, looking at her, Raoul wanted nothing more than to find the people forcing her to do this, and take several hours in teaching them some respect. Well, that and an hour or two comforting her, perhaps slipping into that bed with her, letting her unbutton his shirt….or perhaps just to know her name.

"What are you called," he asked.

"My name is Cherry Atherton. I mean…Lovely Lavender. Yes, Lovely Lavender. That is the name I was given when they told me to come here."

Raoul smiled. "Lovely Lavender is a truly terrible name. I like Cherry much, much better."

The girl smiled and blushed. She had a smile that could melt glaciers, even one that was the heart of Raoul King Jr. He cleared his throat, looked about the room and finally walked over to where she was sitting.

"Now Cherry, I did mean what I said. I truly have no intention of doing anything with you tonight."

She hung her head and nodded acceptingly.

"That err....that being said, I suppose after you put your clothes back on, we could just lie here together and sleep. The people outside don't have to know we didn't do anything, I could just tell them we did. They would pay you that way."

Cherry raised her head, her eyes wide with excitement. She slipped on a scarlet tunic lying on the floor beside the bed and smiled with relief.

"Good," Raoul chuckled. "Now...let's get some sleep. It's been a long day, and I have a feeling tomorrow is going to be pretty interesting."

CHAPTER SIXTEEN

The lorb lights were fading as Clayton darted back inside the tavern. The bartender, who was sweeping up the floor and humming some unknown tune, glanced up as he heard him enter. The balding man smiled, briefly, before noticing the look of terror stamped across the Red Hand's face. The broom dropped from his hands and clattered down onto the stone floor. His brows knitted tightly together as he reached his hand into the back of his belt.

Clayton didn't hesitate. Leaping forward, he jerked out his fist and managed to catch the bartender squarely on the right side of his jaw. Given his haste, however, the blow did not land as fiercely as he'd hoped. The barkeep stumbled back, immediately regaining his balance and lashed back with a swing of his hand. The bludgeon clenched inside it landed on Clayton's forehead, causing him to temporarily black out. After tottering violently back and forth, he managed to gain his footing just as the bartender swung again.

On an average day, the son of Thatcher Hogg had always considered himself a fairly adequate boxer. But, as he ducked down, throwing out a punch to his opponent's abdomen, he experienced a surge of energy that seemed to enter his body out of nowhere. The bartender cursed aloud, his free hand groping his stomach as he doubled over in pain. Clayton didn't wait a second longer. Taking a step back, he landed a swift kick into the bartender's face, making perfect contact with the man's mouth and nose. The bartender flew backwards, shooting across the stone floor and crashing into the bar as if he'd been thrown by a catapult.

A consummative rush of power swept through Clayton to his very core. He had never been so in control, and yet so simultaneously overwhelmed. The feeling confused him. What was even more puzzling was the uncomfortable sensation rising from his chest. He looked down to behold the Acryptus Tree, grim as ever, fiercely burning on top of his skin. His body shook and heaved at the sheer magnitude of the event. A thousand sensations rushed through every vein in his body. The muscles inside him ached mercilessly and the very hair on his head seemed to stand rigidly upright. In that moment, he wasn't just Clayton Hogg of Havendale. He felt…more.

It was only when he heard Jade's malignant laughing rise from down the street that he snapped out of his momentary daze and darted up the stairs. Every new question penetrating his mind was stored away as he hurried past the first marked door, assuming it to be his, and began knocking repeatedly on the second.

"Adelaide! Wake up! We need to go, now!"

Clayton kept pounding away, his heart racing inside his chest. It took some time, but at long last a shuffling sound could be heard from inside and the doorknob began turning. The door opened to reveal Adelaide. Her hair was washed and groomed, and her body was clothed in a pair of tight, black leggings and woolen grey sweater left for her on the dresser inside her room.

"Clayton? Do you have any idea what time it is?"

"No and I really don't rotting care. Where's Finn?"

"Why? You think he's in here with me?"

"Yes, we…wait, he isn't?"

Adelaide laughed merrily at Clayton's apparent distress.

"Hey," she told him. "I do have my restrictions. Don't think so little of me."

"What…I don't…listen, Adelaide, I don't know what you are going on about, but we have to leave this place right now. There isn't time to rotting chat."

"Why? I was just getting ready for bed. Besides, I thought we all were speaking to Oderheim more tomorrow."

"Adelaide, please," Clayton pleaded. "You really need to trust me on this. I've been talking and listening to…well some people, and this….this place is not what we thought it was. I think the townsfolk are going to lock us up tonight and hold us prisoner for Huglund. I don't know how yet, but they're in cahoots together."

"What? Oh come on, you're being a wink," she stated flatly. "I'm tired. Go to bed and we'll talk in the morning."

"Adelaide Stokes, I swear to….."

From downstairs there was a loud scream. Clayton immediately recognized it as Jade.

"What the rot is this?! What happened here?" she yelled.

"Heth dead, or cloth to it," Puck replied. "Probably thell and hit hith head."

"You think he propelled himself across the rotting room?" Jade hissed at him.

"Drunk, most likely," threw in Garrick.

"C-c-c-can we just g-g-get upstairs and g-g-get those squirms now?" Boras inquired, freshly joining the party.

"Fine," Jade growled. "We can deal with this dip later. I call that lovely looking boy. He's all mine."

"I want the girl," said Garrick. Clayton could hear the eagerness drooling from his voice as he spoke.

"And I will t-t-t-take that Raoul. He looks like he c-c-could be t-t-t-t oh, rot it all, t-t-tasty."

Clayton didn't wait for the rest of the conversation. He forced his way past Adelaide, grabbing her arm as he did so. Without warning, he jerked her towards the bed and pulled her down towards the floor.

The faint sound of approaching footsteps could be heard as he joined her.

"Clayton," Adelaide hissed. "What are you doing?"

"Just trust me. I'm telling you we are in serious trouble if they find us."

"Why?" she pressed him. "What about Finn and Raoul?"

"I'm working on that. All I know is that if any of those...winks get their hands on you they'll....they'll....I don't want to think about it. If they get taken, we won't be any good to them captured or dead. Better they are taken first than all four of us getting locked up in some cellar."

The voices outside were now very close. Jade and Garrick were right outside Adelaide's door, while Boras could be heard giggling and humming in anticipation directly next door. Puck, Clayton assumed, was another door over, preparing to break it down and subdue whoever was behind it.

"Alright, here we go," said Jade. "Oh, and Puck....should I want to get naughty with mine before we take them over to holding, just please understand this time: looking is fine. No touching. Got it?"

Clayton and Adelaide both closed their eyes, holding their breath.

All four doors flew open simultaneously. There was an immediate scuffling noise from the fourth room down, where Clayton quickly assessed Finn was sleeping.

"I can't believe I am saying this," he whispered, "but I would have preferred to find both of you in here when I came; even Raoul too, if it meant us all sticking together."

"Rot, rot, rot," Garrick cursed as he scanned the empty room. "She isn't here!"

"Oh shut it," Jade laughed, walking past the open door, her hands supporting Finn's unconscious head as Puck supported his legs. "We got the lovely one at least. It looks like he had a glass or two of Honeydrop after all."

"They're probably out hathing some fun," said Puck, grinning maliciously. "I would hate to be thith boy when he wakes up…for more reasons than one."

Suddenly a loud yelp of pain came from Raoul's room, followed by the sound of something shattering and a despairing cry from Boras. The one called Garrick darted past Jade and hurried next door.

"It's empty," he exclaimed.

"Where ith Boras?" yelled Puck.

No response.

"Where ith my friend, you guys?"

There was a loud thud and a grunt from Finn as Puck dropped his legs to the floor and rushed down into Raoul's room. Clayton and Adelaide heard him gasp loudly before bursting into tears.

"What the …..Boras? No. No. That little rath, I'll cuth him up. You didn't deserve thith! I'm going to find thath little rother and….oh I'll…"

"Close your mouth, Puck. We'll bury him later," Jade yelled from down the hall. "In the meantime, could you two kindly help me carry this meat sack downstairs before my arms fall off?"

Puck emitted a gurgling sob as he returned, once again picking up Finn's feet. Soon, everyone except Garrick had made their way back down the stairs.

"Come on, you rotter," Clayton whispered as the man paced back and forth across the floor. "Just leave."

Adelaide started to breathe again as Garrick finally exited the room and moved towards the stairs. Suddenly, his footsteps stopped abruptly. The floorboards creaked as he quickly made his way back. The bedroom door slammed wide open as he reentered, briskly walking over to the bed, grasping both sides of it firmly with his hands.

"Clayton?" Adelaide whimpered as she clutched his arm, tears streaming down her face as she did so. Clayton wasn't listening.

"No…." he muttered loud enough for Garrick to hear him. "Not…going…to happen!"

The bed flipped onto its side. Adelaide went with it with a helpful shove from Clayton before his fists thrust up, catching Garrick in the face. His opponent tried to back away, but to no avail. Clayton simply jerked himself upwards, following him as he stumbled backwards, crying in agony. His back finally crashed into the wall. With an adrenaline fueled pull, Clayton managed to force him to the ground, allowing him to be briefly stunned as he grabbed a pillow lying nearby and stuffed in onto his face. Garrick's cries for help were immediately quelled as he struggled to free himself. Adelaide crawled over to where they were fighting and wrapped her arms around his legs, preventing him from breaking free. Clayton applied all the strength he could muster onto the pillow, snuffing out any free air. Helpless, Garrick continued to struggle, his arms flailing back and forth and his torso twisting in all sorts of unpleasant manners.

"Garrick?" called out Jade from downstairs. "What are you doing up there?"

"*Just a few more seconds,*" Clayton thought.

"Garrick," Jade called again, this time with growing frustration. "Come on!"

Adelaide could hear her footsteps swiftly coming up the stairs.

"Clayton?" she asked waveringly.

Jade was nearly to the top.

"Die, you rotting dip. Please…just die," murmured Clayton, pressing down with all his strength. The body stopped twitching. Garrick let out a quiet sigh as his life finally left him.

"Come on, Adelaide," Clayton whispered. "It's time to leave."

Jade turned into the open doorway just as Clayton pulled Adelaide towards the nearest window. Grabbing the lamp next to the bed, he cast it into the glass, shattering it through the pane just as Jade started screeching at Garrick's body. Clayton turned to help Adelaide make her way out of the room as the madly deranged Jade lunged out to grab her. She tripped in her haste and sliced her hand wide open on one of the sharp pieces of glass still stuck in the frame. This didn't stop her from grabbing Adelaide by the ankle with her other hand. Adelaide screamed, struggling to maintain her balance on the slanted roof outside. Jade's grip didn't loosen. Trying to pull away, Adelaide fell against Clayton, nearly knocking the two of them into the air before he stopped them at the roof's edge.

From inside, Jade was now struggling to breathe in between cackles of winked laughter and screeches of pain as she pressed her bleeding palm up to her chest. She continued to yank on Adelaide's foot and even managed to drag her halfway back into the room before Clayton came to her rescue. Looking about, he picked up a piece of glass lying beneath the window and swung it at Jade's unprotected face. It sliced across her forehead, cutting it wide open. She let out a bloodcurdling scream and loosened her grip. Now free, the two of them braced themselves for impact and leapt off of the roof. The ground beneath them was soft and muddy, making their landing less painful. Jade continued to shriek and curse above them.

Clayton carefully urged Adelaide along out towards the open street from the alley they had landed in. Already, many of the townspeople were making their way outside their homes, drawn to the loud commotion, which included the uncontrollable blubbering of Puck as he stumbled about in a circle nearby. As they convened onto the street, not a single citizen noticed the pair of them standing there at the alley entrance with their clothes covered in mud and their faces stamped with terror. For the first time in her life, Adelaide wanted nothing more in the world than for Clayton Hogg to protect her.

"What do we do?" she asked him. "We have to find the others. We have to find Finn and Raoul. They could be anywhere."

"Yes they could, and we don't have the time," Clayton stated solemnly. "We have to find a way out of this place before we can save them."

Adelaide was about to slap him hard across the face for suggesting that they should abandon their friends. Then his logic struck home. As terrible as it sounded, they would be no use to their companions if they wandered blindly around Pinewood looking for them. Once outside the town, they could make a better rescue mission while Freud Blankis and his cronies were busy checking every crack and corner for them. It was the safest way.

"Well, come on then," she cried, pulling him along the walkway towards the docks. "We have only a few minutes before they start closing down the whole town and we get trapped in here."

With all the commotion, no one seemed to notice the two mud soaked Red Hands edging away from the tavern. Covered in sweat and wearing dirty clothes was the perfect disguise for the two runaways. Clayton realized this as he accidentally brushed against a pair of young townsman who paid him no heed. The only thing peculiar about them now was the way they were shifting along down the walk as if to elude something. It was suspicious to see.

"Run," he hissed under his breath.

"What? What do you mean?" Adelaide whispered.

"Start running. Don't look scared though, just like you're winked. We look like locals in this natural balm, and if we act like them, we might get out of here without a fight."

Together, they made their way into the middle of the street. Townspeople were running about in every direction, some crying out in agony at their recent stint of unfortunate luck, others cursing the Red Hands they had just welcomed with open arms. Even Clayton managed to yell out a rude comment about the "curly haired meal ticket" as he jumped past a group of blubbering women and yanked Adelaide towards the docks.

"Be ready," he warned her. "Those three rotters in cloaks might be guarding it."

Once they arrived, they both found that the docks were abandoned. The raft remained tied to a post, the oar lying idly in the center. There was no one to be seen.

"We will have to move quickly," Clayton stated. "Remember, they have those maps to navigate through the mines."

"I just hope Huglund isn't close by," Adelaide murmured. "We'll need more than a couple hours to figure out a plan for getting Finn and Raoul back."

"It's nice to know you both weren't going to leave us long term," a voice from the darkness chuckled.

Clayton whipped around, expecting an ambush.

"Who is that?" he growled. "Come out and get a taste of what I gave your friends."

"Oh," the voice sarcastically replied. "You mean accidentally killing a clumsy bartender and disfiguring a winked female? Yes, I heard about those ones just a minute ago. I wonder if that tops my defeating a cannibalistic stutterer. Then again…I did have some help."

With that, two figures made their way into the light of the lantern from beneath the dock. One was Raoul, his gloves and shirt splattered in dried blood. Cherry stood beside him, still wearing her tunic and a pair of tattered moccasins on her feet.

The group's supplies and knapsacks were clasped tightly in her petite fists. She looked up at Adelaide and smiled.

"Raoul, is that you?" Adelaide gasped. "How did you escape? And....who is that supposed to be?"

"This is my new friend, Cherry. Had she not struck that Boras character over the head with flower vase, I wouldn't have had the time to jab my letter opener into his neck. You should have seen the expression on his rotting face. Anyways, we were barely out the window and onto the street before that givie from the Lambshead pulled us into the shadows. She had collected all our things and added a few extra items from this rotting town's pantry."

"You mean Taz?" exclaimed Clayton. Adelaide shot him a look of contempt.

"Yeah, that was her name," Raoul remarked. "She said that if you two escaped, you would most likely head for the docks, planning to steal the raft and head for other side of the lake. She also told me I had to cut you off and tell you it would be pointless. With those maps in the mayor's office, they would be through the mine fields and upon you the second you reached the other side. She said to give you this and tell you that she would handle the rest of them."

Raoul tossed up a small wad of paper to Clayton, who upon unraveling it broke into a smile and passed it to Adelaide.

"Is this what I think it is?" she asked.

"I believe it is, Miss Stokes," Clayton laughed.

"But it's no use," Adelaide moaned, shaking her head. "Blankis and the town will just follow us through."

"Taz said she would take care of it," Raoul informed them. "Cherry, here, says she's known her for years. She trusts her completely."

"Yes I certainly do," piped up Cherry. "Her parents would always take me in when my other family would try hurting me. I liked them a lot, until they were lost in the woods and eaten of course. Those two men Boras and Puck said they found their bones and buried them for me. Boras couldn't stop drooling and cackling as he tried to lift me up from the bed. That's when I hit him with the vase."

"Well what about Finn?" asked Adelaide, her lower lip starting to quiver. "We can't just leave him in Pinewood for Huglund to take at dawn. I don't want to think about what those rotters might do before he gets here."

"Oh don't worry, miss," Cherry comforted her. "Taz said to be out of the woods before sunrise. She would save your Finn."

"And that means unless we go right this second, we will be running behind the mob they're raising at the moment for us, instead of the other way around," said Raoul. "So, if we could all just grab our own plugging bags and hurry along, that would be great."

According to the map, there were approximately sixty eight mines scattered around the surrounding landscape, spreading out for just under a quarter mile. In order to start from the correct point, the group would first have to make their way past the back yards of several houses until they reached one with a red painted fence. Once there, a shallow creek bed would stem out into the woods, leading them on until it reached a small mound of earth with a rock shaped like an eagle's beak sunken on top. Then it was a straightforward, yet perilous, trek zigzagging around a field covered in mines, which the map accurately depicted, moving quickly and carefully along until they were beyond the dangerous terrain.

As they finally reached the rock, the group all took a second to gaze out at the open field before them. One wrong step, a loud boom, and there wouldn't be much left to see.

The voices of townspeople giving chase were closing in behind them. There was nothing else to do. Clayton took Adelaide's hand. She, in turn, seized Cherry's, who clasped Raoul's. One by one the group slowly jogged forward. Clayton constantly checked the map for the next set of instructions. They hadn't been in the field for less than two minutes before a disturbing, yet joyous, sound reached their ears from not far behind them. It was the sound of mass confusion and panic as multiple voices started screaming behind them.

"What ith wrong with these maths?"

"They're all wrong."

"What the rot did they do?"

"Mine is still good, I just know it. Follow me."

A mine exploded near the rock. The panic grew more intense.

"Those little rotters, I'll kill them all! Watch your step…"

Another explosion followed.

"We need to go back! Please. Someone help!"

Two more mines exploded. The field immediately flew into chaos. Members of the mob started running blindly in every direction. A dozen more explosions followed, some at the same time, others five or six seconds apart. The bloodcurdling screams and curses of frightened townsfolk chilled Adelaide's blood as she struggled not to look back.

Suddenly, there was a loud screech close behind the group. Cherry cried out in terror as she turned her head to behold a figure closing in on them. The figure screeched again, this time with a cackle that would raise the hairs on a warrior's neck. Clayton shivered as he recognized its owner: Jade. She was still in the chase with her forehead bandaged up and her hand wrapped with a blood soaked rag. Her shrieks grew louder and louder, gaining ground as it outpaced the rest of the mob and started to close in. She couldn't have been more than ten yards behind the group now, drawing closer with every leap.

"Ha! Hold on now, little pretties!" she screamed frantically. "Come on back. We aren't so bad once you get to know us. Come on now, please. Come cut me some more. I like it! Cut me good. I won't ask again, you rots! Now come…back….here…"

An explosion permanently ended her rant. Raoul felt his body jerked forward as the blast caught him off guard. He soon regained his footing and hurried on.

Freud Blankis was still alive, trying his best to coax the rest of the mob back to the safety of the beak shaped rock. Every now and then, he would cast a threat out at the fleeing group. His voice soon became inaudible as the field ended, and one by one, the fleeing Red Hands started laughing in uncontrollable relief.

"We made it!" Adelaide exclaimed. "We're free."

"Not yet, we aren't," Clayton bluntly stated. "We still have to clear these woods by dawn, and it can't be more than twenty five minutes to sunrise. Raoul, watch our backs. Adelaide, would you please watch our little friend here? We aren't losing anyone else tonight. Now let's go."

Adelaide grabbed Cherry's hand and pulled her along. Raoul brought up the rear, his small blade still clenched tightly in his hand. Clayton spoke comforting words to the group as he led them along, his arms lashing out at oncoming foliage. He didn't seem to be following any sort of determined path, just urging them on northward, where he knew the woods had to end sometime.

The trees vanished abruptly before them and the various tunes of the forest night life grew silent and still. The road they had seen the day before lay stretched before them. Beyond it rose the same wall of freshly grown corn stalks that had blocked their vision the day before. There wasn't a barn or farmhouse in sight. The slumbering sky above them was melting away to reveal the pink hue of an early morning, a grey haze still lingering as the sun's rays creeped up over the tallest corn stalk and illuminated all that was around them.

"Maybe there's help nearby," Adelaide suggested, grabbing her sides as she struggled to gain her breath. "They might even be someone who is not on Huglund's payroll."

"Perhaps," Clayton replied, "but after our dealings with strangers lately, I would rather take my chances relying on ourselves. Let's cut through this field here until we find some secure ground to make camp. From there, we can await Finn and Taz."

"If they make it, that is," Raoul chuckled.

"Don't even start, Raoul King Jr!" Adelaide snapped at him. She was terrified about what might have happened to Finn, even before Taz had gotten there.

"Look. There are horse tracks on the road," Cherry exclaimed, pointing downward. "They look fresh, too!"

"Huglund," muttered Raoul. "That eerie rotter is really starting to annoy me."

"We'll deal with him soon, Raoul, I swear to you. But for now we need to focus on staying alive, that's all that matters," Clayton told him.

"Here, here!" exclaimed Cherry.

Raoul glanced over at Adelaide, who nodded gingerly. He sighed and shook his head.

"Right then," he muttered. "Let's get moving off this open road before someone spots us."

With that, the group hurried into the corn field. The early morning sun peaked above the crops and brought with it the full light of day.

CHAPTER SEVENTEEN

Adelaide awoke to the late morning sun beaming above her head. She found herself curled up on a bed of corn shucks with Cherry lying close beside her. The little girl was making cooing sound as she nestled her face into Adelaide's shoulder, her hands lightly wrapped around her arm.

As she lay there, still the hunted convict she'd been several days before, Adelaide couldn't help but feel immensely calm. Perhaps there was just no more fear left in her body to use. It just felt good to finally stare up at a bright cloudless sky, the sun blinding her eyes as she enjoyed the warmth settling down upon her face. The first few weeks of spring had always been her favorite time of year, ever since she was a squirm. The way the cool crisp air blended with the gentle heat settling down from the sky as the sun shone bright and unchallenged above. The grass was as green as it ever would be, freshly grown out of the enriched soil that was, until recently, imprisoned by coats of malicious frost and snow. The buds of various flowers were popping their heads out as well, not quite ready to reveal their lovely untouched petals, but confident enough to tease their onlookers. Everything just felt more alive this time of year, and had that wondrous feast continued on uninterrupted, and those rotting Tibris Guards on an errand of violence had never come to Havendale, it might have felt all the more marvelous. So, it was with a saddened and wounded heart that Adelaide took in the beauty of that early spring morning, allowing it to consume her mind and soul as she quietly hoped it would last forever.

A loud grunt of discomfort grabbed her attention. Raoul was lying asleep in a wheelbarrow several yards away, his head cushioned against his shoulder and his legs hanging awkwardly over the side. He mumbled something inaudible and twisted himself into a more comfortable position.

Clayton was standing guard nearby. Adelaide guessed he had been up ever since they'd set up camp several hours earlier. Tired as he must have been, his posture was unwavering.

Adelaide couldn't help but feel a deep respect growing for him as he stood there, staring sleepily out at the surrounding corn stalks. Sure, she liked giving him a hard time, but inside she had always known he would be there for her…for all of them. Why did she always give him such a hard time? As far back as she could remember, she'd always been quite prejudiced against him and his many accomplishments.

Shaking off the small blanket across her, Adelaide decided to offer to stand watch for a while, in order to give him some much needed rest. As she rose from the ground, she gently placed it under Cherry's head. The little girl smiled happily, as if falling into a beautiful dream. Looking down upon her, Adelaide suddenly found herself wondering what life would have been like if she'd had a little sister.

"Good morning," Clayton said. He had turned at the sound of her movement. Adelaide noticed his finger lightly touching the spot on his chest where the Acryptus Tree was. His eyes seemed troubled and full of questions.

"Good morning," she replied softly as to not awake Cherry.

"How did you sleep?"

"Well enough, considering."

Clayton nodded solemnly.

"Has Finn returned yet?" she asked.

"Not yet. The sun hasn't been up long now. Let's wait a while and see what happens. I'm sure he and Taz are on their way."

Adelaide looked down as Cherry fluttered open her eyelids and yawned loudly beneath the warming spring sun.

"Hey there, little one," Clayton laughed. "Sleep well?"

"Oh so very well, thank you," she exclaimed. Her face was shining and her eyes were full of gratitude. "Do you guys think it would be alright if I woke up Raoul?"

"Well, I sure as rot wouldn't do it myself. Maybe your face is exactly what he needs to see before I give him next watch duty."

"Nonsense," Adelaide objected. "I will gladly take a shift if you want some rest."

Clayton shook his head. "No, your charge is to keep track of this little girl here and make sure no harm comes to her. We owe her our lives, as well as our freedom."

"Don't forget Taz," Cherry reminded him.

"True," laughed Clayton. "I will have to extend her my fullest gratitude once she arrives with our friend. I know Adelaide will be pleased."

Adelaide smiled. She couldn't show to the group how concerned she was about Finn and what had happened to him. After finding out the town's true colors, not to mention the unspeakable habits they indulged in, it was not worth dwelling on.

Her fears were soon put to rest. Not five minutes after Cherry had successfully awoken Raoul from his awkward slumber and helped him rub the soreness out of his legs, there came a rustling noise to the south. This was followed by a series of loud sneezes and snorts.

Adelaide smiled broadly. She had just started writing away into her journal, making it several sentences in before closing it up.

"That would be Finn," Clayton laughed. "He gets the fits from corn, you see. Little rashes and bouts of sneezing strike him every time he passes it."

"Sounds like a real keeper," grumbled Raoul.

"Oh shut up," Adelaide retorted savagely. "He made it. He's alive."

Sure enough, Finn Wessel soon stumbled out of the corn. His hands and legs were bleeding from constant scratching and his eyes were both swollen and red with inflammation. Taz followed behind him. She had switched her risqué outfit for a pair of leather pants, a v-neck tee shirt, and a bomber jacket.

"I tried….I tried to tell her I was all-all-allergic," Finn said, gulping for air, "but she just, just shoved me inside and called me a b-b-big squirm. Even after I couldn't…even after I couldn't breathe she still wouldn't let….let me stop."

"That's because if we had stopped, we might have rotting died," Taz replied sarcastically. "You were the one who insisted on staying long enough to see what Huglund did to Pinewood after he discovered our escape."

"So Huglund did show after all?" asked Clayton.

"Oh yeah," Taz laughed. "He showed not long after I freed your companion here."

"How did you escape?" Adelaide asked.

Taz smiled over at Clayton. This smile lingered, something that made Adelaide feel a little riled up.

"After I gave the map to your friend Raoul," she declared. "I decided to go back and mess around with the others I left on Oderheim's official desk. A little spilled ink and some additional drawings proved pretty effective."

"How did you get in?" Clayton inquired.

"Well," Taz started. "About a week ago, I fell into it with this guy from town. He was in love with me from the start, but I wasn't that type, given my occupation and all. Anyways, one night after a good plugging, he gave me a spare key to meet him in Oderheim's office on future evenings. I guess he was a custodian of sorts. He up and left Pinewood some time ago, and I've held onto it ever since. I thought it might be useful."

"This fellow of yours," Finn chimed in. "What was his name?"

"Hollis Pearl."

Adelaide gasped quietly and cast a glance to Clayton. He reached into his pockets and pulled forth the locket from the woods.

"I think…I think this may have been meant for you," he solemnly stated, handing it to Taz. She looked down at it and shook her head.

"That's just like him," she muttered. "Spend more shine than he can afford on worthless trash with some winking jargon scratched inside. I told him over and over it wasn't necessary."

A moment of silence passed. She stared down at it without flinching. Adelaide thought she saw the makings of a tear forming in her right eye. Feeling one forming, Taz blinked and quickly changed the subject.

"Rotting oaf took off without even giving it to me," she chuckled. "Anyways, I'm sure he's better off. Much more I'll wager than the whole of Pinewood."

"What do you mean?" asked Adelaide.

"I placed the maps back in the drawer and locked it up before Blankis arrived to collect them," Taz informed the group. "As he and half the town went running off to find you, I freed Finn from the cellar and snuck him out a back way. We could hear screaming and loud explosions, so I reckon plenty townsfolk got what they had coming. The rest suffered Huglund's wrath not long after. We camped out on the edge of town just as the Tibris Guards rode in. Oderheim's face went white as his hair when he realized you'd all escaped. He blamed it all on Jade, Boras, Garrick, and anyone else who was already dead. When that didn't work, he blamed it on Freud. So Huglund had that sidekick Kobal take Freud's head. And then he took Oderheim's. Anyone who tried to flee was cut down or trampled. They would have burned the town to ashes if there wasn't risk of a forest fire."

"Oh," Adelaide murmured. Knowing the grief of losing one's home flooded her with pity for their newfound ally. "I'm so sorry about your town. I really am."

Taz looked at her curiously.

"Why? Anyone I ever loved in that rotting place split or got killed, except for Cherry here. Good riddance, I say. They all got what they deserved." Her tone was cold and unwavering.

"Isn't that a little harsh?" Finn murmured to Adelaide.

"Harsh, you say?" Taz exclaimed, shooting them both an unnerving look. "Tell me, have you got any idea what they made me do back there? What happened when I didn't comply?"

"Well," Clayton began, clearing his throat. "I don't know about any of you, but I think...."

"We didn't mean anything by it," Adelaide assured her.

"No, of course you didn't," Taz retorted. "I'm convinced. How could I ever have misjudged you?" The sarcasm in her voice was piercing and direct.

"I like this givie," Raoul chuckled.

"Thank you," Taz replied coldly," but you see, that is precisely the problem. Your friends here imagine me as the sort of shameless plugger who enjoys a good toss for a couple shine. Rot, why even a couple? You think I'd bend and stretch for less, don't you?"

Adelaide bit her tongue as sharp retorts struggled to emerge. Finn shook his head and waved Taz off.

"Well, let me promise you this," she continued, her hands shaking and shoulders quivering. "I remember every time I said no, and the burns, cuts, and beatings that followed. The loss of anyone who stood up for me strikes my rotting heart again and again. This life isn't the one I chose. So, I don't want you or anyone else looking at me like I asked for it. Are we clear?"

A biting chill descended on the group as darkening rain clouds swiftly appeared overhead.

"Are we clear?" Taz repeated.

A quiet sigh broke the following silence. All eyes turned to Cherry. She was shuddering uncontrollably as the cold air brushed her skin.

"I suggest we get a move on," Raoul growled, wrapping his blanket around her. "That is, of course, unless anyone here has anything else to say?"

Finn started to speak, but a nudge from Adelaide silenced him.

"Good," Raoul said. "Now, what comes next?"

"The Tibris Guards will be scouring the road once they've cleaned up at Pinewood," Clayton announced. "By then, I'd like to be as far away as possible. I reckon this storm will brew another hour or two before downpour. If we strike out now, we can find a barn to wait out the torrents."

"I never imagined we'd get this rotting lucky," Taz remarked, casting a pleasant grin upward towards the thunderous turmoil.

"You call this lucky?" Adelaide asked sarcastically. Clayton coughed loudly at her tone.

"I do," Taz replied. "A storm like this will wash away any tracks we leave behind. Neither Huglund nor Necrya herself will be able to follow us then."

"Know-it-all," thought Adelaide.

"Alright then," Clayton announced. "Let's pack up everything and head out."

The morning sky, once blue and illuminated by the pleasant spring sunlight, was now overwhelmed by tumultuous wave upon wave of growing grey chaos. One could hardly tell it was midday anymore, and not a ray of light could penetrate the storm. Low growls of thunder sounded from deep within the thick sheet blanketing the sky, soon followed by a series of violent bursts of light and cracks of lightening striking down into the surrounding fields. The group had been walking less than half an hour before the lightening bursts started touching down not a hundred yards away in every direction. As unnerving as it was, Clayton led on, his expression grim but resolved.

"How long have we been walking?" shouted Raoul in between a few claps of thunder. "Cherry needs to rest."

"Oh no, please, I am quite fine," Cherry exclaimed, even as she swayed a little to the right, "I could walk a thousand miles."

"Yeah well, I wouldn't let you," stated Raoul dryly. "Come on now, hop on my back. I'll carry you a bit."

The rain started a few minutes later. A gentle drizzle soon became a reckless torrent. Both lightning and thunder were battling for supremacy in the skies above, lighting the way for Clayton as he led the group along with a lorb in his hand, his clothes soaking through to the bone. Adelaide did her best to keep her hair from obstructing her vision. Finn seemed at ease by the storm, it was certainly doing an excellent job of taking his mind off the growing rashes from the corn stalks. Quiet snores confirmed to Raoul that Cherry was fast asleep, her arms still wound tightly around his neck.

"We have to stop!" Raoul exclaimed. "I'm not leaving this little girl out in the rain any longer."

"Oh give it a rest, Blondie," Finn yelled over the sound of the growing storm. "Just try keeping it in your pants, will you?"

Raoul turned to face Finn, his face dark with fury.

"If I wasn't carrying her right now," he hissed. "I'd…I'd kill you, Wessel. I'd kill you right where you stand. I wouldn't hesitate."

"Go ahead and try," goaded Finn. "Even with these rashes, I'd kick your rump."

"Are you two really doing this? Right now?" asked Taz.

"Stay out of this, givie!" Finn yelled. "This little issue doesn't need your guidance."

"Look, we just need to keep calm, guys," Clayton said, turning around. "I know you're both exhausted. Just a little further and we'll rest, I promise you."

"No, Clayton," Raoul growled. "It isn't about the storm, or the fact we're out of food, have no map, no idea where the rot we're going, or even proper weapons to defend ourselves with. It's about this rotter and his attitude towards me, one that I've had it up to here with. Now, I've put up with a lot of things, especially on account of you and Adelaide, with her girlish desires and winking taste in men, but I am drawing the line now. This is where it stops."

Finn laughed sarcastically. Even Adelaide couldn't ignore how horrid he was acting.

"Oh, how adorable," he threw at Raoul. "Some little squirm shows you affection and you practically glue yourself onto her. Goes to show just how desperate you are for some human kindness, you….you sad, lonely wink."

"That's enough now, I mean it," warned Clayton.

"By Sorra, how have you all survived?" threw in Taz.

"Rot off, Wessel," Raoul growled.

"Come on, King, bring it. I'll send you home weeping to your father. Oh, wait…..I'd forgotten….he's not much for taking care of you, is he?"

Raoul stopped abruptly. His mouth flew open, a loud scratchy sound emitting from his throat. His eyes bulged, his lips quivered, and his hands trembled violently.

"You…..you…..are….a dead man. You…..you don't get to….to…"

"What?" Finn sneered. "I don't get to do what?"

"Finn," Adelaide said. "That's enough."

"Back off now, Finn," Clayton said. "I'm warning you."

Ignoring them, he took a step towards Raoul.

"Come on, Blondie. Bring it."

"No!" yelled Taz, stepping forward. "I'll bring it."

She struck Finn across the mouth with a closed fist, throwing him back several steps and causing blood to gush from his lip. Adelaide cried out and rushed to his side as he fell.

"Is that what you want?" Taz shouted down at him. "Huh? You want a little blood on your lip? You might be sick and itchy and tired right now, but frankly, so are the rest of us. You're nothing special, you raven haired rot! Now shut your mouth and deal with it. I doubt your friend would have been that kind to you if you'd pushed him any further."

"Rotting right I wouldn't have," muttered Raoul quietly.

"Clayton, please, we really have to stop and rest," Adelaide pleaded. "We've been at this all day, and we'll drown if we don't find someplace now."

"I agree," said Taz. "We can't risk pushing on any further. Tensions are too high."

"I know," assured Clayton. "But we can't just plop down in the middle of a field. We need some shelter to stay out of this storm."

"Hey everyone," said Cherry, a trembling yawn escaping her lips as she spoke. "What's that over there?"

All eyes turned. A hundred yards down the road, a tiny, flickering light could be seen.

"Maybe someone lives there," Adelaide suggested.

"We should check it out," said Clayton. "They might be able to put us up for the night."

"Or turn us in to the local authorities," Taz threw in. "Have you all forgotten Pinewood already? We should see if we can hide out somewhere on the property instead of just knocking on the front door."

"It's a chance we have to take. We have a little girl here and no good protection from this storm. A cold barn with no food isn't going to cut it."

"This storm isn't going to let up," Adelaide said. "We need to be out of it for as long as we can."

Taz looked from one to the other, her expression one of cynical discomfort.

"Alright," she said. "This is your group. I'll follow your lead."

Clayton slowly led the group along the road towards the light. A loud crack of thunder shook their senses as the skies rumbled and roared continuously. A bright bolt of lightning struck down in the field behind them, causing Adelaide and Cherry to shriek out at its close quarters. Any more time out in the open and the next one might land a little too close. They had just a few minutes before it would strike again, and no time to seek alternate shelter. Whatever that light meant, it had to offer them sanctuary. All their lives depended on it.

Out from the darkness loomed a tall structure. It was faint at first, but became more distinct as the group drew closer. A poorly constructed fence started to the right of the road, carrying on for several yards before veering away into the field. As it did so, the crops parted away and revealed an acre of open land. The tall building stood positioned squarely in the center of it, rising two stories tall with an arching roof that measured half the height of the house itself. A solitary lorb glowed faintly from inside a glass lantern. It hung from a small hook attached to a long strand of cable, attached securely to the ceiling of the house's front porch. The walls were colored in egg-white paint that had peeled due to lack of upkeep and care. The roof was layered in swamp green shingles that looked loose and slippery in the falling downpour. No lights could be seen behind the window panes, but even in the darkness it seemed like all the curtains were drawn and the shutters closed. If there hadn't been a light burning out on the front porch, the group could have easily walked right past it and not known it was there. The front yard was covered in scattered tall weeds, the grass newly green, but barely visible under the long shafts of dry yellow plants. At the foot of the road there was a picket fence coated in a fine oak glaze, which intensified the coat of the wooden planks. From what could be seen, it was the finest attribute to the entire premises. A broken gate swung loosely on its hinges, leading to a brick layered path that crossed across the lawn up to the front porch. The house, as a whole, appeared deserted.

"I don't like this," Taz stated.

"There's a lorb," Adelaide said. "Someone must live here."

"Or maybe it's haunted by a ghost that consumes little squirms," Finn laughed.

Cherry whimpered quietly. Raoul gave him a violent shove.

"If someone does reside here, we won't make the mistake of spooking them," Clayton said. "I'll go first and make sure it is safe."

"Alone?" Adelaide asked.

"Sure," Clayton laughed, tucking his mallet into his belt. "What's the worst that can happen right?"

"I should go," said Raoul.

"No!" Cherry cried.

"Don't be winked, I'll do it," Clayton told him. Raoul smiled and shook his head.

"Take a look at yourselves," he laughed. "You all look like the Red Hands you're accused to be, and I certainly wouldn't think of sending up Cherry. I'm unarmed, smartly dressed and locally known. They'd see me as less of a threat…if they saw me as one at all."

"I don't know…" Taz began.

"Raoul, are you certain?" Clayton asked. "You don't have to do this."

Their companion looked down at Cherry clinging to his shirt and sighed.

"After what we've just been through, who knows what we might find." With that he stood upright and marched towards the house.

CHAPTER EIGHTEEN

The walkway leading up to the porch was made of grainy sand and the occasional stone pebble. Each small step brought Raoul a little closer to the door, his eyes ever scanning the windows for signs of movement. The group watched from behind the gate. Clayton's hand rested on his sword hilt. Adelaide was clenching Finn's hand in hers. Cherry stared after Raoul longingly, her eyes wide with terror as she watched him cover the path without much difficulty and stroll up to the front door. All seemed to be going well, so far. Even Raoul couldn't help but sigh in relief as he considered the strong possibility that this house would be empty and open for them all to enjoy.

His foot was barely on the front step before the door before him swung open. He froze in his tracks, unable to react further. The outline of a tall, muscular figure stood before him, barely visible in the dark atmosphere of the stormy night. In his hands was a long barreled rifle. Raoul heard a loud click as the figure pulled back the hammer, intent on firing should he attempt to flee. He could feel the cold wind curling the hairs on the back of his neck as he stood there helpless, hoping the person before him didn't have a series of homemade graves in the back yard specifically for visitors like him.

The weapon was pointing directly at Raoul's chest. The figure holding it took two steps forward, leaving the shadow of the house and revealing himself. He had wild gray hair that fell down around his neck. He was built with sinewy muscles that bulged from inside his tight, weathered coat. He had piercing brown eyes and bits of stubble all around his cheeks and chin.

His expression was grim, and his hands steady as he lifted the gun closer to Raoul's face.

"What's your business here, son?" the man asked gruffly.

"I....I was....I was just looking for some....some shelter from the rain."

The man shook his head and jerked the gun briefly to the side.

"No room here, tonight," he declared. "We aren't running a bed and breakfast."

"Please…I'm cold and hungry. We all are. I mean…..just me. It's just me here."

The old man raised an eyebrow and grasped the trigger more intently.

"What sort of game are you playing?" he snarled.

Raoul closed his eyes in fear. There was no point in running away. He wouldn't make it five feet before getting gunned down.

"I…..I don't know," he cried. "I am so cold and hungry. Please don't end my rotting life!"

"No! You leave him alone!"

Raoul's head jerked around at the sound of Cherry's voice. She had leapt to her feet and run through the gate, stopping halfway down the front path before anyone could stop her.

"Get out of sight," Raoul hissed.

The old man looked up at Cherry, and then returned his gaze to Raoul. His expression didn't change, but his lower lip started quivering quite noticeably. The sight of Cherry out in the rain seemed to have struck some hidden nerve, one that caused him to lower the gun and blink back the makings of a tear.

"Sal, what's going on out there? Who are you talking to?" a voice called from inside the house.

"Just some passing travelers set on stealing our hospitality."

Another figure made its way out onto the porch. It was a woman. Her face was cringed and wrinkled, but also lovingly kind. Around her shoulders was a tattered grey shawl, covering part of a long, white night gown. She gasped in surprise when she saw Raoul standing with his hands thrust into the air, and exclaimed in horror when she witnessed Cherry shivering close behind him.

"Oh for Sorra's sake, Sal, they're just squirms. What are you thinking, pointing that…that cannon at them?"

"Well, I didn't know they were squirms when I heard them outside, now did I?" the old man grumbled.

"You do now, you old wink," the white haired woman exclaimed, slapping the back of his head with her hand. "I swear you'd lose your common sense if not for me. Just put the gun down and tell them to come on in before they drown out there."

"We uh…..we have some friends too," Raoul stated, his hands still thrust high above his head.

The man turned away and shook his head.

"It's like we're running a bed and breakfast out here," he muttered.

"Now Sal, that's enough," the woman demanded, before turning back to Raoul. "Come right on up, son, you must be freezing. You as well, little one, and anyone else hiding out there."

Clayton walked out from behind the fence. He stood there silently for a second before ushering Adelaide and Finn to join him. Taz followed them, ready for anything.

"You'll have to excuse my husband," the old woman said smiling. She reached down and offered them each a quilted blanket from a bamboo chest next to the open doorway. "He's always grumpy when it rains. You could pack an umbrella by his attitude."

"If she calls us little critters...just once...I am out of here," whispered Finn to Adelaide. "I don't care how cozy these blankets are."

The man reappeared at the door, his brow stern and unwavering.

"Well," he began. "I suppose as long as you're going to be using up valuable space, you might as well come inside. We've got some leftover stew in the pot and some warm coffee in the kitchen. Help yourselves."

The house was much more pleasant from the inside than the group would have guessed. The floors were of stainless oak, and the walls were composed of plaster and coated in peach-colored paint. Pieces of furniture dotted the small living room, including a couple of antique couches, a hand-carved coffee table, some stools and chairs, and a record player in the corner, playing a beautiful combination of harp music and violin symphonies. To Adelaide, it felt like if she had ever met her grandmother, this is the kind of house she would have lived in.

The kitchen was simple enough. A table stood on the center of the cement tiled floor with two long benches placed on both sides of it. There was a small sink for washing in the corner, next to the back door, and an icebox standing against the wall. The woman pulled a brass pot out of it, steam still rising from a crack in its cover. She opened it to reveal its contents: a mixture of pork, beef, potatoes, and white rice swimming in rich gravy.

Every bowl dished out was emptied in a matter of seconds. Taz and Cherry had seconds. Finn had thirds. Adelaide burned her tongue on the stew, burning it again later on with the coffee she swallowed too quickly. All this aside, she couldn't remember having a more delicious supper. Raoul helped Cherry finish her second bowl while sipping a small glass of coffee that the woman had poured them. They swallowed their beverages with ease, sitting back contently once they finished.

Clayton took his time, slowly allowing the juicy chunks of meat and tiny clusters of white rice to roll along his tongue, catching every taste bud on the way down. It was impossible, even as hungry as he was, to wolf down this simple, yet indulgent feast before him. On any other day, a bowl of stew and coffee wouldn't have given him cause for joy, but with the storm rolling around them, the cold sweat of fear from stray bolts of lightning still fresh on his mind, and murderous villains on horseback riding them down...a bowl of stew was more.

After he'd finished, he politely placed his empty bowl on the table, allowing his stomach a few seconds to process this bulging change in the recent diet of a fugitive. The kind old woman had pulled out a small platter from one of the cupboards next to the icebox, which contained a series of newly frosted delights, ranging from chocolate and caramel flavored cupcakes to a round honey drizzled marshmallow in the center. Its size and depth seemed absurd for a marshmallow, which anyone would say served its consumer better by being small and fluffy. This one, however, had been magnified greatly. It would most likely have taken ten people ten minutes to devour it entirely, a feat which Finn, Taz, Adelaide, and Cherry took upon themselves to tackle. Raoul continued slurping down his bowl of stew while hungrily eyeing the desserts before his eyes. Clayton simply smiled and walked away, leaving them all to finish stuffing themselves off of the old woman's kindness.

He strolled into the living room and took a seat across from the old man. The glowing lorbs in the nearby fireplace illuminated his worn, experienced features. His hand dipped slowly into his vest pocket and pulled forth a round tin of chewing tobacco. He offered some to Clayton after sliding a pinch of it inside his mouth.

"Oh no thank you, sir, I don't partake."

The old man nodded with a grunt. Almost a full minute of silence passed before he spoke again.

"Rotting habit to get into, I'm afraid. Started on my fifteenth birthday and haven't stopped since. Drives the wife winked to watch me do it, but we all have our private pleasures, don't we?"

"That is quite true, sir."

The old man shook his head.

"That's enough with the sir. I may be old, but it doesn't help with you rubbing it in. My name is Salvatore Martello. Call me Sal."

"Alright," Clayton replied, "and your wife?"

"It's January, but she prefers Jan. We met back when I was helping her father build dams up north. She was all alone without a mother, and he wasn't much for parenting. Anyhow, I introduced myself, kept her safe, and before long, we were married and off to find our own way of things. We've been tied down here going on forty years now."

"You got any squirms?" Clayton asked.

Sal gazed over at a framed photograph sitting beside his armchair. From where he sat, Clayton could make out a woman's face, full and plump, reddish bangs falling across her forehead.

"That's our daughter, Lark. She'll be almost thirty now."

"She's lovely. Will she be joining us later?"

"No, son, I'm afraid she won't be. We haven't seen her in almost ten years."

"I...I apologize for bringing it up, sir," Clayton stammered. "I didn't honestly know..."

"It's Sal, squirm, how many times do I have to tell you? You got wax in your ears, I suppose. Don't worry, you couldn't have known. We've made peace with it, the parts we understand anyhow."

"What do you mean?"

"Not much of it made sense," Sal grunted. "One day she was here with us, her life as perfect as we could make it, and plenty of time to plan a bright future for herself, and then....then the next she was gone. No note, no reason, no explanation. Then again, I suppose there was a thing or two off before that day arrived."

"Off?"

"Little things, I guess. She was acting a bit strange, like she was concerned about something she didn't really understand. She also started keeping her arm well hidden, always wearing long sleeves, even in warm weather. When we asked her about it, she always made a hurried excuse and walked away."

Clayton pursed his lips, a dark theory crossing his mind as he stared off at the window.

"What happened next?" he finally inquired.

"That was it. She was gone. We asked around, and I searched every road and field for miles, but found no trace of her. I was even willing to walk all the way up north and ask our new lord for help, but I imagine as big as it was to me and the missus, it wouldn't have mattered a bit to someone like him."

"You mean Lord Tiberion?" Clayton asked. "He was in charge when she vanished?"

"Elected not three weeks before the peculiarities and such, I'd bet my life on it. It wasn't long after she disappeared that we started hearing stories and such."

"What do you mean by stories?"

"Nonsense about cursed tattoos, half dead soldiers, storybook trees, and a conspiracy that reached as high as Sanctumsea royalty could go. It was all rumors from travelers and distant friends, not much to put any stock into."

"Did you hear anything else? Anything about…well, a time before we came to Sanctumsea? Possibly something about those storybook trees…glowing for some reason?"

Sal raised an eyebrow.

"Now son," he said. "I won't lie to you, it doesn't exactly ease my old bones that you and your friends are alone and half starved, fleeing from whatever it is you fear so badly, and lost out there on a night like this with knives, mallets and the like. Quite frankly, I'm also a little puzzled by those strange images you're all working so hard to hide on your persons."

Clayton coughed uncomfortably.

"I guess you could say it's a bit…complicated."

"Well, I don't appreciate things that are complicated," Sal declared. "I might be swayed though. You could say I have good old human curiosity."

"Mr. Martello....err I mean Sal, I really have to ask....have you ever heard of Tibris Guards?"

Sal's face went momentarily dark.

"I don't know what troubles you have, son," he replied. "But if Tibris Guards be involved, Sorra herself needs to lend you all a hand. I met one once.....not two days after our daughter left home. He was a monster, if ever was one in human form, who just happened to be passing along that morning as I was tending to the front lawn. I'd been out searching for Lark all night and Jan recommended some work to ease my mind. He was dressed like some ancient warrior, garbed in shiny gab with a hairless face and head, except for some nasty inky veins. His name was something peculiar, like Harland, or Hugo…I can't rightly recall. He had a small patrol along with him; all dressed the same as he was. He rode straight up onto my land and asked me where he could find my daughter. I asked him what his business was with her and he said….I swear he up and looks me straight in the eyes and says she had to pay for something she'd done and it was in your best interest to let things be as they are. His voice was like nails on a rotting chalk board. I almost ran in for my gun, but he up and rode off before I could."

Clayton nodded and glanced over at the kitchen door that was still propped open slightly. Adelaide and Finn were sharing a hand in the card game while Taz and Cherry each giggled over their own hands. Jan Martello was watching over them, her face beaming with joy, as if having children once again in the house was the greatest thing she could ever have asked for.

"I need to protect them, Sal. I need to keep them alive and….and I just don't know how I'm going to do that much longer."

"It seems like you've had it well handled so far. Frankly, I don't think I could have done as well."

Clayton shook his head; his eyes dimming as a tear slowly grew in the corner of each. No one had know it, even Adelaide, but he hadn't allowed himself one minute to grieve the death of his friends and the loss of his home, and it was killing him every second he put it off.

"My name.....my name is Clayton, sir, Clayton Hogg, of Havendale, near the lower edge of the Wallowing Woods."

Sal's hand rose, prompting Clayton to leave his seat and shake it warmly.

"It's a pleasure to meet you, son; you and all your company."

As he returned to his chair, Clayton allowed himself a quick glance around the living room. The walls were empty of portraits or photographs, which didn't surprise him given the lack of connection he assumed the Martellos had with the outside world. He did, however, notice the gun his host had used to threaten Raoul when they had first arrived, hanging on a pair of pegs hammered in just above his head, behind the sofa he'd been using. It was no average hunting rifle, at least not one that Clayton had ever seen. Its barrel was shortened extensively and heated for expansion. If required, it could fire a bullet larger than most rifles could handle.

Clayton recognized it as one of Hammerstahl's inventions, recently banned along with all other forms of firepower. Heinrich Hammerstahl had been a small town gunsmith whose fruitless attempts at joining in with such big names as Smith and Wesson had caused him to seek fortune elsewhere. Once a citizen of Amber, he had set to creating a powerful weapon that yielded more damage than other models found in Memoriam. Naturally, his work had lured some angry criticism. Ultimately, any version of a Hammerstahl gun had been met with caution and legal allegation. Heinrich himself had died a wealthy, but despised individual, who met his end considering himself to be a handler of death. Seeing one of his works resting on Sal's wall made Clayton wonder how the Martellos had gone so long without meeting violent prejudice.

"That's a real piece of equipment you have there," Clayton remarked. "You planning on hunting some bear this season...maybe a whale or two?"

Sal allowed himself a light chuckle as he walked over to where the weapon hung.

"No bear troubles in these parts. I bought that gun special for something bigger....and a lot more dangerous."

"You mean....you mean Firetongues?"

"That I do."

"I thought they never burrowed this far east of Lumos."

"I did as well, son, until a few years ago when a neighbor found one popping up in his own back yard. It was a big one too, over four hundred feet in length. The fool wet himself just seeing it. Fortunately for him, the big digger hadn't matured enough to breathe fire. It just sat there, trying to hock up a mouthful of venom, but ended up only hurting itself. Before long, the thing dug its way back into the ground. Peculiar things, those Firetongues: big flame-throwing worms with poor eye sight and deadly spit."

"And that gun will kill it, then?" Clayton asked.

"It will come close. You see, a Firetongue has scales most weapons can't put a dent in. It's impervious to fire, and just about anything sharp will bounce right off it. That gun up there throws a punch of chemical proportions. A little buckshot coated in grease and filled with just a few drops of Firetongue venom hits their armor like a blue bolt of lightning, shatters the outer scales and cuts right through them. Takes a few rounds to bring it down, but those bullets were designed specifically for Firetongues."

A melodious laugh drew their attention, once again, towards the kitchen. Finn and Adelaide apparently had won their first hand in the card game. She leapt to her feet in delight and danced around in a circle before Finn planted a victory kiss on her lips. Taz couldn't help smiling at this display. Raoul even accepted a high five from Finn, turning briefly to smile over at Cherry.

"You got a good group there, Clayton," Sal remarked. "Don't let anything happen to them."

"I swear, I'll do my utmost, sir, err I mean Sal," Clayton assured him. "I give you my word."

"Good enough for me," chucked Sal. With that, he took a quick peek through a nearby window.

"It looks like the storm is still on. I imagine now that you've eaten our stew and drank all our coffee, it's only fitting you stay the rest of the night."

Clayton smiled. "Thank you again for everything. You really have no idea..."

"I'm not much for gratitude, son. Don't take it personally. There are blankets upstairs to keep you warm. Those girls can bunk up in Lark's old room. I expect you fellows will be down here. I don't appreciate any lude behavior in this house. That's my first rule and it's non-negotiable."

There was another laugh as Jan entered the room, a tray of fresh coffee in her hands and the rest of the group trailing right behind her. "This is all so much fun," she exclaimed. "We must have some music."

"A bit late isn't it?" grumbled Sal.

"Oh please, sir! Please," Cherry pleaded.

"Oh come now, husband," said Jan. "We haven't had a night this fun in quite some time. It's his fault, you know, children. Mr. Gruffles here hasn't had a good friend in years. Lark always told you as much. Come on Sal; let's show our guests a wonderful time."

"Yes," Adelaide laughed. Cherry continued bobbing her head up and down towards him.

Sal heaved a heavy sigh. "Alright, I haven't got a choice, do I? Anyone here know how to play the fiddle?"

Taz slowly raised her hand. "I know a few tunes to pass the time."

"Then kindly grab it out of that drawer yonder. Clayton, there's a worn down old guitar sitting in the closet by the front door. With any luck, we can make this a real party."

Several minutes later, the assembly was ecstatic. Sal sat in his chair, a smile growing on his lips as he played a lively tune. Taz had perched herself on the sofa and was tooting her lungs out along on the fiddle, her eyes focused intently on Clayton as he twirled Jan around and around. The old woman laughed merrily as Adelaide and Finn nearly fell on top of each other with their clumsy dancing. Raoul sat beside Taz, his eyes tired, yet at ease. Cherry clapped her hands happily from across the room, her gaze longingly directed at Raoul. At one point, Taz couldn't resist nudging him as her eyes darted towards the eager squirm. Still, he didn't dance that night, not with Cherry or anyone else. The hours slowly rolled by until the coffee ran out and the group made its way to bed.

"I prepared some pajamas in Lark's room," Jan informed the girls. "You leave your clothes out and I'll have them washed before you awake."

With that, she ushered Adelaide and Taz upstairs. Cherry followed close behind them, stealing a quick kiss on Raoul's cheek before she did so. As she followed their host, Adelaide thanked her for all their hospitality. Jan placed her hand on her shoulder and sighed.

"It's just....it's just so wonderful having children in this house, again," she whispered, more so to herself than to Adelaide.

Sal saw to it all three of the boys received blankets and pillows. Clayton took the couch while Raoul propped himself up in an armchair in the corner. Finn curled up next to the fireplace, a big smile crossing his face as he fell into what must have been an excellent dream. Sal dimmed the lorb lights and bid them all goodnight. As the storm cleared up outside and the stars dotted the skies, the night passed on in peace and tranquility.

CHAPTER NINETEEN

The first thing the boys awoke to the next morning was the smell of frying ham and sausages. Jan was preparing breakfast in the kitchen as they rose, one by one, and stretched out their limbs. Making their way towards the aroma, they found Taz and Sal already seated. There was a plate of assorted fruit, bagels, and bowels of cinnamon sprinkled porridge already laid out before them. Jan loaded a platter with sausage and tender slices of ham, crispy and brown along the edges, before placing it next to the rest of the breakfast feast. A pitcher of ice cold milk sat on the table, along with a series of provisions for their continued journey. Adelaide and Cherry soon came downstairs to join them and the group all dug in.

"I've packed you all deer jerky, dried fruits, four loaves of my homemade cornbread, and a canteen of coffee," Jan informed them. "Once you've all had your fill here, Sal will set you out in any direction you want to go."

"I'd recommend as many heavily populated areas as possible," Sal declared. "As hardnosed as those Tibris Guards are to find you, they won't want to draw any unnecessary attention to themselves. Carrying out orders or not."

"We'll be heading north to Reignfall," Clayton said. "There's more than one question that needs answering, and Tibris Tiberion is the one to do it."

Sal laughed and slammed his hand heartily down onto the table.

"I'd give anything to see the look on his face when your lot shows up," he remarked. "You give him a word or two on our behalf while you're at it."

"You could come with us," Adelaide suggested. Cherry smiled at the idea and pulled on Jan's apron.

"You should," Clayton remarked. "Together, we can uncover this conspiracy. We can see about finding your daughter, too."

Jan looked down at Cherry with doting affection in her eyes. Sal offered Clayton his hand and shook his head.

"We're too old for adventures, son. You all don't need a pair of burdens tagging along. As for Lark, not a day goes by where we don't wonder where she is. If she still lives, which we hope for every day, she won't be our little girl anymore. We'll see her again, either here or in Sorra's bosom."

"You just stay safe," Jan told them. "And stay out of sight. This province is full of rotting sorts, but there are good people in it, too. Seek them out and find a way to right this wrong."

"We will," Clayton assured them. "You have my word."

Sal excused himself and walked away. Jan embraced every one of them. Her arms were wrinkled and strong as they wrapped around them each tightly and fondly. She lingered with Clayton, whispering a short sentence of hope and respect in his ear:

"Be brave young man. Protect them all."

"Here," said Sal. He'd returned carrying something wrapped up and presented it to Clayton. "This here is a handheld Hammerstahl. It's a bit outdated, but still fires true. You'll find some modified ammunition tucked away in your knapsack."

"We are indebted to you both," Adelaide murmured, her voice choking up. "I hope you know that."

"I am glad to have met each and every one of you," Jan said. "My heart is whole again."

Sal walked over and took Clayton by the shoulders, looking him squarely in the eyes.

"Remember what we told you, and try visiting us when all this ends. You were....well, not the worst guests a pair of codgers could have."

The group was soon off again into the cornfields. With full stomachs, clean clothes, refreshed provisions, and a good night's sleep, everyone felt at ease, even Raoul. Cherry and Adelaide began chattering away about the dancing the night before while Taz and Clayton discussed possible supply rationing for their journey ahead. Even Raoul allowed Clayton to spark a small conversation about how many lovely young maidens he had seen tending to the cows and horses on the King estate.

"I'm sure you agree, your family did know how to pick them," Clayton laughed. "Though, I'm sure you had a say in it, too. Come on, don't deny it."

Raoul shook his head, coughing loudly and turned his head. It was hard to hide the grin spreading across his lips.

"Did any of those young maidens meet the real Raoul King Jr, if you catch my drift?" Taz inquired, making a crude, humorous gesture.

"Well...."

"Come on now," Clayton laughed, prodding his ribs.

"A gentleman never reveals his conquests in the presence of a lady," replied Raoul.

"Well, you aren't a gentleman, and I'm no lady," Taz chuckled. "Now out with it, King."

"Ok, fine," he began. "There was this one time..."

"Oh no, where is it?" Adelaide exclaimed. She had stopped dead in her tracks, frantically looting through her bag.

"Where's what?" asked Taz.

"My journal; I must have left it on the Martellos' table."

Raoul mumbled something inaudible and shook his head.

"It's just a short walk back, guys," Clayton said. "We could go get it."

"A rotting diary?" laughed Taz.

Adelaide shot her a look.

Clayton smiled. "It will take us fifteen minutes. Besides, Jan will be happy to see us again."

"Yeah Taz, please, come on," cried Cherry.

Taz bit her lip and nodded.

Cherry clapped her hands together and squealed in joy.

"Yes, yes!" she exclaimed. "We are going to see the Martellos again."

"Just to pick up Adelaide's journal," Clayton chuckled. "I fear I'd never want to leave if Jan fed us some more stew."

"Perhaps we can stay with them again, when all this is over," suggested Adelaide.

"Oh yes! Yes we should," exclaimed Cherry. "And this time, Raoul will have to dance with me."

"Yeah, not on your life I will," murmured Raoul, getting a stern glance cast from Taz. "I mean, sure, of course I will."

Cherry smiled and pulled on his hand. The pair tallied behind to look for caterpillars as the rest of the group continued on.

"What did Sal have to say about the Acryptus Tree?" Adelaide asked.

"Unfortunately, he knew less than we did," Clayton remarked. "It's winked how quiet this entire thing has been kept over the last ten years."

"If Lord Tibris Tiberion is at the head of things, it doesn't surprise me a bit," said Taz. "Before you lot showed up, Oderheim kept things perfectly organized. Tibris Guards came in, executed whomever he'd bagged, and moved along. It stands to reason they perform their duties around Amber without unnecessary fuss."

"Jonah Longstreet knew," Adelaide said. "Somehow, he knew it was all going on. He tried to tell us, maybe even prepare those who would listen."

"I find myself more intrigued by your artsy muse the farther along we trek," Clayton laughed. "I'd enjoy hearing what he has to say on our predicament."

Adelaide beamed. "Maybe we'll run into him along the way."

"He's managed to stay hidden all these years. I doubt he'd surface for a few runaway Red Hands," Taz said.

"Not even for his biggest fan?" Clayton asked amusedly, gesturing to Adelaide. "If he knows a thing or two, I imagine he'll find a way to tell us. With the violence at Havendale and the incident at Pinewood, there won't be anywhere for those against Tiberion to hide much longer."

The Martellos' rooftop peaked above the edge of the cornfield. The group laughed as they considered how pleased Sal and Jan would be to see them again. This pleasant mentality, however, quickly dissipated as Clayton suddenly threw up his hand, signaling an immediate halt. His eyes were strained through the last couple rows of corn, and the look on his face was of absolute horror. Adelaide moaned desolately as she stepped forward to see what he was witnessing. Taz muttered something obscene and clenched her knuckles. Finn stifled a sneeze before retreating back out of earshot.

Not far ahead, standing on the fresh, well kept grass, was a company of Tibris Guards. Huglund was in their midst, staring blankly at the front door. Their steeds were waiting patiently back on the road, their eyes focused solely on their masters.

"How…how the rot did they know we were here?" Taz stammered. "It's plugging impossible."

"What about Sal and Jan? We have to help them," Adelaide quietly sobbed. "They'll be killed if we don't do something."

"What are we supposed to do?" Taz hissed at her. "There are at least twenty riders out there, and we've only got the rotting pistol, apart from those poor excuses for weapons you brought from Havendale."

"Clayton," Adelaide pleaded, ignoring Taz. "We have to do something. Please, I beg of you."

Clayton stared out at the Tibris Guards, his fists opening and closing repeatedly.

"Please!" Adelaide pressed him.

"I'm thinking. Just let me think," he whispered.

"We can't risk exposing ourselves," Taz warned, grabbing his shoulder. "I know it's difficult, but if those pluggers find out we're here, they'll catch us for sure."

Adelaide couldn't believe what she was hearing.

"How can....how can you say that?" she whimpered. "The Martellos...they are our friends! They risked their lives to feed and protect us. You can just...just leave them to Huglund without any guilt?"

Taz turned to face her. Her expression was firm, but bitter.

"No, you winking dip," she growled. "I can't. It's all I can do not to leap out of this field and take them all on right now. But if I did, I'd be rotting dead. And I don't think Sal and Jan would like that, seeing as how we promised them both we'd do everything in our power to stay alive."

Before Adelaide could retort, a loud yell came from behind the front door. Sal came bursting out from behind it, wielding his rifle menacingly.

"Now, what do you all think you are doing here, again?" he barked out.

Huglund took a step forward.

"Now hold it right there! I don't recall giving you and your kind permission to waltz onto my land," Sal gruffly continued. Get on back to that road and be on your way, you unnatural son of a givie."

Huglund turned and beckoned the rest of the Guards to join him. They did so without delay, slowly surrounding Sal, cutting him off from the house. It was clear, however, that he had no intention of retreating. He uttered murderous threats at the Tibris Guards while keeping his gun trained on their faces. From behind the front door, Jan's quivering voice could be heard nervously calling his name. Sal turned abruptly towards the house.

"Jan! You lock that door and stay down, you hear? Let me handle these trespassers."

"Are you Salvatore Martello?" Huglund asked him.

"You know my name, you stillborn toad. You knew it when you came to my home ten years ago looking for my little girl, my innocent Lark. I've half a mind to kill you where you stand. If you did anything to her and I find out, I'll…I'll..."

"You are aware of who I am and what I represent, Salvatore Martello?"

Sal barred his teeth and aimed his gun directly at Huglund.

"I am more than aware. You represent whatever chaos now sits upon the throne of Sanctumsea, this province, anyhow. I moved all the way out here just to avoid trouble like you, but it wasn't far enough, now was it? My daughter was in some sort of trouble, that I know, but she wouldn't tell me of it, wanted to protect me, I'll wager. She had her whole life ahead of her. Your people bring trouble and death wherever you go, if passing rumors are to be believed. So excuse me if I tell you and your Lord Tiberion to go hang yourselves from the underbelly of some aged bridge."

Huglund sighed, his gaze direct and unchanging. He slowly reached into a concealed pocket inside his armor, and drew forth a lorb, no bigger than the palm of his hand. The inside of it burned bright red as he playfully slid his fingers around it.

"Do you know what this is, Salvatore Martello? How could you possibly. This thing in my hand is the very foundation of Sanctumsea and your people use it as a battery. If you knew how powerful any lorb is, then you would cut the throats of a hundred daughters to possess another. Our history…the legends of old…the magic of the land…and you still haven't got a clue. Now, among its many uses, this can also be used as a sort of tracking device. Do you see how it glows? When the holder is a Tibris Guard and on the hunt, it turns brighter the closer we get to our prey. Since our prey is Red Hands and it's nearly blinding, I can only assume our quarry is close by. If you wish to live and spare the life of your old woman inside, you will answer me when I ask you, where are they?"

Sal raised his eyebrow and gave Huglund the widest smirk he could muster. "Where's who?"

Huglund sighed and turned to the rider next to him, a burly fellow with the number four carved into his forehead.

"We don't have time for this. Cut him up a bit, then drag his wife out here and do the same. He will say what we want to hear then."

Sal smiled and shook his head. "You won't be getting that lucky, friend." He cocked the rifle and took aim at the burly Guard. "It's over." Then he pulled the trigger.

From their spot in the corn, Adelaide, Clayton, Finn, and Taz heard the loud crack of the weapon's discharge, followed by the sight of the Tibris Guard flying back off his feet. A burst of blue fire arose from a smoking crater inside his chest. Tiny fragments of his armor flew in all directions as his body arched awkwardly before landing on the dewy ground. Sal prepared to fire again, but not before Huglund had swung his sword, knocking the rifle out of Sal's hands and taking a couple of fingers along with it. Adelaide stifled a scream as she saw the old man stumble back in shock. The other Tibris Guards were on him before he could reach for the rifle, their weapons rising and falling in swift cutting motions. Sal's gruff voice muttered curse after curse, growing small and weak as each blow landed down onto his unprotected body. Clayton cursed under his breath as Taz closed her eyes. Finally, Huglund beckoned the riders aside and strode over to where Sal lay, his body quivering in pain and his mouth overflowing with blood. Adelaide started to sob quietly while Finn drew her close to comfort her.

"Now, Salvatore Martello," Huglund continued as he knelt beside the shuddering body. "If you want your wife to avoid this fate, you need to tell me the location of the Red Hands immediately. Right now, Salvatore Martello, while you are still of use to me."

Sal turned his head towards the house, a small tear growing in his eye. He looked at Huglund's emotionless expression and cracked a broken smile.

"You know….one day….someone is going to hurt you," he murmured hoarsely. "Someone is going to make you feel pain. My one…single regret…is that I won't be there to laugh when they do, you hairless goat."

Huglund shook his head and turned to Kobal, who was standing nearby.

"Place lorbs around the house and burn it down."

Sal spit a mouthful of blood in Huglund's face before finally expiring. A gentle smile remained on his lips, no doubt the result of his final thoughts resting on Jan, and their daughter Lark, wherever she might be.

Kobal smiled menacingly up at the house and started barking orders to several Tibris Guards.

"Make sure all the doors and windows are locked from the outside. Don't let his givie wife escape."

Adelaide shook uncontrollably. She was on the brink of hysterics. "We have to help her," she pleaded. "We have to…to…rotting help her! We have to help Jan. They're going to kill her, don't you see? We need to help her now!"

"Finn," Clayton said softly. "Take her back in the field and find Raoul and Cherry. Wait for us there until we come find you."

Finn nodded and wrapped his arms around Adelaide's shoulders. She struggled in his grasp and started to scream. "No, no, no! Curse you, Clayton Hogg, I hope you rot! I won't leave her to die in there, so get your hands off me."

Taz turned to her and glared.

"You need to quiet down, right now," she warned.

"You can rot, too," Adelaide screeched as Finn struggled to clasp his hand over her mouth. "I hate you both! You are responsible for this."

Clayton turned abruptly, grabbed her and forced her down. "Maybe it is. Maybe it is our faults. And honestly, I don't give a wink what you think of me. Go back with Finn and take care of Cherry like I told you to do, right now."

"No!" Adelaide jerked herself upwards, knocking over Clayton and snatched the Hammerstahl pistol out of his belt.

"Don't you…" Taz yelled, but it was too late.

Before they could stop her, Adelaide had burst onto open ground and wildly fired the weapon at the crowd of Tibris Guards huddled around Sal's body. Each shot resounded across the grounds as she blinked with each squeeze of the trigger. The noise jolted her back in time to the sound of the gun that had killed her father, bringing his startled expression back to her mind. She barred her teeth and pushed it out of memory as she continued her attack on the nearby Guards. Before she knew it, the loud bangs of discharge were replaced with empty clicks. Adelaide's eyes grew large with horror as she finally realized what she had done. Two Tibris Guards lay dead, both shot through the head. A third stood admiring the smoldering hole in his left arm, blue flames still emitting from the wounded flesh. The rest of the group, including Huglund and Kobal, stood unharmed. They stared towards her, their faces like stone. The lorb in Huglund's hand burned brightly as he turned to face Kobal.

"What are you waiting for?" he asked solemnly. "Get her."

CHAPTER TWENTY

Adelaide had never run so hard in all her life. Not on her first night as a Red Hand. Not as a squirm when she heard her father's voice when he came home from work or the tavern, and all she desired was to be in his arms. Dropping the Hammerstahl pistol at Clayton's feet, she dashed into the cornfield, weeping and panting as she went. Her throat choked up from the tears plugging her windpipe. The air around her grew still and eerie as she stumbled away. Raoul and Cherry were examining a green caterpillar with yellow spots as she hurried blindly past them.

"Adelaide?" Raoul called out. "What is it?"

Her feet were automatic. If she'd wanted to stop and respond, she couldn't have. It was as if they had minds of their own and their only present concern was self preservation. She let them carry her on as she struggled to put Kobal and his malicious smile out of her head. She remembered the sound his sword had made as it removed Ronan's head, something that seemed more of a nightmare than reality. She remembered the way his tongue had flicked out and around the side of his mouth like some rabid dog. She remembered his eye, too, that solely functional eye still glaring at her no matter where she ran, haunting her memory by day, and plaguing her dreams by night. It haunted her still as she suddenly thrust her foot into a pot hole covered up with corn leaves and broken stalks. The force tripped her, sending her flying forward to land in a slick patch of mud leftover from the night's storm. She allowed herself to lie on the soggy ground, her eyes brimming with tears. She cried until she felt little Cherry pulling on her arm.

"Leave me alone," Adelaide muttered, turning her face into the ground. "It's all over."

"Adelaide, get off your rump!" yelled Raoul running up beside Cherry.

"Help me get her up," exclaimed Clayton. Finn and Taz were close behind him, their breathing labored and their faces lit with uncontrollable fear.

As Finn wrapped her arm around his shoulder and hoisted her to her feet, Clayton took her other arm and forced her to look at him. His countenance was one of annoyance and ill regard.

"Adelaide, you can disregard my orders, you can knock me down, but I swear if we all die because of you, I will come back from the grave and end yours myself," he hissed through barred teeth. "Now, straighten up and walk."

"Or run. Running might be very good," said Finn.

"I…I can't," she sobbed. "My foot hurts."

"I think she's sprained it," Taz stated grimly after taking a look. "It's already starting to swell."

"Just….just leave me, ok," Adelaide demanded. "I've…I've destroyed everything. People keep dying around me. Ronan, Sal and Jan, everyone I…I…everyone I love. I'm cursed! Kobal knows. He wants me because I'm tainted."

"Clayton, what the rot is she talking about?" asked Finn.

"I don't know, but we won't find out in those cages or under Huglund's blade," Clayton said. "Now, help me carry her along before we end up crow fodder."

The sounds of pursuing Tibris Guards grew more distinct as the group hurried along. With help, Adelaide was keeping a good pace as she hobbled along, her left ankle throbbing in pain as she did so, causing her to cry out now and again in gasps of pain. Raoul was pulling Cherry by the hand, clenching it firmly in his as they slowly broke away from the rest of the group, following Taz deeper and deeper into the field. Clayton strained his ears for the sounds of galloping horses as they all trudged along, their faces drenched in sweat and the itchy scratches of the corn leaves causing Finn to start wheezing again. Whether on horseback or foot, they all knew the Tibris Guards wouldn't be far behind.

"Please...please," Adelaide cried, her leg starting to drag. "I'm begging you."

"Finn," Clayton hissed. "Don't pay any attention to what she says. I don't care what it is, but we haven't the time to be analyzing this nonsense. Now keep going."

Suddenly, the field opened up before them. The trio almost ran over Raoul and Cherry as they found themselves standing at the edge of a short, steep precipice. The ledge overlooked a shallow creek, about a foot and a half deep. Small jagged rocks were prodding their tips above the surface as long strands of runaway plants were being carried by the current. Across the creek was another small incline of loose dirt and gravel, leading up to a wide, open field. In it was what seemed to be short stubs of yellow grass and thin dry ferns, plastered here and there as far as the eye could see. A road cut straight through the field and shot into a collection of scattered maple trees to the east. Not a soul was in sight from either direction.

"How are we supposed to cross this?" Finn exclaimed.

"How do you rotting think?" yelled Raoul angrily.

"Where's Taz?" asked Clayton. She was nowhere to be seen.

"Gone," Raoul said. "Jumped the ledge, waded the creek and took off down that road. I tried calling her back, but she just kept on running."

"She'll return, Raoul!" Cherry cried. "I know she will."

"It doesn't matter. Maybe she is, maybe she's winked, but we have to cross this thing now or Huglund's got us," exclaimed Finn.

"He's...he's right," Adelaide stammered. "I...I can make it. I'm sorry. Let's go."

The water was as cold as freshly melted ice. It stung the legs and sent shivers up the spine, all except for Adelaide, who appreciated it lapping against her swollen ankle more than anything. Clayton reached the opposite bank in a matter of seconds. Finn hurried up behind him, turning around halfway to assist the others. Adelaide saw to it that Cherry made it up the embankment safely before attempting it herself. Raoul placed his hands on her back and gave a weak push. He nearly lost his footing as a loud shriek from Cherry caused him to turn around.

Several Tibris Guards were glaring down at them from the edge of the corn field. Kobal was among them, his good eye widening in a mixture of annoyance, giddiness, and fury. He was so close, so close to having them, and yet couldn't bring himself to leap into the water below. None of the other Tibris Guards seemed eager to do so, either.

"What's wrong with them?" Adelaide asked.

"Who cares," Raoul replied angrily, pushing her back onto the mound. "I'm not waiting around to find out. We have to hurry."

Kobal finally forced himself into the stream just before the pair of them made it to the top. The other Tibris Guards followed, carefully making sure not to get too close to him or trip over something embedded below the surface. The idea of water lapping against their scaly armor seemed to give them both great fear and discomfort.

"What now?" Finn groaned.

"You know there's no way we will outrun those guys," Raoul said. "Huglund is probably on his way with the rest of them on horseback."

"I won't last on that road, not with this foot," cried Adelaide.

"I know," Clayton stated grimly. "Just give me a second."

A second was all he needed. The words were barely out of his mouth before a shrill whistle grabbed the group's attention. From down the road they could see a wagon approaching. It was being pulled along by two overfed, but strong horses. Taz held the reigns, urging them on as quickly as they could.

"It's Taz!" Cherry cried. "I knew she wasn't going to leave us."

Kobal was halfway across the creek. Another few seconds and he would be on his way up the steep embankment. Clayton jerked his head towards the road and immediately took off towards it. Adelaide followed, with Finn following close behind. Raoul picked up Cherry, slinging her onto his back before joining the rest of the fleeing group. Cherry looked down the mound towards Kobal and gasped in terror.

"Don't look at him," Raoul hissed. "Keep your eyes forward."

Taz arrived just as Clayton reached the road. The back of the wagon was filled with assorted farming tools: pots, hoes, rakes, and a chipped wooden plow.

"Where the rot did you get this?" Adelaide exclaimed.

"A farmer down the road was kind enough to lend it to me," Taz replied with a smirk. "I'm sure he'll come to in time for us to thank him."

Clayton laughed and urged the group into the back.

"Is everyone comfortable?" Taz asked.

"Rotting succulent, now let's go!" yelled Raoul.

With a whip of the reigns, the wagon was off. Bits of dirt were flung violently from underneath the wheels as the two horses jolted forward, nearly knocking off Cherry from her perch before Raoul grabbed her hand and pulled her back.

"Quite the habit with you, isn't it Raoul," Clayton laughed, "saving the girl."

Raoul scowled, unable to stop it from turning into a grin as Cherry planted a big wet kiss on his cheek.

As the horses quickened pace, it became difficult to keep track of where the wagon was going. Every small pothole and puddle sent the group bouncing uncontrollably. It was difficult enough to avoid landing on dangerous pieces of equipment without trying to catch the scenery. From what they could see, however, Kobal and his fellow Tibris Guards had given up trying to chase them down, deciding instead to wait on the arrival of their captain. If Huglund was nearby, it seemed only logical that he would collect the rest of his men before giving chase. They were safe, if only for a little while. Finn even allowed a sharp whoop of happiness to escape his lips before being, once again, thrust into the air as the wagon passed over a rather nasty pothole.

Trees flew by as they hurried along. The midday sun peeped through the cracks in the branches as the wagon jolted and bounced about from side to side. Regardless of how far behind the Tibris Guards had fallen, no one felt like slowing down. The more distance between them the better. It wasn't until a crudely built stone bridge appeared before them that Taz cried out in surprise and pulled harshly on the reigns. The group was thrown about as the horses drove their hooves into the dirt with pained whinnies. An elderly woman carrying a basket of dried plums had just crossed their path. She shot Taz a nasty glance and continued on. Past the bridge there were people bustling about in, what appeared to be, one of the largest marketplaces in Amber. Everywhere there were booths and tents set up, every single one of them wearing a long list announcing the goods being sold. Anything from fruits and vegetables to fancy wears and shoes could be found. A nearby tree held up a homemade sign with the words: "Bonanza Square" crudely painted across it.

The group started to stand. From the cart there could be seen the tops of multiple buildings and towers just beyond the market.

"Looks like there's a town just past this fair," Clayton remarked. "There's bound to be some empty places there. We should find one. You agree?" This was directed at Taz, who smiled and agreed.

"I guess we know who wears the slender britches in this outfit now, don't we?" Raoul whispered to Adelaide. She shot him a bitter glance, but quickly turned it on Taz. This look went unnoticed as the group made their way through the marketplace.

"Raoul, buy me something," Cherry laughed merrily.

"So it begins," he sighed, fumbling around inside his pockets.

"We need some fresh supplies," Clayton announced. "Jan's cooking will only last us so long."

"I'll grab some food," Taz replied. "You all head into town. I'll catch up."

The streets of the town were cobbled and worn. Every building was a two story cottage, with roofs covered in thick slabs of pottery tiles painted with black tar. The doors and windows were painted deep auburn with thunderstorm gray. The air smelled dank and musty, and there seemed to be more mosquitoes populating the town than there were people.

"This doesn't feel right," Finn whispered, swatting at a passing mosquito. "It feels like half the town is missing."

"You think they were labeled Red Handed citizens?" Adelaide suggested.

"Unlikely," commented Clayton.

"It stinks here," Cherry said, wrinkling her nose. "Like manure and rotting eggs."

"Good," Clayton laughed. "Maybe it will mask our own stink until we can locate a bath. Not going to lie, we could all use a good scrubbing. Then we'll find a place to rest up for a couple hours. If Huglund isn't here by then, we'll try making a break for it under the cover of twilight."

"You all can rest if you want," Raoul said. "I want to see what the folk here do for fun."

"Raoul," started Clayton. "I don't think we should wander...."

"Oh rot off. I'll be fine."

"Can I come?" Cherry asked.

"No, I'd rather you stay in the group," Raoul told her. "Just until we know it's safe. I'm sure Clayton will agree."

"Alright go ahead," Clayton told him. "We'll find someplace to stay. I'll keep my eyes open for you once we do. Stay away from anyone suspicious and don't venture too far."

CHAPTER TWENTY ONE

Raoul took in his surroundings as he trudged along. There appeared to be plenty of small shops, a couple funeral parlors, a sizable family owned restaurant, and a few empty buildings that once hosted fine businesses before their owners decided to pack it in. The street was nothing more than coarse gravel, lined side to side with shallow ditches dug to hold any rainfall that otherwise would flood the walkways.

"What a rotting dump," he muttered.

Raoul knew in his heart that this town had probably supplied a fair portion of his family's wealth. His father himself had taken several business trips away from Havendale, most likely to towns like this one. Whatever shady dealings he'd had or givies he'd abused, Raoul didn't care to know. No one could ever truly understand the inner turmoil he bore concerning his parentage, and he didn't plan to share any more on the subject than he already had. He soon found himself standing on top of a large mound of dirt, overlooking a productive quarry. Buildings loomed behind him as he glanced out at the scores of laborers digging away at the soil.

"Hey, look what I got!" a voice called out.

Raoul turned around. Taz was making her way up to join him, a sack slumped over her shoulder and a slender, long container clasped in her other hand.

"What are you doing here?" he snapped. "The group's back in town."

"You know you're not the only one who knows how to endure alone," she laughed, finally reaching the top. "I didn't have many friends in Pinewood."

"Plenty of fans though, I expect."

Taz scoffed and punched his arm. "I might have had a dedicated plugger here and there. Look at what I found down in the marketplace."

She withdrew a long metal javelin from its casing. Raoul noticed a pair of triggers along the bottom and an adjustable knob.

"What is that supposed to be?"

"The old man who sold it to me called it "malevolent art," but honestly, I think it's just a rotting spear. If it can pierce the flesh of someone trying to kill me, then I'll use it as one. Apart from that, I found some extra rations and a couple blankets for me and Cherry."

"How many plugs did it take to cover all that?" Raoul asked smirking wickedly.

Taz gave him a skeptical glance and shook her head.

"Anyways," she went on. "The vendor told me this town is called Ditchwater. I never knew it even existed."

"Ditchwater, eh? That seems fitting."

"You know...Clayton says you hardly ever talked to anyone back in Havendale. Since I've met you, I find you rarely ever shut up, regardless of what you say."

"I don't know what the rot you're talking about," Raoul muttered. "Besides, there was never much of anything to say to those....those people back home. Nothing we had in common."

"You don't seem to have much in common with him or his friends either," mentioned Taz, giving him a gentle shove. "Still, you all seem to get along well enough."

"We're all running for our lives. That's something we have in common."

Taz laughed.

"I've seen plenty of Red Hands come to Pinewood over the years. Sometimes alone, sometimes in groups, but they all had one unifying thing in common."

"What's that?"

Taz smiled. "They would have sold each other out to a Tibris Guard for just one more day of freedom. You guys are different. I see…I see trust and loyalty. It's the only reason I've stayed with you for so long. I feel safer with you all than I would on my own."

"Oh that's the reason, eh? You sure it's not something else? Or someone?"

Taz blushed.

"Clayton is a good guy," she laughed.

"And a good leader; one I actually trust."

"He considers you a friend, Raoul, I can tell. I'm sure Finn does too, in his own way."

"Wessel is a rotting dip. I wish only the worst on him."

"I'll admit," Taz said. "There are times he can be a bit…eh…"

"Pathetic? Cruel? Rotting inadequate?"

205

"Immature is what I was getting at. Still...I suppose we all have to stick together. Wouldn't you agree?"

Raoul grunted. A spotted butterfly fluttered around their heads as they made their downhill, passing along the edge of the field and drawing little attention as they did so. The workers didn't give them a single glance as they strode along. Raoul nearly knocked one down. He had a half eaten sandwich in his hand, dripping in some kind of greasy dressing that smelled of goat cheese. His hair was red and cropped, and his cheeks covered in short, spiny whiskers.

"Hey, watch where you walk!" Raoul yelled.

The worker threw up his hands in defeat. "My mistake," he mumbled. His mouth was clearly full of food. "Got yourself a givie there, eh? I'll give you seven shine for a turn."

Taz gasped in surprise. Raoul stepped before her, his hand poking at the worker's chest.

"She's no givie, friend," he growled. "At least she isn't anymore. Show her some rotting respect. Seven shine? She's worth ten at least. Now you can shove along. Got it?"

The worker nodded and walked around them, making his way on back into the clay field.

"Can you believe that wink?" Raoul said.

Taz smiled before placing a wet, sloppy kiss on Raoul's lips.

"Thank you for defending me," she said. "I mean I'd say I could go for at least twenty, but it's all good."

"Yeah well, no one should have to do those sorts of things for shine," Raoul declared. "My father....never mind it isn't important."

"Go ahead, tell me."

Raoul stopped walking, his eyes staring off into the distance as his mind clouded.

"My father....Raoul King...well, what people say about him is mostly true. They always considered him a foul fellow with a taste for affairs and poor business. The TOX, the products....it all went through him. The one thing they didn't know about, or perhaps couldn't accept, was his interest in the givie trade. I never saw much of what he did, but I know he indulged in rewards of the enterprise. Some say he might have even fathered a squirm here or there across the Province. My mother knew too, I imagine. She knew right up until she...well, ended things. Whenever I see someone like you, or someone like Cherry, I just....I won't stand for it. They'll never use the two of you like that ever again. Not anymore."

There was a moment of empty silence, Raoul looking away and Taz looking down. Slowly, her hand slid into his, her fingers clasping together.

"I didn't know," she whispered.

"Yeah, well neither do any of the others. Either that or they just don't care. It's going to stay that way though, I mean it; especially with Cherry. Got it?"

Taz nodded.

Raoul smiled before pointing at a nearby tent. Unlike others surrounding it, this particular one had been adorned in colorful mirages and hand-woven tapestries. A short chain was wrapped around the top of the front flap, a painted side hanging down from it. It read:

"Madam Portia. Palm Reading and Fortune Telling. No Credit."

"Looks like fun," Taz exclaimed, then noticed Raoul's skeptical look. "Fine, I'll go first."

She poked him gently in the ribs and entered the tent. Raoul stood idly by for several seconds before taking a seat on an overturned bucket a few yards away. As he waited for her to finish, he couldn't resist poking his head into the neighboring tent next door. It was too dark to see what was happening, but from what he could hear, it involved two people of opposite genders. Whoever the girl was, she seemed to be trying too hard, a fact that turned Raoul off from spying almost instantly. He turned back to Madam Portia's tent in time to see Taz exit. Her face was dark and confused.

"Well, how was it?" he asked her. "What did she say?"

"What? Oh...a whole lot of rotting dippery."

"Yeah, I figured as much."

"Well," she declared, uneasily. "It's your turn now."

Raoul bowed sarcastically and ducked inside the tent.

The doorway was draped in patterned foreign rugs and black, tattered shrouds. Multiple lamps and burning candles gave off a thick aroma of jasmine and incense. In front of him was a small table, around which were set multiple silk pillows. Past the table hung a thick velvet curtain, falling down to just a couple inches off the ground. The sounds of a woman muttering shreds of nonsense to herself could be heard behind it.

"Um...hello?" he asked.

The muttering stopped and the velvet curtain flew open, revealing Madam Portia. Her hand was lifted casually as if the curtain had moved expressly at her command. She seemed somewhere in her early forties and quite well groomed for a fortune teller. Her hair was braided and adorned with flowers, smelling strongly of vanilla perfume. She had fair brown eyes and ruby red lips. She was dressed in a long, silver gown that covered her from head to toe, except for her bosoms, which protruded out of her chest like they were trying to make a hasty escape.

Madam Portia smiled over at him and bade him sit down.

"Welcome, to Madam Portia's Den of Unexplainable Occurrences," she announced. Her voice was low and luscious. The very sound of it made Raoul's arm hairs stand erect, among other things.

"Are you…Madam Portia?" he asked nervously.

"I am young sir. And what might your name be?"

"You're the psychic, you tell me."

She smiled at his sarcasm. "I suppose I could be like those other psychics out there who can guess your name in a matter of seconds. Would you enjoy that?"

Raoul remained silent.

"Perhaps after that, I could tell you all about how horribly you felt once your mother died. Maybe I could remind you how practically no one back home enjoys your company. I could even comment on how you don't understand why that is, which ultimately makes you bitter and unlikable in the first place. The sad thing is that the more time you spend with people…the less you trust them, even people like your three friends."

No response.

"And after that, we can discuss your hatred of a particular fool you know, one who means well, but continues to drive you closer and closer to some terrible breaking point."

"Well what about him?"

She grabbed his hands, nearly yanking him across the table. He struggled momentarily before surrendering in wonder as her pupils suddenly enlarged and her face started to twitch and quiver. It went on for a full minute before she finally let out a long, labored sigh, sinking back onto her pillow.

"Well?" Raoul asked, leaning in closer. "What did you see?"

Madam Portia raised her eyes to him and smiled seductively. Reaching out, she cupped Raoul's face in her hands, fondling it as she planted a long, lingering kiss on his lips. He didn't even hesitate as she continued to passionately embrace him. His hands crept up her gown in pursuit of what he prayed would be her greatest feature. Before he could find it, she released him, falling back onto her sitting pillow.

"What…what," he started, staring at her mouth retreating from his. "Um…what was that for?"

She smiled, shrugging her shoulders. "I took a peek inside your mind. That particular desire was lodged in a more….oh shall we say "tender" region of your subconscious, but I saw it regardless. It seemed unfair to deprive you of the opportunity."

"Was that all that you saw?"

Madam Portia shook her head.

"I saw how poorly your father treated you," she continued. "I had no idea how cruel he could be. I'm sorry. I saw the nights locked in the closet, the dinnerless evenings, the sarcasm, the hate…..I saw it all."

Raoul shifted uncomfortably in his seat.

"I saw the way you feel when people look at you...all the emptiness you can't control. You don't feel important, and you doubt yourself."

Raoul's palms started to sweat. He hastily rubbed them against his pants.

"You respect your leader....a pleasant fellow. You admire his courage and attitude towards life. I sense....I sense you feel you cannot live up to the expectations he has of you. You should also avoid the one called Finn," she warned him. "You have a dark side that he feeds unintentionally....one I would keep in check, if I were you."

With that, Madam Portia shook her head and rose to her feet. "That's all I found, I'm afraid. Kindly leave a piece of shine on the table before you leave." Before Raoul could speak, she had returned behind the velvet curtain and resumed her quiet mumbling.

Taz was sitting cross legged on a nearby tree stump as Raoul exited the tent. Her head was in her hands and her cheeks seemed red and puffy. She straightened herself up and rubbed her eyes as he approached her.

"How was your turn in there?" she asked him.

Raoul shrugged. "Just a load of rotting dippery, like you said. The woman is clearly winked."

"Yeah...same with me," admitted Taz. She braved a smile, regardless of the obvious traumatic effects still lingering on her face. "You'd think someone like her could have explained all this Acryptus rot. I should have listened to you."

Raoul shrugged again. "Well, it's done now. I figure we should head back. Clayton will want us moving out in an hour or two."

They made their way back up the hill and towards the bulk of town. Each lamented over what Madame Portia had said to them, and each decided it was better never to tell another living soul about the things they'd heard, no matter what. It seemed only right.

As they were approaching the place they had split with the group, Raoul could feel someone following them. He nudged Taz and jerked his head back. They both turned to see a man, about forty or so, with long orange hair and a well groomed handlebar mustache. His neck was lanky and tight, connected to the boniest shoulders either one of them had ever seen. Several of his fingernails were either missing or bandaged up. He smiled as the pair turned to acknowledge him and hurried closer, clasping his hands in gleeful eagerness.

"Splendid!" he exclaimed. "Another Red Hand here in Ditchwater. I wasn't sure you people still existed. Welcome, young fellow, and your friend, too."

Raoul's jaw dropped. Taz cursed loudly and lunged forward. She was at the man's throat with her spear pressed against it in a matter of seconds.

"Don't you speak another word, stranger," she hissed in his ear. "I'll slice you where you stand."

"Who are you?" Raoul demanded. "How did you know what I was? Where is Huglund? Are you working with him? Huh? Speak up."

The man threw up his hands in protest. "Come on, please. This suit is custom made. But if you must spill blood all over it, kindly avoid it being mine. I'm one of the good guys."

Taz raised an eyebrow and Raoul shook his head.

"Prove it," demanded Taz.

The man reached into his suit pocket and pulled out a business card. Raoul snatched it out of his hand and read it aloud.

"D. Pulsipher: Attorney at Law"

"I told you," he laughed.

"How did you know I was Red Handed?"

"When I'm not handling the affairs of divorcees or victims to a drunken squalor," Pulsipher laughed. "I prefer to spend my free time working with those of you our great lord Tiberion has deemed…..unpopular since he took over this province ten years ago. I smelled your group from a mile away."

"Hey guys," Clayton yelled. He had appeared on the front porch of one of the nearby houses. "You might want to bring whatever's going on over here."

Pulsipher grinned. "I can't help but agree with your friend. I've been doing this kind of thing for years in secret…I'd hate to blow my cover with so many people still needing my help."

"Alright," Raoul growled, glancing about. "Let's take this inside."

The inside of the house was tasteless and bland. The wall paper had been stripped and the carpet was torn off of the floor. The only items left behind had been a dozen wooden chairs and a tattered curtain strapped across the only window facing the front porch. Clayton had found some tea bags in one of the kitchen cabinets and had just started to brew some hot water over the stove before taking a minute to get some air outside. He'd been there less than a minute before witnessing Taz and Raoul approaching from down the street.

Once inside, Pulsipher was introduced to the group and made himself comfortable on one of the rickety wooden chairs. Everyone gathered around him, except for Cherry, who slept peacefully in a neighboring room.

"So what exactly is it you do for Red Hands, Mr. Pulsipher?" Clayton asked.

The orange haired man sighed.

"What I do is offer you a second chance; one that contains no peril, little secrecy, and a great deal of possibility. Any Red Handed, man or woman, who finds themselves branded with the Acryptus Tree usually finds their way here to Ditchwater."

"Can you tell us anything about the tree?" Adelaide inquired. "Do you know anything about Jonah Longstreet, too?"

"Longstreet?" Pulsipher asked. "You mean the mysterious inkman?"

"He's connected somehow," Taz told him. "We're hoping to find him before we reach Reignfall and approach Lord Tiberion."

Pulsipher laughed in a fit of uncontrollable hysterics. Taz furled her brow and Raoul grit his teeth. Everyone in the room felt belittled by the lawyer's sudden behavior. After a moment, he ceased and wiped his eyes before speaking again.

"I say," he finally managed to spit out." If you all plan to go marching up to the rotting gates of our Provincial city and knock down the front door, I really must protest."

"Really," Raoul muttered spitefully. "Must you?"

"I certainly must. Every inch of territory between Ditchwater and Reignfall is crawling with Tibris Guards. Scattered villages, solitary homesteads, and all variety of characters in Amber are being harassed, coerced, or monitored. Your village was the first one to be publicly decimated, that I know of. This can only mean their macabre antics will be less stealthy. Any movement towards Tibris Tiberion at this point would be futile. Now I do, however, offer a wiser alternative to those such as yourselves and others like you. For a very reasonable fee, I can supply a map, supplies, and fake papers to start life anew in another province, particularly our closest neighbor, governed by Lord Cassius. He is secretly very concerned with Tiberion's most recent law, especially as very few people around here know of it without experiencing it firsthand. Now, as Tiberion controls this province, Cassius cannot interfere without starting a full out war; however, once Red Hands are out of Amber, Tiberion is powerless to stop them. They are safe. I wish to offer you that same security I've given so many others…..for that small fee of course. I certainly wouldn't recommend the alternative."

"Alternative?" inquired Clayton.

Pulsipher nodded. "Yes, indeed. As a law abiding citizen of Amber, it is my duty to report any conference with Red Handed individuals to the nearest Tibris Guard. Can you imagine the legal ramifications of helping someone like you? I could lose my license, or worse, end up eliminated from existence. From a legal standpoint, the only course of action is to turn you in. Fortunately for you, with a small sum of shine, that little dilemma can be readily overcome."

The group sat in silence.

"You want us to bribe you," stated Adelaide.

"Bribe? Oh, whatever gave you that silly notion? It's expensive to find supplies and have maps drawn up. I'm just covering the bills. Not to mention the risk I am taking by breaking the law for you. The ramifications of going against my loyal conscience can be rather strenuous. Besides, a few shine would barely buy me lunch, let alone make me rich."

"A few shine would have kept me fed for a week!" Taz exclaimed angrily.

"How do we even know you mean to help us?" Adelaide asked. "You're just as likely to take our money and lead us straight to the nearest pack of Tibris Guards."

"Just to be clear, you aren't getting any shine from me," Raoul sneered.

"You've got plenty to spare, Blondie," said Finn. "Don't be a rot. You could cover us all and then some."

"Sure, sure," Raoul whispered. "Everyone here, except you."

"Would you two please knock it off," Adelaide said.

"Now, Mr. Pulsipher," Clayton said. "We aren't implying you're a brigand, or just another card in Huglund's pocket...but let's be serious here, who has spare shine to spare?"

"Frankly," the lawyer sighed. "I'd imagine someone who is out of options. Someone who can appreciate the trials and risky chances a guy like me takes in just offering you people this reasonable deal."

"Stop calling them "you people", you arrogant dip," Taz growled. "They're better than you."

Pulsipher scoffed. "Is that so?"

"Ok, that's it," Raoul growled, rolling up his sleeves.

"Now calm down, everyone," Clayton said. "Let's not get out of hand here."

"I have saved approximately twenty two Red Hands the last few years alone," Pulsipher stated. "I've given them food, shelter, and well heeded advice. I can guarantee you that, unless fallen upon by thieves or wild beasts, every single one of them is safely dwelling in the comfort of another province. Don't seek to lecture me about my terms. I don't promise you freedom from the terror that haunts your dreams each night, I deliver it! How can you think so little of that? Why don't you all think about that little girl back there, sleeping so soundly. Think about her life. Why should she suffer an early end because of your involvement in political conspiracy and malevolent trees?"

Raoul leapt to his feet. Clayton held him at bay with an extended hand.

"I'll say this piece and then leave you to decide," Pulsipher continued. "You have a lot going on at the moment. I am impressed and revere of your ability to survive, thus far. However, pride and hope only benefits one for so long. The sooner you all realize your present dilemma will land you all under a sharp blade's tip, you will stop trying to be the noble sort and attempt to endure this in the best manner possible. Living like animals isn't wrong if you are being hunted like them. My deal is the last true chance any of you will have. As for those of you unmarked by that cursed tattoo, don't get excited. Anyone even remotely involved with a Red Hand is treated just as bad, death upon capture. You signed your death warrants the second you tagged along for the ride. Now, I might be a greedy, winking rotter, but I can guarantee I am one of a very, very small group of folks in Sanctumsea who will help you, regardless of the costs on both ends. Thirty shine each, that's my price. I'll lower it down to ten for non marked members of your party. You all got a decision to make here: take your chances out there, alone, cut off from any help or open society....or enjoy a new life someplace else. Any family you had or have here....you're going to have to let them go. The choice is yours. I'm not saying it's an easy one, but it's one you're going to have to make soon." He glanced down at his pocket watch. "If you were being pursued, I give it an hour before Tibris Guards arrive. I'll be in my office down the street across from the bar should you all come to your senses." With that, he walked out the front door.

"Maybe we should try to get Cherry out of here," Taz suggested. "One of us could go with her and keep her safe."

"Meaning me?" Raoul asked. "Forget it! I'm not going anywhere."

"It makes sense," Taz continued. "She trusts you the most out of all of us."

"Not going to happen," Raoul said.

"First off," threw in Clayton. How much shine do we even have amongst us?"

"I've got nothing," Taz said. "Oderheim wouldn't allow us to keep our own. Freud just came along every week and confiscated it for himself. Hollis gave me a couple for food before he went missing. I just wasted them on a modified javelin and listening to some winked fortune teller."

"I don't have any either," Adelaide sighed. "I had ten saved back home, in a box under my....my bed. I didn't grab it, I...I should have grabbed it. And I should have grabbed my journal this morning."

Finn put his arm around her shoulder.

"I've got one, I think," Clayton announced, digging his hands into his pockets.

"I got some," declared Raoul, "but I'm not leaving the group. I don't care what you all agree."

"How much?" pressed Clayton.

"Fifteen...plus two pellets of TOX; those are worth around five each."

Finn laughed and shook his head.

"So we have enough for Cherry," Clayton remarked. "That much is clear."

Stifled whimpers from the next room immediately silenced the group.

"Cherry?" Taz called out. "What's wrong?"

""You...you guys aren't going to leave me here, are you?" the girl's voice cried out.

"Of course not," Clayton exclaimed. "We wouldn't abandon you, little squirm, I promise."

"We just...." Taz said. "We were just thinking maybe...maybe it would be safer to send you away, you know, someplace safe until all this blows over."

Cherry responded with another whimper.

"I don't want to leave you guys," she cried. "You....you watch out for me."

"And that's what we're trying to do right now," Taz said.

"I don't want to leave you! I can....I can keep up, I promise. I'll cook every meal and stand watch every night. Please you guys, I'm begging you. I....I know the risk. I can accept it. I'd be in that bed in Pinewood if you guys hadn't saved me. Running with you is...it's where I belong."

"I say she goes over the border," Finn said. "That's my rotting vote."

Clayton sighed. "I wouldn't feel good knowing she was anywhere we couldn't help her. I'm willing to allow her to stay….if the majority rules."

Raoul glanced over at Cherry's room and sighed. "I wouldn't trust her out of my company. There's a bunch of winks and rotters out there. She can come along."

"Well, I say she's in danger here," Taz announced. "With Raoul's money, we could get her away from all this. I stand with Wessel."

"Alright, 2-2," summed up Clayton. "Adelaide has the last vote."

Adelaide looked over at Finn. He nodded towards her, as if to say she was expected to side with him. She could hear Cherry purse her lips together in uncontrollable anticipation. As eager as she was for the tension between Finn and Raoul to end, she couldn't bring herself to tell that little girl she had to go. Besides, strength in numbers seemed the better option no matter how she viewed it. She finally shrugged her shoulders and sighed.

"I say…she stays. We need all the help we can get without splitting up the group."

"Alright then," Clayton sighed, shouldering his pack. "So be it."

CHAPTER TWENTY TWO

The group decided to head east, to avoid running into any patrols. Clayton estimated a day's march would bring them right to the edge of the Obrillo Forest, which was over twice the size of the Wallowing Woods. Once inside, and under the shadow of the trees, they could then move safely north towards Reignfall. This plan was quickly put into motion as the group made its way out of Ditchwater and onto open land. Swampy mush beneath their feet quickly disappeared and was replaced with coarse crabgrass and horned weeds that scratched and tore at their feet. The ground turned rough and rocky, with patches of slippery moss coating stones and small boulders. The landscape sloped and rolled about them, slowing their pace down quite considerably. There was always a babbling brook or flowing stream to top off their canteens and console their tired feet. The air grew denser as they trudged along. The longer they walked the harder it became to breathe. The entire wilderness seemed to be turning against them, as if to delay their escape or turn them back towards civilization and certain capture. They would not be swayed.

As the hours dragged on, Clayton slowly turned their course inch by inch towards the east, intent on reaching the edge of the Obrillo tree line before sunset. Several short stops were made, during which the group struggled to catch their breath while nibbling away at small fragments of the provisions supplied by the Martellos.

"Cut it," Finn groaned. Raoul had just broken into a quiet whistle as they cleaned up after a short rest.

"I can do what I like," Raoul chuckled. It greatly annoyed Finn that he was in a rare good mood. Even his latex gloves had been removed, tossed onto the ground back in Ditchwater. There was also the fact that it had been quite some time since any supply of Honeydrop had been found along their journey, and Finn's craving for it had only magnified.

"I'm tired, Blondie. Try giving it a rest."

"He's so good at it," laughed Cherry. "You should appreciate his talent."

Finn grumbled and turned away. It was going to take more than water to quench his thirst.

"I appreciated him better when he wasn't so chipper," he muttered.

An hour passed and nothing changed. The ground sloped and slid about with no sign of changing. The rivers and creeks grew less and less as the afternoon sun rose high above the group's heads, adding to their growing thirst and depression. Taz and Clayton kept themselves upbeat with casual jokes and playful nudging; acts which helped them cope, but unfortunately only increased Adelaide's irritation and inner fury. At Cherry's request, Raoul kept whistling away, every now and then hurrying up close behind Finn, clearly with no other purpose but to bother him. He didn't have to do it long to get results.

"There," Clayton finally exclaimed, pointing his weary finger up towards a growing cluster of trees in the distance. "There it is. We've made it."

The trees loomed above them as they drew closer to the edge of the Obrillo. They seemed duller and darker, like old weary soldiers who had seen the worst of battle. Anyone who knew anything about the Obrillo Forest knew it to be deadly and dense, home to packs of wandering bandits, and haunted by the spirits of their victims. No one ventured there unless they had no other choice. As Clayton saw it, it may have been the only place Huglund wouldn't be able to follow them with such ease. There they all could plan for their future trek to Reignfall while distancing themselves from their assailants. It was the best option they had.

Cherry, once again, fell asleep, perched on Raoul's back as the group plunged off into the forest. The ground was littered with fallen pinecones and sharp branches poking through the worn out soles of the group's tattered shoes. The sun slowly started to set behind their backs as they headed due east, gradually losing sight of the sloping wilderness behind them.

"This is ridiculous!" exclaimed Finn, rubbing his face roughly with the palms of his hands. "There has to be a break somewhere up ahead."

"The light is nearly gone,' Clayton remarked. "We can camp at the first opening we find."

"One thing is for sure," Taz laughed. "I'd like to see those Tibris Guards follow us in here on horseback. I can barely stand up straight in all this rot."

Clayton smiled and ushered the group onward. As they trudged along, Adelaide couldn't help but notice Taz taking a quick glance at Clayton's backside.

"Ugh," she thought, *"no class."* And then she did the same...... *"hmmm, not bad."*

The forest was alive with the haunting sounds of ravens cawing in the trees. Mice scattered about under the leaves and bark beneath their feet, causing Adelaide to occasionally shriek in fright and dart about the ground nervously. There were no rivers or streams from what the group could tell. The air around them was all but suffocating. It was like being in the world's largest coat closet: dark, dank, and musty. There was also a strong scent of pine that stung everyone's nostrils. The longer they walked, the more each craved fresh air, just one breath of it. What dangers were lurking around them seemed insignificant compared to Huglund and his Tibris Guards. Adelaide couldn't help but wonder what was worse: being set upon by thieving bandits who most likely hadn't seen or felt a woman in years, or finding themselves standing face to face with a Tibris Guard, a sharp blade in hand, and a malevolent smirk on his face. In the end, it was just better to focus on trying to breathe while not losing sight of the person in front of her. She could feel Finn behind her, his hand squeezing her shoulder as they walked along. A loud yawn from the back of the group told Adelaide little Cherry was still fast asleep, her body warm in the stifling air of the forest.

As she walked along, Adelaide's mind again wandered to hidden thoughts of her mother…..that poor, weak woman. There was a chance she had made it out of Havendale. None of the Tibris Guards had seemed interested in killing her, or taking her prisoner. Maybe she was somewhere safe, living off berries and roots in the Wallowing Woods, or perhaps she had come across some good fortune in the form of a passing traveler curious about the rising columns of smoke. Deep in her heart she wished this, and that she might one day see her again, alive or dead.

"Adelaide?" Cherry interrupted. "Are you crying?"

"No, little squirm…I'm fine."

It wasn't long before the group found themselves leaving the thick forest brush and walking onto an open grassy knoll. A spring of water sat nearby, the clear, undisturbed liquid calling out to them as they gazed longingly towards it.

"We'll camp here tonight," Clayton announced. "We can rest up and get an early start in the morning."

"I'll lay out the blankets," Taz replied. "I don't want Cherry to freeze."

"Oh, I should be fine," the girl laughed. "I have Raoul here to watch over me."

"Oh, good for you," Finn muttered sarcastically. "If I wanted warmth, I'd turn to Raoul, too. He's my hero."

"Finn," Clayton hissed sharply. "Why don't you help Adelaide find a comfortable place to sleep while Taz and I go check the perimeter? Raoul, I trust you to guard the camp and our supplies while we're gone. You're in charge now."

Raoul nodded with a grunt. Cherry stoutly saluted him, an action that yielded more than one chuckle from the rest of the group.

"I'll be your second in command," she stated.

"Um...yeah," Raoul said with a reluctant grin. "That's exactly what you'll be."

The group spent their evening in lively and pleasant company. The sky above eased from pinkish gray to a star studded blue, while distant owls and chirping crickets serenaded them. As she lay curled up next to Finn, Adelaide tried desperately to not notice Clayton and Taz laughing together as she drilled him with question after question about his life in Havendale, his dreams, and the many wondrous stories about his past. Raoul showed Cherry the finer art of whittling wood by carving her a small statue of himself, presenting it to her as a gift. She attempted to make one of herself, which came out looking like the victim of a savage mauling, but he smiled broadly and accepted it all the same, praising her for her effort. Finn relayed some of his earlier childhood pranks to Adelaide as the night passed on. Try as she did to pay attention, Adelaide couldn't help occasionally turning her head back to watch Taz and Clayton. Every now and then Taz threw a playful punch at his shoulder. He'd return it with a ticklish prod of his fingers to her rib cage. They were bonding quite quickly from the looks of things.

Cherry finally nestled up against Raoul's chest, an act which he didn't seem to mind. He allowed his right arm to fall onto her waist and his left he used to stroke her hair as she hummed to him a long tune she'd been taught as a child by her parents. It was the only thing she had to remember them by. As she gazed around the group Adelaide felt Finn place a passionate kiss on her cheek, one she quickly returned. His cravings for alcohol had apparently abated, or been replaced with something else entirely. She certainly didn't mind. For the moment, all felt as it should be....or well enough.

"It's getting late," Clayton finally remarked with a drawn out sigh. "I'll take first watch."

"Not a chance," Taz laughed. "You always take it. How about letting off for a night?"

"I can watch as well as any of you," Cherry said. "I shouldn't be treated special."

"Yes you should," Raulo said, shaking his head down at her.

"Taz is right," said Adelaide. "I don't care if you can. You shouldn't have to be up for half the night. Why don't we start taking equal shifts instead of just putting four or five hours on just two people?"

"I can do it," Clayton laughed. "With all that's happening....I'd just prefer that every one of you be as refreshed and awake as you can be, should we run into any trouble."

"Well, what about you?" Cherry asked him. "You're our leader. We need you awake and refreshed too."

This remark struck Clayton unexpectedly. Everyone else in the group could see it in his eyes. Even with all that had happened, he had never once considered himself higher above or in charge of their little troop, not even once. Maybe it all had happened too fast, maybe it was just never an issue worth debating. No one else seemed interested in leading the way. It had always been assumed that wherever they went, they went together. He just kept ending up in the front of the group.

"Yeah," Adelaide laughed. "You are our leader. We shouldn't be expecting you to do everything for us. You already saved our lives more than once and stuck with us through thick and thin. I say we give Clayton a night off,"

This was agreed upon by everyone. Clayton allowed himself to fall asleep just seconds after his head touched his knapsack. Cherry wrapped herself up firmly in her blanket, her face content and at peace as she cooed her way to sleep. Raoul lay out beside her and stretched out with his hand resting on top of hers. The moon shined brightly above them as vigilant owls and other nightly creatures moved to and fro around the campsite.

Adelaide woke suddenly as Finn slowly wrapped his arms tightly around her slender trembling waist. His shift had just ended and Raoul had quietly slipped away from Cherry's side to relieve him. A thought came to Adelaide as she felt Finn nestle up against her. It was an odd thought, one she hadn't had very often in her lifetime, but more than once since the attack on Havendale. It was one she had been once embarrassed about, but soon had come to enjoy and even ponder on each night before going to bed. The thought was one of desire, a desire to be comforted. It was not just the protective warmth of someone beside her she wanted. No, it was something else. It was something more....physical. She turned over to Finn, whose eyes were starting to droop.

"Would you kiss me?" she quietly asked.

Finn smiled and leaned in for a short, passionate kiss.

"There," he murmured. "How was that?"

Adelaide inched her body closer to his. "I was hoping for something a bit...more."

Finn raised his eyebrow. "More?"

Adelaide nodded. Her hand was now intertwined with his, her fingers playing seductively as her breathing started to grow deep and heavy.

"Have you....ever done more?" Finn asked.

Adelaide smiled and placed her lips against his cheek. "No. I don't think I'd even know what to do if I tried. You're going to have to show me."

He stared at her for a brief moment, his eyes studying her face, as if he couldn't be sure whether or not she was being serious. He finally gave a slight nod and began to place himself on top of her. "I suppose I do," he murmured, his lips once again returning to hers. "I suppose I do."

CHAPTER TWENTY THREE

Adelaide awoke the next morning fully clothed and alone beneath her blanket. Finn had already risen for the last watch, leaving her to sleep. Clayton was rummaging through his knapsack nearby, fully invigorated from his night of rest. Taz lay curled up nearby. Cherry had nestled against Raoul in order to wrap her hands around his waist. The sun was just beginning to rise over the top of the nearest ring of trees. Already, the sky was slowly clearing of stars as the early dawn crept across it. Clayton crouched beside her with a plate of leftover jerky.

"Good morning, Miss Stokes," he said.

"Morning," she replied, rubbing her eyes. "Is it time to move already?"

Clayton nodded. "We've been here for nearly six hours. I'm afraid what might happen if we waste any more time. I'll give everyone a chance to wake up, and then we'll be on the move."

"I suppose we'd be a lot better off if I hadn't made so many mistakes on this trip," she declared.

Clayton nodded without hesitation. Adelaide gave him a nasty glare.

"Even so," he laughed, throwing up his hands in surrender. "You have been more than helpful with Cherry. Finn really likes you, too. Frankly, I think you're one of the few reasons we haven't lost our heads yet, Adelaide. I'm glad you're here with us. I want you to know that."

Adelaide smiled, looking over to where Taz still lay in deep slumber. The only thing that would have made that moment any better would have been if she'd been awake to hear him say it.

"*Oh well,*" she thought. "*At least he's forgiven me. That counts for something.*"

Before long, the group had been roused. They ate a hasty breakfast and left the open space of the knoll. Clayton took the lead, followed closely by Taz. Finn came next, followed by Adelaide. Cherry walked behind her with Raoul bringing up the rear.

The chilly morning air soon disappeared as the stuffy atmosphere of the Obrillo once again consumed them. The forest was just as dense as it had been the day before. Fortunately, after a good night's rest and relatively full stomachs, it wasn't as difficult to endure the second time around.

Spring was now in full effect. The crisp morning air felt refreshing against the group's faces. Warm rays of sunlight poking through the breaks in the foliage above their heads toasted their limbs. Adelaide and Clayton started talking again as if they'd been close friends for years. Taz herself seemed interested in the stories Adelaide was bringing up as they marched along. She touched on her family, her brother Ronan, and his noble end. She spoke on Gable and how she hoped he had somehow survived the attack on Havendale. She even informed them about her journal of personal works, something she worried she would never be able to hold again.

"Not many girls get published that I've heard of," Taz said. "That's quite an accomplishment."

"I read it over three times," Clayton laughed. "Once I showed it to Lazlo Darden back in Havendale, he insisted it be used as the new activation code for the village defenses. It was the best thing either one of us had ever seen. I especially enjoyed the less than joyful finish. Life isn't always as fair to lovers as it should be."

"It's so winked," Adelaide said. "Even with all the constant tragedy and betrayal the two lovers experienced, they still always ended up together. It's just so…..so corny and unreal."

"Some people like that," said Taz.

"Adelaide here has never been one to bend to the wants of the masses," Clayton laughed. "So, she wrote a poem where even with all the love between them, the man and woman ended up apart. It was one of the most accurate love stories I'd ever read. It's pretty catchy, too."

"Not bad," admitted Taz. "Most stories or poems I read back in Pinewood were about lumbermen and building the ideal house on a small budget. There wasn't much else to do when I wasn't…well, you know, on duty."

"Why didn't you leave?" Adelaide asked. "You had Hollis. The two of you could have run."

Taz shrugged. "I thought about it. Once my family was killed and any friends I had disappeared, I started thinking that was the best I deserved. Hollis taking off was the last confirmation I needed. Then I met you rotting pluggers, and now I know different."

"At least you knew your family," Clayton sighed. "My memories are a little faint.

"Do you know what happened to your dad?" Adelaide asked.

Clayton shook his head.

"One day, he went out exploring a possible breakthrough concerning lorbs and the mysteries of Sanctumsea….and he never came back. After that, his months of research and progress were forgotten and his name blocked from the medical academies of Sanctumsea, given his reckless urges and unsanctioned research."

"What do you think he was looking for?" asked Taz.

"I haven't the faintest idea. Whatever it was, he claimed it was going to change the world as we know it...forever."

For a brief time, the group was able to catch a glimpse of the morning sun through scattered cracks in the branches above. The foliage was starting to thin out as the leaves and bushes changed color from deep green to honey-brown. The atmosphere was so peaceful and serene that if there were any thieving murderous bandits nearby, the group wouldn't have known it. The brush was so thick that it carpeted the trunks and tree branches around them. Blankets of leaves, shrubs, and various other plants padded the soil beneath their feet as they walked on. Eventually, the beams of sunlight faded away, and all but a handful openings in the trees remained. It seemed that the group would be, once again, thrust into nearly total darkness. Just as feelings of melancholy started to take hold, Cherry starting pointing vigorously towards the sky and gasping excitedly.

Not far ahead, through a slight break in the branches above, a tall precipice could be seen. It towered majestically over the surrounding hills and sky bound tree tops with modest nobility. A narrow pathway could be seen zigzagging perilously upward along its jagged face. The band of travelers craned their necks awkwardly to catch a glance of what rested above the cliff's edge. The only visible objects appeared to be some scattered pine trees and dead blades of grass protruding out into the air from their stony base.

"We're not going to climb that, are we?" Cherry inquired.

"Rotting no," Clayton laughed. "Even if we did, another day and a night's march more would bring us to the border of Amber and right into Daroon."

"I knew that Pulsipher was a dip," Taz muttered. "We made it without his help and without wasting a single shine."

"Is anyone having second thoughts?" Clayton asked his companions.

"About abandoning our quest to confront Tiberion in Reignfall by fleeing our province as Red Hand fugitives?" Adelaide chuckled. "Not a chance."

"Just checking; I reckon we can strike north once we reach that cliff up ahead. A couple more days in the Obrillo should bring us just outside the outer walls of Reignfall."

"I can't wait to sit Tiberion down and have a chat with the plugger," Taz declared. "The tip of my spear will likely prove beneficial in revealing the details behind the Acryptus conspiracy."

Adelaide smiled. Maybe there was hope to resolve their situation after all. She wondered how much Jonah Longstreet knew of their plight. If he was as informed as he seemed, then perhaps he was aware of her as well. It was possible he might even have read some of her work. To be joined in the fight against Tibris Tiberion by her hero almost made the issue seem thrilling. She allowed her clouded mind to mellow as she pictured the reclusive inkman rushing out of the shadows, waving a dozen new manuscripts that only enhanced the clues and curiosities about the brand each Red Hand bore and how their provincial lord was involved in some catastrophical cover up that they would all expose. Her skin rushed with goose bumps as her imagination hurled about like a monsoon. Oh, how she wished she had her journal with her...just one blank page to scribble upon. She sighed as she remembered the Martellos and how their sacrifice would not go unavenged.

She turned back behind her to check on Cherry. It was then she noticed, for the first time, that Raoul and Finn had fallen slightly behind from the rest of the group. Cherry was walking directly behind them, her face livid with concern.

"Look, Blondie," Finn was saying. "All I'm saying is that everyone in Havendale knew why you got nominated this year. You were standing behind some little girl and couldn't get out of the way in time to let her fall on her rump. That's the only rotting reason."

"Maybe I actually meant to help her!" Raoul exclaimed. "You ever consider that?"

"Um, no I didn't. I don't think anyone in the whole village ever considered that thought for a minute. You're a wink, Blondie, you always have been. You can blame it on your dad all you want, but we both know you don't try changing because secretly....you liked it."

"Liked what?"

Finn smiled maliciously. "What do you think? You liked getting beaten. You enjoyed all the verbal abuse, everything. The way he never looked at you with love or kindness, not even once. You grew up believing it was the only way to act, even after you saw how other people treated each other. You still believe it's the right way, even after everything we've done for you since the attack."

"That's not true," Raoul retorted. "I'm changing. Something an immature wink like you wouldn't understand. You think you're some kind of arrogant model of perfection, but you're just a pretty squirm who won't grow up."

"Guys, come on, please," Cherry pleaded.

"I haven't grown up yet, eh?" Finn chuckled. "Well maybe you should speak to Arielle about that." He smirked and started walking ahead. Raoul grabbed him roughly by the arm and spun him around.

"What are you talking about, Wessel?"

"Watch yourself, Blondie," Finn growled. "I mean it."

"Adelaide, Taz, please help," Cherry exclaimed, her lip quivering.

"Hey," Clayton called out, stopping up ahead and turning around. "What's going on here?"

"Raoul has a lower itch for my girl and he's jealous of the excellent progress we've made," replied Finn.

"Hey...I don't have a...lower itch for her," Raoul stammered. "So shut up, Wessel. I'll kick your rump right here and now."

"Go ahead and try. Maybe you can defeat me in TOX consumption."

"Shut up!" Raoul yelled. Cherry was now desperately clinging to his hand.

"I swear Finn, if you don't shut up, I'll rotting slug you again," warned Taz. "Just leave Raoul alone."

"Why is he even here?" Finn laughed, extending his hand towards Raoul's shaking figure. "We never liked him before The Tibris Guards. The minute my lady saw him she practically threw up. He says I'm immature, well he's correct. I might still have some growing up to do, but at least I am not some spoiled, whiny wink."

"You….really….want….to shut up now," Raoul gasped in suffocated bitterness.

"Do you want to know what the two of us did last night, Blondie? Do you?"

"Finn, please," pleaded Adelaide.

"That's enough, everyone," Clayton threw in.

"Come on. We're…we're all just tired," Cherry pleaded. "Let's just take a break."

"You should listen to her, Wessel," Taz hissed.

"You secretly want her," Finn continued, "but you don't like her the way I do. You want her because…because in your winked mind she is some kind of beacon you crave to make your life more bearable. I just hope you don't have your hopes too high, because last night she and I…"

"Shut your rotting mouth!" Taz yelled walking forward. She didn't make it in time. Raoul's clenched fist ripped out of Cherry's clasp and connected with Finn's left cheek. He stumbled sideways, falling just as Raoul leapt upon him, laying punch after punch on his unprotected head.

"I'm going to kill you, Wessel!" he screamed. "You're going to die! Die! Die! Die!"

"Raoul stop!" Cherry cried in horror.

"That's enough Raoul," Clayton told him. "He's had enough."

Raoul's punches persisted and only increased in magnitude.

"Someone stop him!" Adelaide exclaimed.

There was a bright light burning in the young heir's eyes. His face was red and his mouth had a twisted smile of terrifying glee. He started to spit and sputter as he kept wailing down upon Finn's head and kicking at him with his feet. Clayton finally managed to grab his arm and jerk him back out of hitting range.

"What the rot is wrong with you?" Adelaide yelled. She dropped to her knees and tried tending to Finn's blood drenched face. His lips and eyes were already starting to swell up.

"You think he didn't have it coming?" yelled Taz. "I was seconds away from beating the plug out of him myself!"

"That doesn't give him the right to…to try to kill him," Adelaide cried. "Are you winked? Look at his face."

"Now everyone just stop! I said now, rot it!" Clayton yelled at the top of his lungs. The entire group froze.

"What is happening here? We are supposed to be working together," he continued. "Once we start turning on each other, we won't last another day! You got it? Raoul, you have Cherry to keep track of, so spend more time taking care of her and less time getting into fights. As for you, Finn, I consider you a good friend, but if you don't grow up right now and stop causing trouble in the group, I'll kick your rump harder than Taz and Raoul combined! You hear me?"

Finn nodded, his eyes glaring up at Raoul as he spit out a mouthful of blood. Cherry pulled Raoul away, trying to draw his attention to a colorful butterfly she'd found resting on a small branch. Her eyes were still swimming with tears, but she was doing her best to smile and stay calm as she spoke. Raoul kept muttering something under his breath as he walked along with her, his available hand opening and closing into a fist.

"Clayton…" Taz started as Adelaide and Finn marched up ahead.

"I know," he whispered. "I won't let it get this way again."

The group soon arrived at the base of the cliff. Pockets of open ground sat positioned between clusters of boulders, both big and small. The group started setting up camp, laying out their blankets and knapsacks in forced silence. As they all finished, Taz finally declared her intention to go hunting.

"Hey King, feel like joining me?" she asked.

Raoul shook his head, his eyes cast downward at a line of ants perfectly synchronized as they marched diligently between his feet. He whispered something in Cherry's ear as she ran her hands through his thin locks hair. She blushed bashfully and skipped over to help Clayton dig the rest of the lorb pit.

"You know, with any luck, we'll be eating deer, squirrel, or rabbit tonight," laughed Taz.

"Clayton here has some masterful trapping skills," Adelaide replied.

Clayton chuckled and shrugged modestly. Little by little, the events concerning Finn and Raoul were being put behind them. Kind, yet cautious smiles were spreading from face to face as various colors danced for supremacy across the landscape under the quickening call of dusk.

"Oh, come on, now," Taz said, seductively beckoning Clayton over to her. "Let's see what you can do. I'm going to need all the help I can get."

Clayton threw up in hands in surrender and followed her back into the forest. Adelaide prepared a plate for Finn and did her best to clean up any remaining crusted blood on his forehead. As she did so, Cherry walked slowly up to them and tapped the back of Adelaide's shoulder.

"Look, Adelaide....I know you're busy, um, cleaning up your....Finn, but could we maybe talk?"

Adelaide smiled up at Cherry before turning back to Finn. She placed a kiss on his cheek, handed him the cloth, and followed Cherry over to behind a nearby boulder for some privacy.

"Ok," Cherry started, her hands clasped together in a nervous fit. "I have a question for you, and I honestly don't exactly know how to ask it."

"Is everything alright? Has...has Raoul done anything to you?"

"Oh goodness, no, far from it; he has been nothing short of kind and wonderful towards me."

"I see." Adelaide had expected a different answer entirely.

"I have been trying to get Raoul interested in me ever since we slept together back in Pinewood. We didn't do anything, of course, just laid in the same bed and talked. I know I am young and he is a gentleman, but I would like his attentions to become more...feral. I was hoping, since you and Finn have already done it, that you could teach me how to get him more physical with me."

Adelaide was taken aback. Apart from her childhood friendship with Mimi Varrow, she had never been approached before on matters of female concern. She could not, in a hundred years, have anticipated that one day a young squirm like Cherry would ask her what she had to do to get a boy to want to "be" with her. The question caught her completely off guard. She took a moment to compose herself while struggling to find an appropriate answer.

"Um, well……you see, the thing is….do you really want to hear this from me?"

"Of course I do," Cherry sweetly declared. "I don't like talking to Taz about it. It really upsets her, you see, given what she had to go through back in Pinewood."

Adelaide nodded and ushered Cherry to sit down on the ground, squatting down beside her.

"Well Cherry, there's something you should know. Finn and I didn't do anything last night."

"What do you mean? He said you two…"

"Yes, well he was just mad at Raoul and wanted to hurt him. We did fool around a bit, of course, and got a little further than I'm used to, but in the end we didn't go all the way. I do like Finn, and he likes me. At the moment though, it just didn't feel right."

"So you're an Untouched?"

Adelaide winced at the name and nodded. "Yes, I still am. I plan to be for a long time, too, from where I stand at the moment."

"Why?"

"Look…what you're thinking about isn't something you can just jump into. It is a special act that happens only when two people are very much in love, or at least that's the way it should be. Sometimes, people tend to get a little carried away with it and forget its importance. I suppose I just believe in it too much to just have it whenever the feeling takes me. That is what I believe."

Cherry smiled and hugged her arm tightly. "I like that you told me the truth. I know I can trust you now."

Adelaide smiled and patted her head gently. "So, you still want to try your luck with Raoul tonight?"

"Not just yet. I do like him, I like him a lot! He's the manliest man I've ever met. But maybe we should wait a little bit before making something big out of this…given the present circumstances. You know, I've never had a sister, but if I did…I'd want her to be like you."

With that, Cherry rose to her feet and started humming a lively tune as she skipped back to camp. Adelaide remained behind the boulder, contemplating their talk for a couple minutes before getting up to join her. It felt good to be needed in such matters. The only advice anyone had ever asked her before that day concerned little more than cooking tips and good reading recommendations. A relaxing sigh escaped her lips as she made her way back to Finn, feeling fulfilled and thoroughly pleased in herself.

Clayton and Taz returned half an hour later with a pair of dead rabbits slung over their backs. Cherry ran to greet them and stifled a laugh as she beheld the dried leaves still stuck in Taz's disheveled hair and the teeth marks lingering on Clayton's neck. Regardless of the success of their hunting, it was fairly obvious that a rough, passionate encounter had transpired as well. Adelaide bit her tongue as she too witnessed the results of their activities. She muttered something rude against Taz under her breath before returning her attention fully back to Finn, turning her back entirely to Clayton. It was then that she saw Raoul approaching the camp, ducking in and out from behind a collection of boulders at the base of the cliff.

"And where have you been?" she asked him.

Raoul merrily laughed, which was an action very unnerving to Adelaide, and glanced upwards toward the majestic wall of stone.

"What? Don't tell me you did some climbing," Taz exclaimed from nearby. "One wrong step and you're dead."

"True, true," the pasty Red Hand chuckled. "But the thrill of it all, I swear….it's the best thing I've felt since TOX."

His newfound sense of contentment, though unusual, seemed genuine. This led to calmness throughout the group, as the earlier event finally drifted to the back of everyone's mind. The rewards of Clayton's trapping were swiftly skinned, cleaned, and laid out over a shallow, lorb-filled hole. Each wondrous sphere gave off a natural heat that readily cooked the group's dinner without added effort. As with so many other things in Sanctumsea, this curious feat again went over everyone's head. It might as well have been an everyday occurrence, like the rising sun or chilling wind of a winter storm. And so the food was sufficiently prepared and readily devoured. Every meaty bone was picked clean and every piece of fruit was nibbled down to the core. With smiles as full as their stomachs, the six travelers discussed past regrets, future hopes, and various strategies in dealing with the cause of their present situation. There were gleeful laughs, somber tones, wistful propositions, subtle flirting, and above all else, ease and gentility. Hours rolled by as, one by one, the companions began drifting off to sleep. Taz volunteered to stand watch till midnight, and then pass the task along to Finn.

It was around halfway through the night when Adelaide woke up and groggily noticed a shadow darting past one of the closer boulders in the distance. She quickly dismissed it as a trick of the moonlight and dozed back off to a slumber of poisoned dreams.

CHAPTER TWENTY FOUR

Adelaide awoke the following morning with a sudden unease. Clayton was sleeping soundly a few yards away while Taz snored gently beside him, her arm resting gently over his shoulder. Cherry was nestled nearby, her face one of comfort and ease. The ground around the camp site was moist with early morning dew. The lorbs burned ever brightly from within the hole, releasing soft, soothing waves of warmth that coated the sleeping travelers. For a second, Adelaide could have sworn there was one missing. Heaving a great yawn, she rubbed her eyes and passed it off as a mere miscount. Before she could drift back to sleep, nearby footsteps drew her attention. Raoul was strolling around the campsite, his eyes darting up and down peculiarly. A low, scattered hum sounded from between his lips. He turned towards Adelaide with a start and broke out in nervous laughter.

"Good morning, Adelaide. Did you sleep well? I slept like a swaddled squirm. Nice morning we're having, wouldn't you agree?"

Adelaide nodded. Her restless feeling remained as she scanned the campsite in search of someone.

"Raoul…did Finn go somewhere?"

The heir's back rigidly straightened. Adelaide attempted to catch a glimpse of his face as he hastily turned away.

"I don't know," he finally said, shrugging his shoulders. "He said he was going to check for paths or nearby markers to the north, but that was a while ago. He could be anywhere up ahead by now."

Before long, the rest of the group had risen. Raoul retold her story concerning Finn and suggested they all shoulder their supplies and try catching up to him. Clayton readily agreed, making it a public opinion that Finn needed to be more careful about sticking together, even in the security of the Obrillo Forest. They had barely set a course before Adelaide suddenly stopped dead in her tracks and gasped aloud.

"What's wrong?" asked Clayton.

"His...his bag was still there!" she exclaimed. "I saw it!"

Raoul, who was walking directly in front of her, turned around and shook his head vigorously.

"No it wasn't," he brashly declared. "It was gone, just like he was. I already told you."

Clayton turned to face the rest of the group. Taz started to look from him to Raoul curiously, while Cherry stood at the rear, the same innocent and excited smile livening up her face.

"Yes it rotting was!" Adelaide continued frantically. "It was next to one of the boulders, up by the base of the hill. I didn't think much of it when I noticed it after breakfast, but it had to have been his bag!"

"He...he probably forgot it." Raoul replied, laughing nervously. "A winking guy like him wouldn't remember his own head if it wasn't screwed on right."

Clayton shot him an uneasy look.

"Alright look," Taz said. "Finn has obviously disappeared. Whether by his will or someone else's, we don't yet know. I'll head back to the knoll and see if I can find any trace of him."

"No. I want you here with the group," Clayton told her. "I have my mallet, so you take the Hammerstahl and continue on. I'll go look for him. You all keep moving. If we passed him up or he got lost, I'll find him and bring him back."

"You know, he...he could be just ahead, waiting for us," Raoul suggested. His brow was now started to moisten, something he seemed adamant to ignore.

"Maybe, but I'll go fetch his bag regardless. I should catch up to you guys fairly quickly. If you haven't come across Finn by the time I arrive, we can plan our next move to locate him."

Everyone nodded. Clayton wished them all luck and began retracing his steps. They had only been walking for fifteen minutes, and even now as he looked up towards the distant sky, he could see the tip of the massive hill they had all slept under. Taz took control of the group as he disappeared back towards the knoll and ushered Adelaide to walk close behind her. Cherry stayed behind with Raoul, clasping his hand firmly as she pulled him along.

"I'll stay here with you," she announced. Raoul gave a slight nod before kissed her hand.

As they walked along, no one noticed the dark ominous shapes slowly growing visible behind the trees around them. Not a sound could be heard in the forest, not a bird singing or animal running. The silence should have interested them, but with the early light of dawn still growing in the sky and their goal nearly achieved, these oddities went unacknowledged. They strolled on as the shadowy figures became more and more exposed, their bodies catching brief rays of sunlight that reflected off their scaly armor.

As minutes passed, Raoul's face began to soak. Neither Adelaide nor Taz seemed to notice, but every now and again, Cherry would look up at him curiously.

"It's alright," he murmured down to her. "All this exercise is catching up to me. I'm fine. I just….I just think we need to move a little faster, that's all. We are just going so rotting slow."

Cherry stood on her tip toes and kissed his sweaty cheek. "Don't worry," she assured him. "We'll get some water and you'll feel much better. You'll see."

As she spoke, Taz stopped ahead, her hand jerking upwards in a halting motion. Adelaide hurried up beside her and reached for her knife.

"What is it?"

"I don't know," Taz whispered uneasily. "Something doesn't feel right."

A branch cracked behind them. The group swung quickly around with weapons raised. Nothing was there.

"Please," Raoul begged. "I think we should hurry now."

"Quiet," Taz hissed.

"No…no, no I am being serious," he continued shakily. "I've….I've done a really bad thing." He looked hastily to his left, and then to his right, his hand squeezing Cherry's until she winced and pulled it away. "We have to…to leave. I've…I've…doomed us all."

Taz edged her way back towards him, her hands gripping the Hammerstahl. The forest seemed peaceful, but somehow she felt like a dozen eyes were watching them, hidden securely behind the trees and bushes.

"Raoul," she growled. "You better come clean right now. What's happening? Who's rotting out there?"

Raoul shook his head vigorously and started to sway, his knees weakening as tears started brimming in his eyes.

"Please…..please believe me," he sobbed. "This wasn't supposed to happen."

A rustling noise could be heard behind one of the bushes.

"Who's there?" Taz yelled loudly. "Clayton?"

No response. Adelaide raised her knife.

"Taz, we should go," she whispered. "We should go now."

Cherry's eyes turned big with fear as she clung at his shirt sleeve. "What is this? What's happening?"

Raoul looked down at her, his look one of guilty despair.

"Take care of her," he said, shouldering his pack and pushing her towards Adelaide. "I would do anything to take back what I've done."

"What have you done?" Taz screamed. A head poked around a large pine trunk momentarily in the distance, then darting back out of sight.

"Raoul, what did you do?" Adelaide yelled. "Tell us!"

Raoul took a step back. His eyes were streaking with tears and his lips quivered uncontrollably. He turned and darted back towards the hill, his legs carrying him away is if hounds of darkness were nipping at his feet.

"Taz," Adelaide said. Her voice broke as she started trembling. "What do we do?"

Taz pointed forward and darted away. Adelaide followed close behind as she grabbed Cherry's hand and pulled her along.

Twigs, leaves, and branches behind them started to snap and break as the group of Tibris Guards who had been quietly following them leapt into the open and gave chase.

CHAPTER TWENTY FIVE

Back at the boulders, Clayton had arrived to find everything as they had just left it. Finn's bag lay propped up nearby, just as Adelaide had claimed. He called out his name, but to no avail. Scanning the landscape, he finally turned his gaze up towards the cliff Raoul had scaled the day before.

"Worth a look," Clayton thought and started to climb.

Soon he had reached top, barely breaking a sweat along the way. The precipice ledge was open and bare, covered in small patches of dying brown grass. As he reached the top and paced around it, Clayton could see for miles across the forest. Faint wisps of perspiration rose above the trees, signaling the presence of a waterfall not far away. Glimmering colors drifted towards the sky as the low rumbling of rushing water reached his ears. He smiled and sighed deeply before turning his attention to the ground beneath his feet. Multiple scuffle marks littered the ground. Though it was obvious they were left by Raoul, their patterns were baffling to say the least. It almost appeared as if he had been dragging something with him, something heavy.

It was then that a low moan arose from behind a nearby stump. He rushed over to discover a shallow grave dug by hand. Inside it was a struggling figure bundled up tightly with a blanket and some rope. In its lap sat a solitary lorb, burning bright red like the one Huglund had held several days before at the Martello house. Clayton reached cautiously inside and pulled up on a free piece of rope. The blanket rolled off to reveal Finn.

His eyes were flickering open and shut as if he'd been unconscious for most of the night.

Clayton cursed aloud as he pulled apart the remaining bondage. He was about to reach down for Finn's hand when he felt the Acryptus Tree on his chest again start to burn. An uneasy sensation reached across his back as well, signaling the presence of someone watching him. Straightening himself up, he drew in a deep sigh and turned around.

A pair of Tibris Guards stood at the edge of the cliff. One had a long piece of barbed wire sliding in and out of his face, revealing itself at multiple breaks in the skin. This project of self mutilation fell short of his companion's work, which consisted of shards of bloodied glass jammed into his gums where teeth should have been. Each stared forward with the dead glint of malice in their eyes. Clayton, his hand reaching down to where his mallet hung from his belt, addressed them with what courage he could muster.

"Good morning, gentleman. Now, let us pass and....I'll spare your lives. What do you say to that?"

The two Guards charged. One flanked his left. The other lunged right. Clayton let out a loud cry as the facially mutilated opponent's blade pierced his arm, causing him to temporarily lose focus. Together, the attackers succeeded in subduing him, forcing him down onto the ground and kicking his weapon out from his grasp. Finn struggled to help, but only succeeded in being forced back down into the hole in which he'd been laid. As the dentally impaired Guard kept Finn occupied, the other one dragged Clayton by his hair towards the stump and firmly placed his head upon it. The Tibris Guard took his sword in his hand and held it high.

"Wait for Huglund," growled his companion. Fresh blood trickled down his chin as he spoke.

"No. He is occupied elsewhere. We can do what needs to be done with these Red Hands. Worthless filth, they all deserve to die." With that the Tibris Guard swung back the blade, intent on striking it down across Clayton's exposed neck.

Before he could, a loud war cry suddenly sounded from the edge of the cliff. The hand holding Clayton down suddenly jerked away, allowing him to raise his head. His barbed tormentor was lying on the ground, his body twitching and thrashing around as Raoul King Jr proceeded to smash his face apart with a rock. The glass-toothed Guard hastened to his companion's aid, but tripped forward as Finn clasped onto his legs, hitting the ground hard and remaining still. His partner struggled to stand as Raoul struck him again and again, caving in his face until there wasn't much left. At long last, the Guard stopped struggling, his body going limp and slumping to the ground. Raoul turned to his companions, that same fiery look in his eyes that they contained when he had attacked Finn. Just as he opened his mouth to speak, a slow, agonizing cry escaped his lips. His body jerked slightly forward as the tip of a blade poked out from his chest. Clayton saw his shoulders sag and his legs start to quiver. His head dropped to the right and a short gurgle sounded as he stumbled to the ground. The Tibris Guard he had so savagely beaten rose above him, his blood soaked weapon in hand. Only one good eye was visible underneath the swollen flesh of his face. The wire looping throughout his cheeks and forehead was almost entirely exposed. Anyone else would have died from the pain, but there he stood over Raoul, as if in perfect health.

Clayton cursed loudly and charged forward. He narrowly ducked in time to miss a swipe of his opponent's blade, before connecting his hands to the Guard's chest. The same consummative energy that had filled him up back at Pinewood returned in full force. His hands struck with powerful, dangerous momentum. The Tibris Guard flew backwards, soaring over the edge of the cliff before plunging down onto the jagged rocks below. Even with the protection of the Firetongue armor, his spine snapped in half like a dry twig. His body twitched and squirmed before finally growing still.

Clayton and Finn quickly made their way over to where Raoul lay. His chest was rising and falling in slow, labored breaths. Clayton, his lip quivering, tried to slip a pellet of TOX into Raoul's mouth. The wounded Red Hand shook his head and spat on the ground.

"No. I'm going out clear," he murmured.

"What about the pain?" Clayton asked.

"I'll live....I'll....well I guess, I won't." He laughed quietly, coughing up some blood as he did so.

"I..." Clayton stammered. "I don't have anything....maybe, maybe I can....I could always...."

"Don't worry about it."

"No! I'm not going to let you die. I won't. No one else is going to..."

Raoul smiled. The light in his eyes was fading, slowly, but steadily fading.

"Wessel," he began. "I suppose it goes without saying that I owe you an apology."

Finn looked at him suspiciously.

"You see," Raoul continued. "After I climbed up here yesterday to clear my head, I noticed a patrol of Tibris Guards moving through the forest, maybe a day and a half's ride behind us. When I realized they would be here by dawn I...I let my anger guide me into concocting a plan of revenge. I was so rotting consumed with it that I....I wanted you gone. I hoped if I left you up here with a lorb to attract them, your fate would be sealed before anyone decided to return to the knoll. In the end, I got what I deserved for it."

Finn sat still, his eyes scanning Raoul's face before resting on his gaping wound. He shook his head and forced a sympathetic smile.

"You just saved my life," he declared. "You saved Clayton's too. "I'd say we're even, Blond...we're good, King."

"His lungs are filling up," Clayton determined solemnly as he checked the wound. "I can...I can apply pressure, but I can't stop the bleeding. His...his breathing will...."

Raoul shook his head and raised his other hand to silence him.

"I never figured I'd die this young...out here in the middle of nowhere," he whispered. "The worst part, of all this is...is me dying a....rotting traitorous fool. My plugging dad would be proud of me now. I brought this on myself...I deserve it."

Clayton shushed Raoul and took his head in his hands.

"Now you listen to me; you acted on an imprudent rush of hate, which led to the endangerment of not only Finn and me...but of Adelaide, Taz and little Cherry too. Even so, you came back at great peril to yourself to save Finn and ended up saving both of us. That final act of selfless courage has defined you in Sorra's eyes. I am proud to call you my friend. You die in good company."

Raoul's eyes were closing. His face lost color as his head moved slightly from side to side.

"You...you tell the girls whatever you want, Clayton. Tell Adelaide I...well, just tell her, alright? Please tell Cherry....tell her thanks, thanks for making me feel more…just more. And Taz, she….she always…she always stood…"

Clayton nodded, his hand clasped on Raoul's shoulder. He and Finn remained by his side, comforting him as best as they could in his final moments. At last, a quiet sigh left the heir's throat, drawing long and low for several seconds, before stopping all together.

The ever steady calm demeanor of Clayton Hogg had disappeared. Rising to his feet, he squeezed the handle of his mallet firmly in both hands before walking over to where the glass-toothed Tibris Guard lay sprawled on his face.

"You should know," he began, raising the mallet above his head. "I'm usually not a violent sort. It takes something personally painful and deep to push me to such extreme measures. So thank you, thank you so much for burning my home to the ground, for pursuing me and my friends and killing countless innocents along the way. And thank you for assisting in the death of that noble young man over there, my good friend, Raoul King Jr, of the village of Havendale, who was as honorable a man as I ever hope to meet. Remember him as he labels your fate, you sullen piece of rot."

With that, he brought the weapon down onto the Guard's unprotected head.

CHAPTER TWENTY SIX

Adelaide could hear Kobal's laboring breathing and fearsome howls behind her. There must have been four or five Tibris Guards alongside him. Too afraid to turn, she plunged forward with Cherry's hand grasped in hers. Taz was just up ahead, ripping aside foliage with one hand while waving the Hammerstahl wildly in the other. She turned abruptly and fired a shot past Adelaide's shoulder. Bark shattered off a nearby tree as the bullet struck widely off target.

The Guards grew closer with every step. Cherry screamed as Kobal lunged out his hand trying to grab her. Adelaide jerked her out of reach just in time as his fingers brushed the back of her tunic. A few more paces, and he would be on them. They had to come up with a new plan, and as quickly as possible.

Just up ahead was an accumulation of thick, unyielding bushes. Taz disappeared from sight as she heedlessly leapt into the middle of them. Adelaide followed after her, ignoring the sudden cry emulating from where Taz had landed. A second later she found herself teetering on the edge of a steep decline. Cherry swung past her, screaming aloud as Adelaide pulled her back. Several feet down raged a swelling storm of foamy water. It was a river, well concealed by embanked trees and wild shrubbery. Air and water merged repeatedly to form dancing blankets of color that inspired turbulent awe. Forty feet to the left the torrents flowed over a stone wall beneath a thin veil of mist. The deep blue water dropped an unknown distance onto what Adelaide assumed to be a collection of slippery sharp rocks and frightfully shallow water. In any other situation, such a momentously colorful display of natural beauty would have given joyful goose bumps to any beholder. In that moment, however, even surrounded by all that wonder, Adelaide's emotions were raw with panic. A splash to the right drew her attention to Taz. Her hands were gripping a moss covered branch half submerged below the water as she attempted to regain her footing. Her grip was the only thing keeping her from being dragged over the falls.

As Adelaide turned around, she let out a horrifying scream. There was Kobal, his face still as pale as the day she'd first beheld it. Not one drop of sweat was visible on it, nor did he seem particularly out of breath. His face was just inches away from hers as he jumped for her, his hands outstretched and his dead eye focused entirely on her. Cherry's lips parted and the beginning of a yell escaped them before Kobal's armored form collided into them. Together, the trio went crashing into the rushing river below. Taz's yells were lost as Adelaide went beneath the surface, her hand being ripped away from Cherry's by the impact of the fall. The first thing she felt as she submerged was her head striking down against the rough gravel riverbed. She could feel traces of blood gush from her scalp as she tried desperately to find her footing. The river was already pulling her along towards the waterfall's edge before she could even reach the surface. When she finally did so, she saw that Taz was doing her best to reach for Cherry, who appeared to be floating unconscious just outside her grasp. There was no sign of the one eyed Tibris Guard anywhere.

"Adelaide," Taz yelled, her mouth filling up with water. "Grab onto something!"

Adelaide could see that in a few seconds she would go over the edge. She had no idea what lay at the bottom. She darted her head about looking for a rock or a branch to hold her back, but saw nothing. She reached underwater in the hopes of snatching a stable weed from the riverbed below. The water was a good five feet deep, but the current made it nearly impossible to stand upright, let alone keep from being pulled towards the swiftly approaching drop. Starting to panic, she finally threw her hand into the gravel, yanking a handful of it up without finding anything useful. *"Just a couple more seconds,"* she thought. *"This is it....I'm going to die."*

A cold, clammy hand reached through the water and grabbed hers. She felt herself being hoisted to the surface, her body no longer being pulled towards certain doom. Whoever had grabbed her had managed to beat the current and was successfully standing still against the water. She rose from the current, her eyes still blurry from the foaming cold water. Kobal maliciously grinned down at her, licking his lips in greedy anticipation.

Adelaide stared back at him solemnly. His face was just as eerie as it had been in her dreams. The same empty glare came from his dead eye as he smacked his colorless lips together giddily and smirked. It was as if every nightmare she had ever experienced since that wretched night in Havendale was coming to life right before her. This time, however, she felt remarkably in control. She could hear Taz screaming from her branch as she kept losing her grip on Cherry. On the bank overlooking the swell, the remaining Tibris Guards were staring down at her, their eyes occasionally darting to where Kobal stood gleaming over his prize. Slowly, Adelaide reached down into her belt with her free hand. With a swift jerk, she whipped out her knife and jabbed it into Kobal's remaining eye. The Tibris Guard released her hand and began wailing and cursing as he flopped around in the current until he was finally swept over the edge. Adelaide had a brief second to look up at Taz and smile before she followed him down. The mark of Acryptus glowed fiercely on the back of her neck as she fell, going unnoticed as she clenched her eyes shut and awaited the impending impact.

CHAPTER TWENTY SEVEN

As she descended, the air around Adelaide grew still. Her heart slowed the pace of its beats. A strong warming sensation ran through her. She could feel Ronan alive, his stylish grin still livening up her day as he danced around in her head. She could see Gable darting about their house in Havendale, playing a game with Pallard. Her mom was cooking in the kitchen, preparing meat pies for lunch, steaming with gravy and freshly cut vegetables mixed with fresh cut venison and tender beef sirloin. She could feel her father watching them from his favorite chair, laughing along with some joke she had just thought of.

She heard Clayton and Finn chatting in the living room while Taz played her flute nearby. Even Raoul was close by, his hair fixed perfectly and Cherry's hand gently stroking his blushing cheek. She could feel the world breathing around her, the voices of everyone she had ever known or loved laughing and playing together in harmony. The whole of Sanctumsea felt at ease, no orders from Lord Tiberion or villainy by Huglund and his rotters to upset it. All felt peaceful within her, and she was glad. It was then that she struck the water harder than she could have ever imagined and all feeling of joy and security she had shattered into a million pieces, leaving her cold and alone in total darkness.

When Adelaide finally opened her eyes again, she was propped up against a fallen tree trunk on the opposite shore. Her feet were still floating in the water and her back felt funny as it sunk down into the soft muddy bank. Her grey sweater was torn, with the sleeves ripped all the way up to her elbows. Looking down, she could see her knees were beaten and bruised, all color having left them in the water's frigid temperature. She could taste blood in her mouth and licked her tongue across her lip, feeling a nasty gash running down the middle. She looked groggily down the river in search of where she had fallen and saw the waterfall just off in the distance. There were small dark lumps dotted around its base, like the tips of jagged rocks. She guessed that she had fallen straight into the depths without striking a single one. Her entire body was numb, and apart from the warm trickle of blood on her lip, she couldn't a thing. There was no sign of Kobal, the other Tibris Guards, Taz, or Cherry anywhere. The sky above her head was cloudy and grim, as if marking the passing on of an innocent soul. Her father had always said cruel weather soon followed on the heels of a cruel death.

Suddenly, there came a loud rustling in the bushes behind her. Adelaide looked around desperately for her knife, but it was nowhere to be found. She reached weakly out for a sharp stick lying nearby as the sounds of approaching footsteps drew nearer. Her fingers finally clasped around it as the newcomer emerged from the brush. She winced as she stretched her arm out as far as she could, grasping the stick loosely with her fingers, preparing to strike out should she be attacked. She braced herself and turned her head out, giving a sharp cry as her neck pulsed in agony.

"Are you alright, wet fish?"

Adelaide blinked her eyes, rubbing traces of water from of them as she beheld the identity of the speaker.

"Mimi?"

Mimi Varrow laughed and shook back her long frizzy locks. She had changed since Adelaide had last saw her back in Havendale. The petticoat and skirt she'd worn to the Guild ceremony were gone. Her outfit now consisted of a worn down pair of leather slacks and a ragged poncho. Brass welding goggles covered her eyes and a checkered handkerchief covered her mouth. The entire ensemble resembled something a Red Hand would be expected to wear. Adelaide even noted the way Mimi's hands were stained to the wrist with some form of berry juice.

"Adelaide!" she exclaimed. "I thought I'd never see you alive again. Tripper said he'd found you floating down under the waterfall and I....I just couldn't believe it. I couldn't rotting believe it! I'm so glad you're here."

"How did....Tripper? You mean Tripper Wetherby?"

Mimi nodded her head. "Yes. Dakota and I found him killing off one of those mangy dogs just inside the Wallowing Woods the day after Huglund arrived. Together, we cut north around the corn fields until we reached the Obrillo Forest. Once inside, Tripper figured we could avoid being seen until all this chaos blew over. He is truly wonderful, Adelaide, really he is. After that, we soon found ourselves fearing the worse. There were no signs of life here and no one knew how to hunt. It was days before someone came to help us."

"Who helped you?"

Mimi smiled.

"Have you found your Acryptus Tree yet?"

Adelaide looked at Mimi, completely dumbfounded. "You know?"

"Of course we know. They've been collecting information on the mark for nearly ten years. It turns out to be the workings of someone you admire, Mr. Jonah Longstreet."

"Have you found him?" Adelaide asked ecstatically. "Has he revealed himself to our plight?"

"By Sorra, Addy; keep your squeezer dry!"

This remark bewildered Adelaide, who had no recollection of Mimi using such crude lingo. Apparently living on the run had influenced her as well.

"No," Mimi continued. "The man has not come to our aid beyond some hasty scribbling on paper. But through his work, we identified the mark and have attributed it to the story of the Two Mothers and the eternal struggle betwixt all good and all nefarious."

"Have you got any idea what it's got to do with us?"

"Not at the moment. Mason has been actively pursuing leads all over Amber."

Adelaide's look of curiosity caught Mimi's eye.

"Who is Mason, you are wondering? Mason Ware, the Red Handed King of Sanctumsea. He's been living here in the Obrillo secretly for almost ten years, building an army. It's an army of us, Adelaide, of marked Red Hands. He's kept them all safe from Huglund for years, always staying out of sight. As long as they stay past the falls, they cannot be detected. I don't know why. Neither does Mason. No one really gives a rot as long as we can all stay safe and survive."

Adelaide's head was still throbbing as she struggled to make sense of everything being said.

"Don't you see?" Mimi laughed. "We're fighting back. Mason has armed us all with confiscated weapons and put us to work. Take me, for example. With these goggles, I can handle highly unstable lorbs and use them as missiles. There is so much we don't know about them yet, Adelaide, you wouldn't believe. When projected at an adversary, they react in a truly magnificent way. There is normally a flash of white light followed by a powerful blast of energy that incapacitates and often annihilates anyone around it. We've been using them as household generators and they can truly supply us with so much more. I am a member of the movement against Tibris Tiberion. The Red Hand Army protects all of Sanctumsea…or at least Amber, anyway."

"What about Clayton, Finn and Raoul? We all made it out together. Have you found them yet?"

Mimi shook her head. "I haven't seen any of them yet, sorry. We have patrols out scouring both sides of the waterfall day and night. If they're out there, we'll find them."

"There were two others; a givie with a spear and a little girl," Adelaide continued. "They weren't Red Hands. They came along with us from a town in the woods and I lost them both over the falls."

"You're all I've found today. A few friends of mine were scanning above the falls a while ago, perhaps they had better luck. Our camp is just north of here. Can you walk?"

"I think I can; maybe with some help."

Mimi nodded and placed Adelaide's arm around her shoulder for support. Together, the pair marched off into the forest.

CHAPTER TWENTY EIGHT

The afternoon sun beat down on Adelaide's face as they walked along. She struggled to stay awake as Mimi rambled on about her adventures, and what had transpired between her and Tripper.

"I mean, who knew that he and I would find all these hidden feelings, you know? I honestly felt terrified from the start that Dakota was going to snatch him right up. But, after some time, he just came out and told him how he felt. I could have swooned right then and there, Addy, I swear I could have. It went so well, right from the start, he couldn't keep his hands off me. I actually started feeling rotting guilty about it all in front of Dakota. Thought about inviting her in for some of the fun, but the idea scared Tripper half to death. It was so cute to watch, he really is a gentleman. At least in public company, anyhow. I always hoped Clayton would make a move on me, but now…now I wouldn't have anyone less than Tripper. He truly is one in a….oh wait, look at that. We're here."

A pair of towering oak trees stood before them. Mimi whistled a sharp tune and immediately two men appeared. The left one was a husky fellow with an outfit that stretched across his form to the point of tearing. Even with his uncombed hairstyle and second-hand clothing, Adelaide picked up a subtle attitude of prosperity, hinting at a previous lifestyle that involved shine and multiple luxuries. The man beside him stood over seven feet tall. He had a sharp, stubbly beard and a grizzly head of hair hidden under a tattered, black bowler hat. His skin was coarse, leathery, and freckled, which whispered of a life spent on the open seas. The heftier man carried a double edged broadsword with various runes inked along the blade, while the taller one supported a homemade shillelagh, the top dipped in molten iron, strapped across his back.

"That there is Arbus Spyrbank," Mimi announced, pointing to the man in tight clothes. "His pap is one of the wealthiest fellows in all of Sanctumsea. Their family was Raoul King's competition in the selling of lorbs. Rumor is that Mr. King had to reach into illegal sales of TOX just to stay ahead. Arbus doesn't say much about his pap. He's been with Mason and the Red Hand Army, or as we call it, the RHA, since the beginning."

"I see."

"And that colossus of flesh is Hagan. He arrived in the Obrillo not long after Arbus. They are two of Mason's top fighters and trusted comrades, and practically inseparable. Now fellows," Mimi continued, placing her hand on Adelaide's shoulder and calling out to the two figures. "This is Adelaide Stokes, from Havendale. She was my neighbor and my friend. I trust you both can show her as much respect and courtesy as you can."

Hagan looked Adelaide from top to bottom, mumbled something quietly, and nodded.

Arbus whipped off his cap and gave a tremendous bow.

"Welcome to the Obrillo, milady," he declared. His voice was enriched with culture and education. "Any cherished acquaintance of Mimi here is a one to us as well."

"Thank you," Adelaide said. "Please, do you know anything about my friends? There were five of them and they couldn't be far from the falls. Have either of you heard anything?"

"We sent out a patrol across the waterfall almost an hour ago," Arbus informed her. "They'll find your friends before nightfall, I'm quite certain."

This seemed to contend Adelaide and the group headed on towards the camp.

A few minutes more brought them in sight of a hundred small lorb filled pits, each with three or four people crouched beside them. Every man, woman, and squirm appeared to be exhausted. They huddled together and murmured quietly as they saw Adelaide limp alongside Mimi through their midst. It appeared that every single one of them had stained their hands in the same berry substance which Mimi, Arbus and Hagan has used.

Dotted amongst the camp stood multiple wagons, much like the one Taz had borrowed to aid their escape back at the creek. From what Adelaide could see, most were overflowing with various confiscated Hammerstahl firearms. One or two of the wagons appeared to fully stocked with crates containing lorbs and complicated equipment, somewhat resembling the fiery mechanisms involved in constructing the Flammeau-11. Curious as this was to see, it was the collection of Red Hands huddled fearfully together than completely grabbed Adelaide's attention.

"They look starving" she murmured to Mimi.

"Mason has been scraping these parts clean looking for food. It's never safe to leave the Obrillo, even at night. He puts himself at great risk leading out expeditions outside the forest."

"Look there, Mimi," Arbus laughed. "I think someone wants to wish you salutations."

Up ahead, a young woman could be seen kneeling in front of a small tent waving her hands.

"That's Sevigne," Mimi informed Adelaide. "She's been a Red Hand for a couple years now. Mason found her wandering alone in the dark somewhere outside Obrillo and brought her here. He claims the moment he saw her, he understood every ballad, sonnet, and painting about love. She felt the same way, but could hardly understand his affections for her. Some people had…well she didn't get a lot of help on the run. Those that did made her do things no one should ever have to in order to survive. By the time Mason rescued her, she had been…well, see for yourself."

As they drew nearer, Adelaide was taken aback. Sevigne had to have been one of the most tortured beauties she had ever witnessed. Her hair, once surely full and luscious, had been hacked crudely off and all remnants scraped away with a dull razor. A hundred healing scars covered her face and arms, some too violent for even her sun-kissed skin to hide. Her smile was deformed in part to a slight divot in her bottom lip, the result of some sadist with a fish hook and an unhealthy imagination. Adelaide wanted to rush ahead and embrace her without saying a word. Instead, she offered Sevigne her hand. She shook it kindly and looked to Mimi for information.

"This is my friend, Adelaide Stokes. She comes from my village," Mimi informed her. "She made it out just like me."

Sevigne smiled and clapped her hands together.

"Oh and Adelaide," Mimi started. "One thing you need to know about her is…."

She was interrupted as Sevigne began forming shapes and symbols with her fingers.

"She's a Hush?" Adelaide asked.

Mimi nodded.

"Since birth, I've been told. We've all done our best to learn her language. Some things still go misunderstood in the odd conversation, but we're getting along."

"Mimi...I don't know a word of it," Adelaide whispered awkwardly.

"It's fine. She's very understanding. Just pick up what you can."

"Um....well......she's saying she's...she's happy to meet me and....welcome me here?"

"Not bad," Arbus grinned. "You're a born natural."

"You'll learn soon enough," Mimi assured her.

Adelaide smiled. Sevigne pinched her cheek amusedly and beckoned to another nearby tent. Adelaide almost leapt with joy at what she saw. Clayton and Finn were being tended to by a pair of Red Hands, serving them plates of dried fruit and applying warm bandages. She rushed over, embracing them both with tears in her eyes.

"I thought you were both dead," she sobbed. "I thought Huglund had found you. What happened back there? Where's Raoul?"

Finn cleared his throat and looked away. Clayton cast his gaze downwards and shook his head.

"What? Where is he?"

"When I was looking for Finn," Clayton began, "some Tibris Guards followed me up the cliff. Raoul saved us both. He's a hero, Adelaide, he really is."

"What are you saying?"A sick feeling was growing inside Adelaide's stomach.

Clayton ushered over to a nearby tree. At its base rested the body of Raoul King Jr, wrapped tightly in a ceremonial shroud. Adelaide gasped as she nearly toppled over.

"I've spoken to some of the Red Hands here and…and they've agreed to give him a proper burial," Clayton announced grimly. "We'll lay him to rest at sundown."

"I…I wish," Adelaide stammered. "I was so cruel to him…he never heard me…I never got the chance to…"

"He forgave you, Addy," Clayton smiled, resting his hand on her shoulder.

Adelaide wiped her eyes and nodded. Her attention was quickly drawn behind her by the sound of approaching footsteps. She turned to see Arbus and Hagan come to a halt with looks of concern growing in their eyes.

"What is it?"

"Deepest condolences, milady Stokes, on the loss of your friend," Arbus solemnly remarked. "I know you must be in a state of shock but…it's only that your other friends…the residents of Pinewood…they've just been brought in."

"Taz and Cherry are here?" Adelaide laughed. "I knew they'd make it. Where are they?"

Before Arbus could speak she tore past them both and glanced anxiously about the camp. She called out Cherry's name several times, expecting her to leap out from behind some tree and embrace her happily like she always did. Finally, she saw the back of Taz's colorful head looking down at something in her arms. Adelaide smiled broadly and rushed over to see what it was.

The same, innocent smile that Cherry had always born with unending joy was still visible upon her cold, dead lips.

"I....I lost her." Taz began. "I had....I had her, she was so scared, you know. I had her and then...then when I saw you and that Tibris Guard go over, I cried out and I...lost her. She just slipped away and...and disappeared. I tried to grab her again, but she just....she just..." and then she started shaking and sobbing. Her tears dropped down onto Cherry's marble white forehead.

"They found her floating among the rocks below," said Arbus. "She died on impact. There wasn't any pain."

Adelaide stared down at Cherry's corpse. A thousand screaming voices rang throughout her head. Loud as they were, she failed to heed them. Her thoughts were merely paper now, being ripped apart again and again while her swayed from side to side, admiring the image before her. She saw Cherry's eyes shoot open, her pupils soaking with blood. Time froze around her as the painful ringing from long before returned with a fury.

"Milady Stokes, are you alright?" Arbus asked.

Adelaide sighed, the ringing slowly abating and the unusual smile on her lips retreating from sight. She laid her hand down on Cherry's hair, stroking it fondly one last time before turning to face Arbus.

"Take me to Mason Ware," she whispered. Her voice was frightfully relaxed. "We have a lot to discuss."

CHAPTER TWENTY NINE

As the group awaited an audience with the Red Hand King, Arbus gave them some background. Before his time in Obrillo, Mason Ware had been a rather successful thespian roaming the lands of Amber in the company of likeminded performers. Their leader had been Alfredo Morelli, a jolly orator from a shoe-shaped land somewhere in Memoriam. Alfredo, who felt like a father to Mason, had brought him up to be his heir. When the Tibris Guards had come for him, Mason's comrades had sacrificed their lives to give him a head start. Morelli himself had tackled Huglund to the ground before being executed. Ever since that day over a decade ago, Mason Ware had sworn to aid any like him and those who had the courage to protect those cursed with the Tree of Acryptus. He estimated around four hundred Red Hands in the camp, all whom had Mason Ware to thank for their survival. He asked for no shine, no favors, only that anyone choosing to stay as one of his army dedicate their lives to helping out fellow victims, and any who sought their aid.

"He's managed to keep us all breathing," Arbus laughed. "Everyone here was found by him. All our weapons, food, and drink come from loyal supporters or are confiscated by those who try turning Red Hands in for profit. Mason has no tolerance for rot."

"Any luck finding Longstreet?" Clayton asked.

"Mason has sent out small patrols to inquire about his whereabouts. So far as I know, there has been no luck. All we have is what the story tells us before…"

"Before ending abruptly," Adelaide coldly finished.

Mimi nodded. "A tree is planted by a man fueled by ambition. The more good the man accomplishes, the greater the fruit it bears. The naughtier his actions, the more it withers. Finally, after succumbing to a life of selfishness and arrogance, the tree dies."

"We all know the story," Arbus said. "Just when all hope seems lost for Acryptus, Longstreet had to go and end the tale on a rotting cliffhanger."

"Well, until we find the man and ask him ourselves, we won't learn anymore about why the rotting tree is tattooed on our skin," Arbus concluded. "Mason has made it a priority, right behind saving more Red Hands, of course."

"What's taking him so long anyhow," Finn grunted.

"I imagine he's seeing to important issues within the camp," replied Clayton.

"And just about done from the looks of things," Arbus declared. "Here he comes."

A man approached them. Like everyone else in the camp, his hands were stained from the tips of his fingers down to the wrist with berry juice. He wore a flashy salmon-colored vest over a well pressed white shirt. His hair matched the sandy color of his slacks, which fell down just below the knee where they met the tops of his boots. His chin was rich with stubble and his jaw was firmly locked. Adelaide could clearly see the appeal many might have seeing a man like him striding along a well lit stage.

"Good evening to you all," he began. His voice could calm a tempest. "Please know that you have our deepest condolences for the loss you have sustained. We the RHA are at your service."

He turned his focus entirely on Adelaide and smiled.

"Since the day I found this mark on my person, Miss Stokes," he began. "I have learned to appreciate the courage and skill one acquires when facing a Tibris Guard. It is an honor and a privilege to meet you."

"You as well, Mr. Ware," Adelaide replied. Her voice had become oddly cold since she had seen Cherry's body.

"Sir," Clayton said. "We have lost two companions whom we care for very much. They need a proper burial."

Mason nodded respectfully. "You have my word, Mr. Hogg, they will have it. In the meantime, you and your friends will be fed and rested. Once we have laid your comrades to rest, I shall personally secure you safe passage wherever you choose to go. It goes without saying, of course, should you decide to, you and your companions are welcome to stay. I cannot promise you luxury, but you will be amongst friends."

"Oh yes, you have to stay!" Mimi exclaimed.

"I fear we cannot," Clayton stated. "I have business with our Lord Tiberion. It is by his order we are all being hunted."

"This has been known to us for quite some time," Mason replied. "We've considered sending spies to Reignfall in search of answers, but I fear to permit anyone passage that far north. Whatever dangers reside in these parts are only multiplied once you enter those gates."

"So why not go together?" Adelaide asked. All eyes turned to her. "I mean really, why not? With mighty numbers, your army here could march on Reignfall and demand an audience with Tibris Tiberion. You could end this once and for all."

Mason pondered her statement briefly before extending his hand out towards the camp around them.

"We may look ferocious in counting, Miss Stokes, but I can assure you the RHA is in no fit manner to be knocking down the gates of our provincial city. What roots and berries we can muster here in the Obrillo, combined with the meager rations supplied by allies outside the forest grow smaller every week. The Tibris Guards are cracking down more now than ever. Before Havendale, they had never openly attacked a whole village before. They seem to be in a hurry now, struggling to meet an important deadline. For the time being, we can stay here and endure. The time for greater action will arrive soon, I can assure you. Now feel free to rest, fill your stomachs, and quench any lingering thirst. We will lay your companions underground at sunset."

An hour passed by as afternoon turned to evening. Clayton spent the time learning more about the camp from Mason. Adelaide managed to pick up several battle maneuvers from Taz, including several defensive stances that could easily save her life in a tight skirmish. Finn chose to stand guard over Raoul's body, as if leaving it unprotected would result in its immediate theft. It wasn't until a quick call from Clayton that they all converged together beside a nearby tent.

"Mason has made all the arrangements," Clayton informed them. "The ceremony is starting. The whole camp has gathered at their burial ground."

The place in question was a nearby meadow. Countless friends and loved ones bearing the Acryptus Tree were spread out honorably across the flowery landscape. Two fresh plots sat side by side, awaiting their patrons. As the sun began to set behind the forest trees and the sky turned a pinkish hue, the RHA collected around the open graves humming bits of solemn tunes and noble melodies.

The remains of Raoul and Cherry were carried on homemade stretchers, each by eight Red Hands wearing scarlet hoods. Adelaide, Clayton, and Finn walked directly behind them, with Mimi, Arbus, and Hagan following close behind. The bodies were gently placed and buried, after which Mason stepped forward and cleared his throat.

"You know," he loudly spoke. "I never had the pleasure of meeting Raoul King Jr of Havendale, or Cherry Atherton of Pinewood. From what I've been told by friends and companions, to know them would have been an unparalleled privilege. I know we all here feel their end and wish them swift, unheeded passage to the serenity of Sorra's bosom."

The crowd nodded. As one, they each placed their juice-stained hands in front of their faces, positioning their palms facing outward. Mimi quietly explained that this was a sign of respect in the RHA to a fallen comrade.

"I can't believe they're really gone," Taz whispered. Her face was still flushed and salty with unchecked tears. It was strange for the group to see her so vulnerable. Clayton placed her head onto his shoulder, running the tips of his fingers along her hair and whispering comforting words into her ear.

"They were lucky," Adelaide muttered.

Finn cocked his head curiously while Clayton shot her a skeptical look.

"What?" she continued, so loudly that several Red Hands turned their attention towards her. "They were. We're the ones still stuck here, on the run without a rotting clue as to why or what to do about it. How many more of us do you think need to die before this is over? How many of these people? We tried to take the safest route to Reignfall and look where that got us? Raoul and Cherry are dead. If we don't take a stand and show the whole of Amber what we can do, we won't complete this mission. We simply can't."

"What exactly did you have in mind?" asked Clayton.

Adelaide's eyes grew large and passionate as she pondered his question. It was time to change their strategy. She could somehow see that now, more clearly than ever.

"We should attack," she finally declared with a hint of giddiness. "Yes...yes we should."

"Attack the Tibris Guards?" Finn whispered, taken aback. "Alexis, are you winked? You want to just take them head on right here in the Obrillo?"

"We aren't just a handful of Red Hands anymore," she replied. "Now we're an army."

"Adelaide, look at them," Clayton hissed, glancing about. "The RHA isn't ready to engage in great conflict."

"They aren't ready?" she growled. More than a dozen Red Hands had gathered around them. "Clayton, when Huglund came to Havendale, how many of us had ever fought Tibris Guards or vile animals? When faced with death, people can do almost anything. I think we can take down Huglund's forces here and now and leave him waned. That, alone, should inspire anyone else out there trying to survive. Can't you understand that?"

Before he could respond, Adelaide brushed past him, acknowledging the closing of Mason's speech. It was time for someone from the group to say a few words. Her eyes shifted sharply from one Red Hand to the next, finally resting on Clayton. He shifted uncomfortably from one foot to the next as her gaze burned through him. It was obvious to her what had to be said. Now was the time to show Huglund that the Red Hands would no longer be afraid of him. Armed, fed, and unified, they could unleash a scourge of retribution that would have Tibris Tiberion leaking himself by the time they reached Reignfall. She smiled as she imagined the words flowing from her lips to the sounds of hearty applause. Something of that magnitude could crush her previous work, like a grape under a boot heel. She allowed her smile to fade, slowly, away as it dawned on her that it wasn't her place to say anything. She wasn't their leader. She cast Clayton one final look of disappointment before turning away.

"Clayton," Mason sighed. "Anything you wish to say?"

Clayton looked at his companions, his eyes dark with conflict. Clearing his throat, he took a step forward.

"I can only imagine," he said, "how many brave friends, family and comrades you all have lost. For ten years, whether in secret, or openly without regard, the lord of Amber, Tibris Tiberion, has destroyed countless lives through unsanctioned execution and unjustified propaganda."

Murmuring grew amongst the crowd.

"Why is it happening? What does it mean? Apart from a rotting tree stamped on our persons, what other clues have we found?"

Heads started shaking.

"I thought so. For all our suffering and investigation, nothing can be truly yielded without finding the source."

"Jonah Longstreet!" several viewers exclaimed. "He is the source."

"No!" Clayton yelled. "Though his part in this has yet to be truly revealed, it is not the inkman we seek. We must confront the person who labeled us all Red Hand rotters without right or representation. I will not lie down until this man's forces trample me into dust. You all know of whom I speak. He is a wink, a dip, and a political incompetent. He sits in Reignfall shouting orders that are carried out without question, no matter how much suffering is caused. It is by his hand that our lives will be forever altered and only by his hand that we can be at peace again. We must speak to Tibris Tiberion! And we must speak to him now!"

"Here here," Adelaide cried out. Finn nodded assertively and Taz struck the ground repeatedly with the butt of her spear.

Clayton thrust out his hand and pointed towards the direction of the falls.

"Just out there are Huglund and his lot. They will find a way across the water and attack this camp. What can you do about it?"

"We can run!" a voice cried out. "We can hide!"

"You can stand," Taz replied boldly.

"Before we can march on Reignfall and demand some answers," continued Clayton. "We must deal with the immediate threat. I know you are all scared, I mean rot, so am I. Sorra and Necrya are calling our names, and who knows which one will be there when the sun falls from the sky, but I would rather die here for something than spend the rest of my life living for nothing. What about you?"

The entire forest seemed still. Not a bird, bee, or woodland creature stirred as the RHA and company stood before Clayton. It was Sevigne who at last spoke, signing a message as she turned slowly around in a circle.

"What, um..."Clayton began nervously. "What did she say?"

Mason placed his hand on his shoulder and smiled.

"She said you took the words right out of her mouth. We will deal with Huglund and his men. After that, I believe a trip to Reignfall has been about ten years overdue."

Clayton smiled. As he did so, a loud call echoed from across the camp. Everyone turned to witness a trip of Red Hands making their way towards them. One was Tripper Wetherby, a woolen scarf around his neck and a double-edged battleaxe in his hands. Beside him strode Dakota Browning, holding a glistening scythe, and sporting a ruby red beret that complimented her pearly white blouse and polka dot skirt. The third figure was a man in his late fifties with streaks of white running throughout his wild, grey hair. A long range Hammerstahl rifle hung strapped to his back. A slender elkhound ran next to him, his tongue lolling out of his mouth in spirited but labored pants.

Mason laughed and turned to Clayton.

"I believe you already know Tripper and Dakota of Havendale. May I then introduce to you, Rade Sorenson, the finest tracker in all of Amber. This, of course," he pointed to the dog, "is Leto, his loyal companion."

Leto licked Clayton's hand as he gently ruffled his fur.

"Rade, our new friends here have proposed we launch an offensive against Tiberion," Mason informed him.

"Well," the grey haired man stated. "They'll have their chance soon enough. Huglund and a whole army of them are slowly making their way across the falls."

"There's been more showing up every hour," Tripper threw in, removing himself from Mimi's overpowering embraces.

"I had to count like a few times, but I like reckon somewhere around like two hundred and fifty of them," Dakota finished proudly. Adelaide couldn't ignore her overuse of prepositions.

"With those odds, we still outnumber the rotters two to one!" Arbus exclaimed. "We have the means to set up a glorious trap for them as well."

Hagan snorted something unintelligible and nodded assertively.

"They'll be expecting you to run, Mason," said Clayton. "If you stay, we'll stand with you. I even know a way to pierce their armor."

"How is that possible?" Rade asked.

"A trick taught to us by an old friend. The bullets in your Hammerstahls can be enhanced to cut through the scales, so long as you can get your hands on some Firetongue venom. I don't suppose you have any around?"

Sevigne signed something to Arbus, who nodded with a smile.

"I'm sure we can scrounge up a few jars of it," he informed Clayton.

"Excellent! So what do you say, Mason? Will this be the time for the RHA to avenge their fallen?"

All eyes turned to the Red Hand King. Adelaide knotted her hands, painfully awaiting his decision. It wasn't until Sevigne walked over and placed her head on his shoulder that he smiled and spoke.

"If the Tibris Guards are crossing the falls, they will either walk the length of the river to find a dry crossing, or build a makeshift bridge. Either way, I imagine they won't be across until early tomorrow morning. So tomorrow, we take Huglund on. After that, I vouch my services and sword with any who follows me to help you reach Reignfall. Consider the RHA fully behind you and your friends, Clayton Hogg. Now, tell us about this trick of yours concerning Firetongue venom and enhancing our weaponry."

CHAPTER THIRTY

The next day, Huglund and the Tibris Guards found the camp completely deserted. Only a few dirty plates and abandoned tents remained.

"They are trying to escape," murmured Ptolemi as he examined some nearby footprints.

"Perhaps they are," replied Huglund. "These tracks are still fresh. They cannot be more than a mile or so away." With that, he reached into his saddlebag and pulled out a lorb. The red light flickered briefly before disappearing entirely.

"Just out of reach, Captain," Ptolemi said. "They are quite clever."

"I do not suspect these Red Hands planned on being clever. Blind fortune, no matter how short lived. It will be over soon enough."

"What are your orders?"

"Ride on. They will be close."

Suddenly, a small rock flew out of the bleak fog just ahead and struck his armor, bouncing harmlessly off his chest. Another soon followed it and hit the snout of Ptolemi's horse. Loud cursing arose up ahead as unseen figures proceeded to bombard the Tibris Guards with rocks and debris, all the while berating them with verbal ridicule.

"Captain," Ptolemi said, his mouth curving into an amused grin. "However will you quell this dangerous rabble?

"Ptolemi," Huglund murmured, his hands sliding gently down towards his sword. "I neither respect you as a soldier, nor consider you a true Tibris Guard. As for Kobal, he was the best of both. Do you believe I enjoyed ending his life this morning? Do you think I wanted to snap his neck when we found him, crawling around on the riverbank, blind in both eyes? He had his purpose taken from him. I did what had to be done. If you believe I would spare your life when I so easily took his, you have not an ounce of brain in your head. Now let us go find our Red Hand friends and end this nonsense once and for all."

Ptolemi nodded and signaled for The Tibris Guards to draw their swords. Huglund dodged a jagged throwing stone and grit his teeth.

"Charge!" he exclaimed.

The riders urged their horses onward. Within seconds, they were moving at full gallop. Just up ahead, a dozen hooded Red Hands cast their final stones and fled. Huglund pointed towards them as he bound over a grassy knoll revealed their quarry. Each Red Hand seemed fit and fleet on foot, but it wouldn't be long before they were overtaken. As they all rushed deeper into the woods, it seemed their retreat would be short lived.

Suddenly, from above, there sounded a loud bang. A Tibris Guard toppled back from his horse and plummeted to the ground, blue smoke emitting from his chest. A second bang commenced, and then a third, followed by a series of falling lorbs, which shattered on impact, causing bright flashes that knocked nearby Guards to the ground.

"They're in the trees!" Ptolemi yelled. He ducked as a hurled lorb barely missed his head. "They have found a way to pierce our armor!"

Whoops and victorious calls emerged from the branches above, signaling over fifty Red Hands strategically perched for optimum accuracy. Multiple Tibris Guards fell off their mounts as they drove deeper and deeper into the forest, meeting aerial opposition with every leap. Armed with only swords and daggers, there was little they could do to defend themselves. Huglund successfully cast a blade with expert precision into the heart of a visible Red Hand, killing him instantly, but all the riders could do was continue the chase, even amidst the rain of dangerous objects above. Any who dismounted and tried climbing the trees were swiftly disposed. At last, the twelve grounded Red Hands seemed to be slowing down, due it seemed likely to unmanageable exhaustion.

"Hurry," Huglund yelled. "Now we have them!"

The words were barely out of his mouth before the smell of kerosene reached his nostrils. He had only a second to comprehend its meaning before the horse beneath him exploded in a burst of smoke and fiery ash. The Tibris Guard officer flew several yards down a steep decline before striking his head against a tree stump. He turned to watch as one by one his fellow riders hit the Flammeau-11, obviously rigged along an impromptu tree line with makeshift equipment and handcrafted mechanisms. The horses vanished into thin air amidst the smell of burnt meat and singed fur. Their riders joined Huglund on the ground as they were roughly flung into the air, landing roughly onto decaying logs, sharp, protruding branches, and jagged boulders. Many backs were broken, necks were snapped, and heads were bashed as, one by one, each Tibris Guard plummeted to the ground. Only a few riders managed to stop their beasts in time, staring down at their companions sitting awkwardly around the forest floor.

A loud battle cry erupted from just beyond the rising morning mist. Huglund leapt to his feet and strained his eyes as the RHA tore into sight, wildly waving their weapons and bellowing bloodthirsty battle cries at the top of their lungs.

"Should we run?" Ptolemi asked. Huglund struck him across the face before turning to his men.

"You are all Tibris Guards of the great Lord Tiberion. You cannot fear, you cannot care, and you cannot lose. Let us destroy this Red Handed plague once and for all. Everyone attack, now!"

The two forces collided in a spray of sweat and blood. The Tibris Guard's superior armor proved much more effective face to face. They were well trained in the art of sword play and struck down Red Hands left and right as they hacked their way into the thick of the battle. Lack of fear made them almost unstoppable. With no apparent concern for their own wellbeing, each bald fighter dove headfirst into the fight, mindlessly eliminating every man, woman and squirm that crossed their paths. No wound, big or small, hindered their progress. It was only when a tremendous blow was struck to their persons, via Hammerstahl, blade, or club, that each Tibris Guard finally went down, their eyes glazed in eternal sleep. They made sure to take as many Red Hands down with them as they could, sometimes draping themselves over a small collection of corpses before allowing themselves to expire.

The RHA gave as good as it got. Years of loss and prolonged suffering had infused every fighter with an unbreakable sense of fury, which was belated a little at a time with the aggressive disposal of multiple Tibris Guards. With every weapon and bullet drenched in fresh Firetongue venom, the Red Hands wielding them found themselves quickly slicing their enemies apart like scissors through a raggedy shirt. Solid, blue flames erupted across the battlefield with every successful strike.

Adelaide found herself leaping from side to side, eagerly thrusting her knife into every neck and face of a Tibris Guard that she could reach. Her head turned speedily about, taking in the ruthless carnage that surrounded her. Her fears of death were blanketed by strange pleasurable surges as she raised her knife and plunged it into any Tibris Guard within arm's reach. She could hear Finn whooping with delight as he battled a Tibris Guard. Try as she did, she could see no sign of Clayton.

"Adelaide!"

Ten yards away, Taz was lying on her back with her spear out of reach. Above her stood Huglund, shaking his head and muttering something inaudible as he lifted up his sword to deal one fatal blow.

With a bloodcurdling scream, Adelaide collided with Huglund, the force of her leap knocking him to his knees. He instantly leapt to his feet and deflected a savage jab from her blood soaked knife. The Acryptus Tree pulsated on her neck as she flung out her free fist, catching him on the lower lip. Huglund grunted and lunged again, this time forcing her to stumble to the right and nearly lose her balance over the corpse of a fallen Red Hand. She regained her composure and prepared for the next onslaught. Taz jumped onto his back and slammed her free hand down repeatedly on his unprotected head. With a quick jerk to the side, Huglund cast her off just as Adelaide took a chance and again sliced at his throat. It missed by inches as he arched back just in time. The look on his face was grim and emotionless, and yet his eyes were on fire with something she couldn't quite comprehend.....an unchecked supply of murderous rage.

Huglund lashed out with his sword, aiming to take off her head. She ducked down and stabbed out at his chest. Her weapon, still dripping with fresh Firetongue venom, pierced his scaly armor and nicked the top few layers of skin, drawing forth a few drops of blood. Seemingly unphased, Huglund delivered a swift kick to her stomach that sent her falling back onto the blood soaked earth, gasping for air. Taz lurched for his unprotected back with a curdling howl, only to be struck across the face with a powerful backhand. She fell to the ground, twitching about as she blindly felt for her weapon lying several feet away.

Huglund glanced at her briefly before turning his focus back onto Adelaide. He shook his head repeatedly and sighed.

"I cannot understand how you insist upon fighting us. You know you cannot win. You understand all this and yet….and yet you resist your destiny. Why? What drives you to fight for an impossible cause?"

Adelaide cursed aloud. Her knife had disappeared. Everywhere she looked, she saw people fighting for their lives, too involved in the battle to even try helping those who had fallen. She finally turned back to Huglund, her face resolute and firm, and whispered back an answer:

"Hope."

His blade shot up, the edge aligned with the center of her scalp. There was nowhere to run, nowhere to hide. Adelaide smiled and closed her eyes. This is where it all ended. "I'm coming," she whispered to everyone she had lost. "I'm coming."

A terrifying yell erupted from behind her. As she gazed up into the sky, she saw Clayton's form block her vision as he leapt over her and landed beside Huglund. In his hand was the small knife she had lost only a moment before. Huglund turned for a second, just one second, before Clayton ripped the blade across his face, cutting deep through the flesh until it scraped against the bone. Huglund's head turned away, as his sword fell from his hands. Blood sprayed from his face, staining his teeth and lips with gushing crimson. He stumbled away, his hands pressing against the blinding wound.

"Clayton?" Adelaide whispered weakly.

"Yes, it's me," he groaned, trying to catch his breath. "I cannot believe this. I leave you alone for one rotting battle and you get yourself into trouble," he laughed as he helped her up.

"The mark..." she whispered, rubbing the back of her neck. "I felt it...it started..."

"Yes, I know," Clayton replied. "It's been happening to me too. We'll figure it out together, I swear. Come on now, let's get Taz."

"Finn..."

"Finn is with Sevigne and Mason. The battle is over, Adelaide. We've won. It's over."

The battle was indeed coming to an end. Ptolemi led what was left of the Tibris Guards after Huglund, who was staggering away from the battlefield with both hands pressed to his bloodied face. They soon outran the pursuing Red Hands and vanished from sight.

As Adelaide stared at the carnage around her, she found herself emotionally numb. There were no whispers this time, as there had been so many times before on her journey. Instead, found herself standing perfectly still, her hands hanging idly by her sides. The cries of pain from wounded fighters drifted away, brushed aside like a heavy curtain obstructing the light. For a moment, no matter how brief, she felt completely and unwaveringly...still. She smiled as she felt Finn's lips press on the back of her neck. She turned smiling towards him. His face was worn and exhausted. He had a shallow gash on his left shoulder and a dark bruise just above his left eye. His bloodied hatchet hung loosely in his hand. As his arms closed around her, she nestled her face against his neck. She could see Taz shaking nearby as she sunk down against a tree trunk, staring at a Tibris Guard whose throat she'd cut. Tripper and Mimi were tending to a nasty cut on Dakota's hand. Mason and Sevigne were hugging each other passionately. Arbus Spyrbank was on his knees gazing out across the corpse covered ground, his eyes brimming up with tears. Hagan, who had been checking for living Tibris Guards amongst the dead, took a second to rest his hand on Arbus' shoulder. Clayton himself was crouched on a stump nearby, Adelaide's kitchen knife still clenched in his hands. His scalp was bruised and his nose was bleeding. The wound on his arm from the precipice above the knoll was seeping through the bandages, and his pants were drenched in sweat and vomit. He smiled as he saw Adelaide glancing at him. He walked back over to where she and Finn were standing.

"We did it. I wish…I wish Raoul and Cherry had been here."

Taz struggled to her feet and hobbled over to Clayton, her eyes red and puffy.

"We….made it," she sobbed.

Clayton grinned and kissed her forehead. She returned it with a kiss on his lips and together the group began moving across the blood soaked terrain.

"Well," Taz whispered, her eyes turning skyward towards the morning sun. "What happens now?"

"Now, we head north," Clayton declared. "News of this will travel fast. Tiberion will know what Red Hands are capable of. Who knows what he'll do to stop us."

"We'll need more fighters," Adelaide remarked. "Do you think they'll come?"

"I have little doubt, Miss Stokes," Mason announced approaching the group. "And until they do, I offer the loyalty and lives of every member of the RHA to meet the ends of your endeavor. By Sorra's bosom, I swear."

Sevigne signed her agreement as Mimi, Tripper, and Dakota joined them.

"Havendale lives on!" Mimi exclaimed proudly.

"Totally," Dakota concurred.

"We're with you guys to the rotting end," Tripper joined in.

Rade, Arbus and Hagan strode beside them. One by one, the survivors of the battle collected behind the group, marching onward with weapons in hand. Clayton cocked his head with a smile before returning his gaze up ahead. Whatever questions they had, the answers couldn't be far away.

"Alright," he said. "Let's go to Reignfall."

The End

Made in the USA
Charleston, SC
16 November 2015